THE ENERGETICS, BOOK 1

BLAIZE
AND THE
MAVEN

Powerful magic, unexpected desires,
and a threat to their world's existence

ELLEN BARD

BLAIZE AND THE MAVEN

The Energetics Series : Book 1

Ellen Bard

Many thanks for reading! Please consider leaving a review wherever you bought the book, or telling your friends about it, to help me introduce it to new readers. Thanks for supporting my work.

ISBN: 0993439403
ISBN-13: 978-0993439407
Published by Parchment Publishing
ParchmentPublishing.com

Dedication

To my mum, Mary, and sister, Sarah, who support me in all my crazy adventures. And in memory of my inspiring and loving Dad, Chris Bard (1952-2007).

The Chakras and their Energies

Muladhara: The Root Chakra – Earth Element
The energy of nourishment and home, family and safety.

Svadisthana: The Sacral Chakra – Water Element
Fluid and adaptable, the energy of movement and connection, of practical and physical creativity. The energy of pleasure, sexuality and sensation, and emotions.

Manipura: The Navel Chakra – Fire Element
The energy of the individual; of confidence, of proactivity and of drive and passion. Playful and proud.

Anahata: The Heart Chakra – Air Element
The energy of healing, and of balance, located in the middle of the body and the seven Chakras. The energy of love, of relationships, of devotion. Of compassion and empathy.

Vishudha: The Throat Chakra – Ether (Space) Element
The energy of communication, of conceptual creativity, and of truth. Of expression, and of listening.

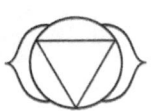

Ajna: The Third Eye – The Mind
The energy of imagination, of visualisations, and insight. Of clarity and wisdom. Of dreams and intuition.

Sahasara: The Crown Chakra – None*
The purest of all the energies. Only experienced through the Grace of the Source (the energetics' name for the creator, the divine).

*Neither a dominant nor auxiliary Chakra for energetics

CHAPTER 1

Blaize stood in front of the Three.

They looked back, their faces impassive.

Blaize needed to wait, to show patience; everything about today was part of the ritual. Even the waiting was a test—a gentle test compared to what was to come—but a test nonetheless, of her self-discipline.

But her skin itched with the need to do something. Dominant Manipura energetics like her often suffered from a lack of patience. Manipura—the energy of fire, of passion, of willpower. But also of pride, arrogance, and a quick temper.

She pushed the impatience down and willed herself to stand in front of them without action. The sand was warm under her bare feet, and the harsh heat of the sun bit even at this hour of the morning. The quiet of the jungle temple provided little to distract her from the waiting.

They stood like this in silence for thirty minutes. She kept her gaze steady and held each pair of eyes in turn as they studied her. None of them moved. *What are they thinking?*

It was unusual for an Adherent to fail the trial at such an early stage, but it could happen. Her stomach contracted and she held herself rigid to keep her face neutral. *Stay confident.*

One of the three stepped forward slightly. "Blaize Blackfire, of the Blackfire clan, you come before us on the recommendation of your Maven, Fai Sweetwater. After a scant five years of teaching, she believes you are ready for your Practitioner trial."

The speaker's robe draped her strong, lean body, and her silver hair cascaded down her back like a waterfall. The only markings on the white robe were the three red stripes across her upper left sleeve, which denoted her Master status in the Manipura Guild. The tiny owl symbol next to the stripes showed she was also a Maven.

"We represent the Manipura Guild, one of the six energetic Major Guilds. Based on your performance today, we will decide whether you are ready to move from Adherent to Practitioner." Her grey eyes held Blaize's. "First, we must ask you. Do you attempt this trial of your own free will?"

Blaize nodded.

"State your answer so the record is clear." The woman's voice was kind, but firm in her admonishment.

"I do."

"Are you aware that if you fail to reach the standard required you must wait a full year before you attempt the trial again?"

"I am." Blaize tried hard not to wince as she said this. *I'm ready. More than ready.*

"Has your Maven taken you through the dangers that await you within the trial? That even death is possible?"

"She has." Blaize's gaze met Fai's, and Fai gave a small smile and an even smaller nod that hinted at their relationship.

Fai. The woman who had been her Maven for the last five years of her life—and had always been her aunt. Blaize was so grateful to Fai, for her love, her support, her discipline, that the idea of failing—of letting her down—was unbearable. Blaize tried not to shiver, but her shoulders twitched anyway. Today Fai wasn't here as her aunt, or even her Maven. She was here as one of the Three.

"Do you consider yourself ready to face the trials that are ahead of you?"

"I'm ready." Blaize squared her shoulders and lifted her chin. She was confident. She was. She'd been pushing for the trial for months, certain she could pass. Fai had finally agreed, and now here she was. Her stomach was a tight ball inside her, and she was grateful that the preparation involved fasting, as she wasn't sure she'd be able to hold food down. *I'll be fine when we start.* Blaize liked action. *It's just this waiting that's killing me.*

"Then we will begin." Serafina, the Italian Maven, stepped back after she spoke. Blaize felt she was being judged, and hoped that Serafina didn't find her wanting at this early stage.

"Your trial will begin with a test of the strength of your energetic power. You must conjure and create Warrior fire, and hold it for one hour. During that hour, we will challenge the strength of the fire that you create. If the fire is extinguished, you will fail," Huo, the male who made up the Three for the trial with Serafina and Fai, said. "If the fire has dimmed at all, you must bring it back to full strength, or you will fail. The fire must be contained within the circle of sand in the temple. If you lose control, and your fire spreads further than this, you will fail. Do you understand?"

Blaize forced her voice to ring out. "I do."

"Then we will begin." The male's near-black eyes were steady and neutral. He was the only one of the three she'd never met before the trial. He was Chinese, and as with the other two Mavens, had the same three red stripes and owl symbol on his white robes. As a male Maven, his stripes were on the right, the Yang side.

An energetic was born a 'Dormant.' Once the energetic started to train in one of their energies, they were given the title 'Adherent.' After many years of training, they faced their Chakra Trial, as Blaize did now, and after successfully completing the trial, they became a Practitioner. After this—and many decades—they might become a Master. Most energetics remained at Practitioner level in their Major Guild, as it took a great deal of power and focus to become a Master.

Only Masters could become Mavens—a title outside the energetic hierarchy, given only to those who helped other energetics develop their own powers.

The Three, all experienced Mavens, moved to worn stone seats at the edge of the sand circle Blaize stood within. This circle had seen many trials in its time. It was the heart of one of Manipura's most important temples, an open-roofed stone sanctuary on a quiet island to the west of Thailand. Hard to find if you didn't know where to look, the temple was surrounded by twisted green jungle, rough terrain, and the clinging wet heat that was the typical climate of the island at this time of year.

With the nearest habitation several miles away, Blaize could use her energy as she liked without any humans knowing.

Blaize stepped into the circle and closed her eyes. She made an effort to loosen her shoulders and took a few deep breaths to saturate her system with oxygen. In her mind, she visualised the shape and size the fire she wanted to conjure would take. There would be time for more showy stuff later. This trial was all about strength, power, and protecting her fire against the challenges that the Three would test her with.

She drew on her energy centre for Manipura Chakra, at the core of her body, where her belly button would be. This was her link to what her people called the etheric plane, or ether, where Blaize needed to draw the energy from to the terrestrial plane, where the energetics lived alongside their unknowing human neighbours.

All energetics had two active Chakras, one dominant, one auxiliary. For most, the dominant was considerably more powerful than the auxiliary.

Blaize's dominant Chakra was Manipura, fire, and her auxiliary was Ajna, the power of the mind. She was still an Ajna Dormant, with little interest in her power in that area, as all her energy to date had been spent training her Manipura. Refining it, honing it, ready for today.

She used her Manipura energy centre to pull energy through from the ether in a steady stream that fizzed and sparked inside her. She shaped and created the fire in front of her with her eyes closed, not needing them to know what she was doing. The flames were strong, powerful and burned from the floor in front of her higher than the top of her head. She could create fiercer, taller flames, but that wasn't required. The trial would also test her pride, another weakness of hers. She always wanted to be the best, the biggest, the strongest. In this particular test, that could easily be her downfall.

Each energetic had their own natural limit for pulling energy that determined how strong they were. Her limit was high; she just didn't know whether it would be high enough.

The fire burned hot, but she kept it within the circle.

The first attack came a few minutes later, from Fai, whose auxiliary Chakra was Svadisthana, the water Chakra. Rain fell on Blaize's fire. At first the rain was playful and fell lightly over the fire. The mix created steam in tiny 'pfts' as each drop sizzled in the fire. But moments later it changed into a deluge that targeted Blaize's flames, and she had to concentrate hard to draw enough energy through to keep her fire burning.

It flickered and dimmed, but Blaize had faced this attack from her Maven many times before in all its variations. Blaize raised her flames high above her head, seeking the source of the rain, and used the fire energy to nullify the water energy. There was some resistance, but in time the rain slowed to a stop, and her fire returned to its previous height, just above her head.

The next attack came before she had centred herself after the first. This was from Serafina, the Italian Master whose auxiliary Chakra was Anahata, the Chakra of air.

Wind whipped around Blaize, and her hair snapped against her face. The wind aimed to drive her fire out of control, and out of the circle. The fire's wild flames danced, and part of Blaize wanted to dance with it, to lose herself to the power and the energy. She exulted as Serafina's air fed the fire more oxygen, and it rose and rose.

Blaize stopped herself just before the fire crept over the edges of the circle. She was now at the centre of a furnace, and she delighted in the heat on her skin. She forced the flames in towards her and lowered them to neck height, so that she stood in a much smaller circle of flames, a witch burning at the stake. But she wasn't burning. The opposite in fact. The more she drew on the power, the better she felt.

The air continued to dance around her, but it could no longer find a way into her tight circle of flames. Fire and air licked at each other, each darting around the other energy, deadlocked. Blaize sighed in pleasure and drew energy through, feeding her flames. A weaker fire energetic might find this air attack a challenge, but for Blaize, air was just fuel for her fire.

After an indeterminable time, the dust and sand that had been caught up in the air drifted back to the floor, and the wind calmed. Her fire was still strong, and sweat ran down the sides of her face and her back from effort and the hot sun.

The next attack surprised her. It was from Huo, whose auxiliary Chakra was Ajna—the Chakra of the mind. Rather than attack the fire itself, he spoke inside her mind, an unusual power even among Ajnas.

<That's enough Blaize. You've passed. You've done well. It's time to rest.>

His tone was soft, persuasive. Blaize frowned. She was sure an hour hadn't passed yet. The trial wasn't over. This must be a trick. She kept her fire burning.

His voice was insistent. *<Relax. Let go of the energy. Sit down. Rest...>*

She shook her head involuntarily and tried to block his voice out. Her flames wavered as she heard the voice persist.

<You don't need to prove anything to us. You're strong, proud. You know your powers are as good as a Practitioner; why do you need our approval?>

Her eyebrows drew together, a crease forming between her eyes. That sounded like a thought she'd had once or twice. Had he taken it from her mind? His powers were an exact match for hers—his dominant energy Manipura, and his auxiliary Ajna, the energy of the mind. Did that connection make it easier or harder for him to speak in her mind? Blaize was a bit murky on what Ajna could and couldn't do, despite it being her own auxiliary power.

<Rest, Blaize. Let the flames die down.>

The insidious voice became harder and harder to block out. For the first time in the trial, she opened her eyes to check her fire. Her eyes widened as she realised it was suffocating. The other two Mavens had joined the assault, creating an environment of damp air in which it was hard to sustain the flame.

Blaize bared her teeth in a fierce grin. He might have taken some stray thoughts from her head, but he didn't know her. She thrived on competition.

The challenge just makes it more interesting.

She tipped her head back and closed her eyes. She focused on the energy she pulled through and tugged harder, using the energy to make her flames burn brighter and hotter, maintaining their height. It took some finesse to keep everything balanced, but she could do it.

For the next ten minutes, she fought off more attacks from the Three, the attacks stronger and more complex each time they renewed their assault. But her flames burned, her focus steadfast.

The attacks ended, and there was quiet. Blaize judged it about the right amount of time for the trial to end, but she wouldn't take any chances. She kept the flames at head height until Serafina said aloud, "This trial is complete. You may rest for a short period before the next trial."

Blaize drew in a shaky breath and opened her eyes.

"It is done," Fai and Huo's voices spoke as one.

Blaize breathed out and let the energy subside. The first trial was over.

Her body buzzed and hummed, and she felt energised, ready for anything. She knew all too well that this could be a trick of her body and mind, and that if she weren't careful she could find herself with an 'energy high,' unable to judge if she was close to burning herself out. So she folded herself cross-legged on the sand and breathed deeply. *In and out. In and out.* She focused on the air she breathed in and out through her nose. She steadied the energies, and grounded and stabilised herself. Waiting.

There were still two tests to go. All three would contribute to her success – or failure. She had completed the test of strength. The next were the tests of stamina and finesse. She was most worried about the last, but both held their traps and dangers.

Huo stood, his hands clasped together in front of him, his face distant. "The next test is of endurance. Use your defensive abilities while we call Warrior fire against you."

She nodded her understanding.

"You may not use your offensive abilities. If you use offensive energy, you will fail. If you step out of the circle, you fail. In this trial, you can end it before time should you wish, by calling stop. This will mean you fail the trial immediately."

Source, there are a lot of opportunities for me to fail. Blaize tried to keep her face as serene at the Three, but inside she winced.

"Do you understand?" Huo finished.

"I understand." Blaize rose to her feet.

"You may have a few moments to prepare." Huo remained standing, and Serafina and Fai joined him, arranging themselves in a line, gaps of about a yard between them, much further apart than the stone chairs. Each of the Mavens closed their eyes and made their own preparations.

Blaize shut her eyes and drew on the energy she still felt within her, and took yet more from the ether. It was almost impossible for your own energy to be turned against you, but an energetic could be hurt by energies wielded by another energetic. This trial was about defending herself from some of the most powerful members of her Guild. As before, she'd had practice. A lot of practice. And over time, she'd had a lot of burns. But it had been a while since Fai had been able to touch her with her Warrior fire, at least without taking her by surprise. Blaize felt confident if they attacked her one at a time she could defend herself.

I hope I can manage all three at once.

She spooled power inside her. She built a defensive wall around her and snapped shields she'd spent years working with into place.

She extended her energy out a little into the temple.

She felt Fai's energy—fire and water—hot but almost fluid. Serafina—fire and air—was warm and light. And then there was Huo, the most mysterious of all, whose fire and mind powers were sharp, laser-like. *Will my powers ever feel like that?* Blaize wanted to learn about her Ajna powers, her mind element, but she could wait. She loved the energy of fire too much to want to focus on anything else right now.

Without warning, the attacks began. Huo slashed fire across her face. Blaize drew in a breath—and her throat burned. As she sent energy to repair the weakness in her shields that Huo's Warrior fire had created, another slash came. And another. She spooled energy, and her breathing increased. She was keeping up so far, but each slash caused her pain and depleted her energies. Her whole body shook with the effort of defending herself.

Fai added to the attack with a fluid fire that flooded the area around Blaize's legs as if she stood in hot water. Though the fire didn't come close to penetrating her defences like Huo's, she knew that if she didn't pay attention to it, Fai's Warrior fire would erode her defences, scraping them away until she was cooked.

Blaize threw a wash of defensive fire along her body and reinforced her shields. Which was lucky, because at that moment, a blast of heat hit her and she staggered from Serafina's attack.

None of the three moved from their solid stances. Blaize was closer to the stone wall behind the circle now, and she used this as another tool, a shield at her back. She parried attacks rather than absorb them, with no time to intellectualise and analyse, just respond.

Attack. Parry. Slash. Parry. Strike. Parry.

She drew more and more energy from the ether, and her body expended huge amounts of energy to keep her shields up. Sweat ran down her body. The drops tracked through the dust that Serafina's wind in the first trial had thrown at her body.

One of Huo's attacks whipped through her defences and created a thin red burn across her shoulder. She shook off the pain and turned up her defences once more.

Blaize was hit by another wave of heat from Serafina, followed in quick succession by several slashes from Huo. Blaize lost her balance and fell to one knee. Burning sand penetrated the thin material that covered her legs. She strengthened her shields. The attacks continued, fast now, so fast she didn't have time to get up. She parried, defended and deflected, and burned through energy at a blistering rate. *How long can I keep this up?*

Huo's insidious whisper crept into her mind once more. <*You can call time on this, Blaize. Just say stop.*>

Source knew, Blaize was tempted.

CHAPTER

2

Huo's barbs kept coming, and his voice inside her head was louder now. <*Your defenses are weakening. You're going to let your Maven down.*>

Blaize stiffened, and her body shot to attention, giving her the energy to push up on her foot, teetering as she stood. *He's wrong. He has to be wrong. I will not fail this test.*

<*You're weak, Blaize.*>

A wave of heat flushed through her body that was nothing to do with her energies. *How dare he?*

<*You're going to fail. You're going to end up just like your parents.*>

At this taunt, Blaize's vision misted, her nails dug into her palms and she stepped towards Huo. But as she did her shields wavered, and she staggered and fell back to her knees, pain smashing through her kneecaps as they hit the rough sand.

Huo sent a flurry of strikes and slashes through the weakness in her defences that had opened when she'd been about to attack him.

Each hit left a raised red welt. Blaize's vision cleared and she caught Fai raise her eyebrow very slightly.

Blaize drew her defences around her, keeping them in tight to her body as she knelt on the sand. *What the hell was I thinking?* If she used offensive fire, she would fail. It had only been the shock of Huo punching through her shields that had stopped her from lashing out at him. Her stomach gave a lurch and she swallowed, her mouth dry.

I need to focus. How can I keep him out of my mind? Can he read mine? She tried to use the same kind of shields of fire energy she used on her body to protect her mind. The energies twisted and pain shot through her head. *Ouch. Okay, so not exactly the same principle.* But the voice stopped. For now.

Her thoughts were slow, but her movements and instincts remained fast. She'd been hit a number of times now, and there were new burns on her shoulder and hip. Her cotton trousers and white cotton T-shirt were torn and covered in dirt and sweat. *At least burns don't bleed.*

She winced as another of Huo's attacks snuck through her defences. She felt lightheaded; the extensive energy use had taken a toll on her body.

She. Would. Not. Call. Stop.

The stone wall behind her gave off heat as it reflected Fai and Serafina's Warrior fire. Blaize protected her body, back and front, with defensive fire. She drew a deep breath in and centred herself even as she pulled a massive amount of energy. The defence she created was almost impenetrable. The attacks no longer reached her skin, and she put all her energy into maintaining the shield and nothing else.

Time stopped. There was nothing but her defences.

She didn't have much left in her. She needed to rest. *How long will this go on?*

She maintained the shield from the floor. She knelt and attempted to ground herself. Managing her physical body as well as her energies was almost beyond her.

And then, nothing.

The attacks stopped.

"It is done," said Huo.

Serafina and Fai echoed his words and the Three stepped back to their stone chairs.

"Rest again. The final trial will begin in one hour." Serafina's words soothed Blaize. She really needed that rest.

Blaize wanted to cry, her body limp and her arms hanging heavy by her sides. There was still one more trial to go. *Did I pass the first two?* It felt like it, but judges were capricious, and they had the last say on her performance.

She got to her feet, feeling like a newborn fawn. She needed a drink. She gestured to the door, and Serafina nodded.

Blaize walked out of the circle and down the stairs that led to a dark, familiar storage room away from the Three. She grabbed a bottle from the fridge in a hidden cupboard. She drank the cool water down, the liquid a balm for her throat, which was rough from breathing in the heated air of the trial. She drank another and washed her face in the sink. She leaned on the edges of the basin and stared into the mirror. She looked dreadful. Her hair hung in wet curls around her face, and her normally bright green eyes were shadowed.

The water helped. She rubbed her hands over her face and sat on the hard wooden chair that sat in the corner of the room. She closed her eyes, relaxed her body, and sank into meditation. She would repair as much of her energies as she could within the hour's rest period.

Blaize had fasted for the last twenty-four hours. She'd taken a ritual bath, and had spent time in meditation, focusing on the fire in her mind, in her body. When she'd come to the temple that morning before sunrise, she was as clean, as purified, as she could be, physically, emotionally, and mentally.

She tried to get back to that state as she meditated. The hour passed quickly – *too quickly* – and soon it was time to head back upstairs. She walked back into the circle with her game face on.

Serafina stood. Her eyes were grave as she held out a solid goblet, as smooth and worn as the stone seats in the temple. "The next trial tests your finesse. You must drink the poisonous liquid held in this goblet. Use your energy to burn every trace from your system. If you do not, it is probable that you will die. The poison is fast-acting. You will have about five minutes from drinking the poison before you feel the effects."

Serafina offered the goblet to Blaize.

She had tried this exercise successfully many times, but never with a substance that could kill her. The worst had been the liquids that made her sick, which Fai believed acted as a definite incentive to learning.

Blaize clung to the conviction that she had enough experience to get her through this trial, and tried to stop her stomach from jumping into her parched mouth and throat.

She cupped her hands around the heavy goblet and looked down at the green liquid inside. Serafina had sunk into the third stone chair without a sound, her face immobile. All of the Three were now still as statues. Blaize met each of their eyes in turn, Fai last.

I can do this. I will do this.

Then she tipped up the base of the goblet and the liquid flowed into her mouth and throat. The taste was bitter and somehow floral, and she gagged, her throat convulsing as she battled to keep it down.

Gah! That was disgusting.

Her throat burned, and her heartbeat sped up, her pulse a physical drumbeat in her body. She fought to keep the panic from overwhelming her as the poison flooded her system and began to do its work. She felt cramps in her abdomen and wherever the poison had passed.

Adrenalin surged through her body as she realised she'd made a major error by not spooling more energy before she drank. *Stupid.* She hastily drew energy from the ether, sending the energy inside her body rather than outwards as she had with her shield in the previous trial. She opened her consciousness up as deeply as possible to her own body, and the stone temple faded to the background of her mind. Her energy raced around her form like wildfire, in corkscrews and spirals. Wherever it encountered a molecule of the poison, it incinerated it before any more damage could be done.

The task was a difficult one. Finding every trace of poison as it coursed through her system was no easy matter. To burn the poison from her throat and stomach was straightforward enough, but the few seconds' head start the poison had was enough to give her some cramps. Her muscles were tight, and she gulped convulsively as she sent more and more tendrils of energy through her system to attack the poison molecule by molecule.

Perhaps the cramps she felt were psychosomatic. *Serafina said I had at least five minutes...*

Blaize tried to ensure her inner turmoil wasn't visible to the inscrutable eyes of the Three. But after a minute or two, sweat beaded at her temples, and her breath had quickened.

She found fewer molecules of poison. *Is there enough left to kill me? Perhaps if there's only a small amount left, it won't kill me even if I miss the five-minute deadline. Hmm.* Not really a chance she wanted to take.

Her stomach cramped again, tighter, and she was grateful it was empty as the spasms turned into a retch. Her right arm throbbed.

The poison saturated her system, a spider-web of pain throughout her body. She could no longer manage the multiple streams of energy around her body. *I'm not going to make it through this in one piece.*

The pain in her stomach, one of the areas where the poison had been at work the longest, was agonising. She made a split-second decision to focus on her vital organs and pushed her energy as hard as her strength would allow into her viscera and away from her arm.

A cramp like multiple stab wounds gripped her organs, and she couldn't breathe. She could think of nothing but her stomach, and she dropped once more to her knees.

The pain worsened.

She was going to run out of time.

CHAPTER

3

"It's not possible." Cuinn gripped the phone receiver in his hand and forced himself to keep his tone even. He kept his eyes on the stunning green view from the window of his workroom.

"Cuinn, please, reconsider. She has spectacular energies," Marius said. Fai's husband, he had called Cuinn from Thailand. Again. "Her Manipura is one of the strongest her Aunt has trained, and we think her Ajna energy is almost as strong—it's unusual for an auxiliary energy to be that powerful."

"I know." Cuinn's reply was dry. His own energies were also abnormally strong. He was one of the strongest Ajna energetics in the Guild. And much good had it done him. He rubbed his face, feeling the stubble that had grown there while he'd been immersed in his books yet again.

"You'd be a perfect Maven for her Ajna. She needs someone strong but grounded. It's hard to find a Maven with Ajna and Muladhara." Marius's Irish brogue had been dulled by time and travel, but could still be heard by Cuinn, also born there, many years ago.

"You know better than most that I can't take an Adherent. I've told you and Fai both for months. Why are we having this conversation again?" Cuinn felt a wash of heat across his chest and put a palm against the cool glass of the window. *Why are they still pestering me about this?* If his friendship with Marius hadn't been so old—and Marius and Fai were two of the small number of people in the world he cared about—he wouldn't have even taken the call. As it was, the temper that others rarely saw was now close to the surface. He took a deep breath to slow the pulse that had sped in reaction to Marius's harassment.

"Her trial's going on now. She'll pass, but her anger is still strong. She can be hasty, proud, quick to flare up. Rogues, in particular, have an … incendiary effect on her."

"It's understandable, given what happened to her parents." Cuinn knew the girl's history. It was a hard one, and he of all people knew how tragedy could change and influence a person. He didn't blame her, but that didn't mean he wanted anything to do with her.

"It was fine when she was young, a Dormant, but she'll be a Manipura Practitioner after the trial. If her Ajna isn't well developed by a grounded Maven, she could easily go off course. She may be a straightforward Warrior now, but one day she could be a Guild Leader. She needs to develop the power of the mind, especially her farseer powers. It may seem as though her leadership won't be required for many years, but the death of her parents shows us that even the most experienced and longest lived of us can be taken by surprise. We want to be prepared."

"Her grandmother is strong, cautious, and adaptable. She's going nowhere. And the girl would have to be voted in by her Guild, which is unlikely. She's ridiculously young for the politics that would be involved. Which is something I can't teach her." *And wouldn't want to even if I could.*

"Please. For us. We need your help." Marius wouldn't budge.

Cuinn sighed. If this was a competition for the most stubborn energetic, he was happy to oblige. And it wasn't as if he was pretending, either. His plate was full. His brain buzzed with the glut of information he'd been taking in recently in an attempt to decipher the prophecies. "There are other things going on. I have things that I'm working on for the Circle."

"You'll always be busy. Your work ethic and your sense of duty determine that." Marius hesitated for the slightest moment. "But it's time for you too. Time for you to take another Adherent."

"That's for me to decide." Cuinn's tone became clipped. The heat now washed through not only his chest, but his neck and head. His forehead joined his palm against the window. "I value your friendship, you know I do, but don't presume to discuss matters with me that are my business alone."

"It's not only your business. You've cut yourself off for too long. Just because you won't take a leadership role for the energetics, doesn't mean you can't do important work elsewhere."

Why won't the man take no for an answer? "I *am* doing important work elsewhere."

"Part of being strong is working with others."

"That's enough." Cuinn's voice had a dangerous edge now. All he wanted was to be left alone, and Marius knew that. Surely that wasn't too much to ask after more than two hundred years of service to the Guild?

He kept silent, reining in the anger, kept staring at the green view, and Marius didn't break that silence.

At the back of Cuinn's mind lurked the debt he owed Marius. A debt that he gratefully acknowledged; Marius had brought Cuinn back from the brink of madness after Cuinn's horrific experience with his last Adherent. But surely Marius would never call in the debt in this way? He of all people knew how unsuited Cuinn was to be a Maven.

After a handful of moments, Cuinn relented, shaking his head. The girl was unlikely to pass her trial this fast. And even if he simply managed to postpone this conversation, at least he'd be able to get back to work now.

"She has to get through her trial first anyway. It's never a given. It would be rare for an energetic to pass their dominant energy's trial with only five years of training. Come back to me when—if—she passes, and we can discuss it again."

Cuinn hung up, slung the phone onto the desk and strode back to the window. His hands clutched the windowsill as he stared out, willing the view to ground him as it usually did.

The gentle hills, at this time of year still dusted with snow, reminded him of the Ireland he'd left many decades before. This kind of view was less common in Canada, his adopted home. But he'd found it in this area to the south east of Vancouver, Fraser Valley. Of course, Ireland didn't have the huge, white-capped mountain that was Mount Baker behind the valleys, but that just added to the view.

Not in the least soothed, he spun around and paced across the spacious room, stepping around the piles of books heaped on the floor.

Damn him. I don't want an Adherent. And not because he wasn't prepared to be responsible for a beginner's mistakes like many Master level energetics who chose not to become Mavens.

My reasons are far more important.

Cuinn's Ajna energy, the energy of the mind, gave him the power to dreamwalk. To visit the ether, and to use farsight to see slivers of the future. His recent dreamwalks had terrified him. So much so, he'd already reported them to his Minor Guild's Circle member. Over recent weeks, day and night, he'd explored the prophecies to try to understand more, but they were patchy, and the feelings of fear and trepidation that came with them had increased.

Cuinn stopped pacing and sighed. He pushed his hair back from his face. He hadn't been sleeping and his body felt as if it had gone three rounds in the practice ring with Adam, his extremely well-muscled and well-trained cousin.

Cuinn didn't want to have to deal with some fiery Adherent on top of everything else. He wasn't cut out to teach. Time had shown that.

He opened the door and went downstairs towards the house's huge kitchen, where, if he was any judge of the smells wafting down the corridor, Tierra, Adam's sister and Cuinn's other cousin, was baking. Adam and Tierra were all the family he had left – he didn't count his father – and they were the two most important people in the world to Cuinn.

He came through the kitchen door and saw her, humming along to the mellow sounds of a saxophone coming from the radio. Her dark hair hung around her face as she bent over the oven and took a mouthful of something from a baking tray. She looked up when he came in, eyes wide, guilt on her face.

"I was just having a taste!"

"Good?" He frowned. Had he missed something? *What was she talking about?*

"It was a small taste. It doesn't count against my diet." She had a smear of chocolate on her forehead. He walked over to her and wiped it off.

"You're on another diet?"

"Yes, yes, I want to lose a few pounds. I saw this beautiful dress in town, and I'm between sizes at the moment. I need to lose a few more pounds to get down to the next one."

"Why don't you enjoy whatever you're eating and go up a size?" He pinched a bit of brownie from the baking tray for himself and tasted it. Hot, a bit squishy, but good. Very good.

Her mouth dropped open. "What's wrong with you?"

"What's wrong with you?" He poked her in the arm and grinned at her.

She smiled back, shaking her head, and he gave her a quick one-armed hug. "I will never understand women. You'd have to go a long way before you found a man who wouldn't appreciate your curves."

"Not much chance of finding a man to ask given the luck I have in that area." She pushed the brownies back into the oven. "They need a few more minutes anyway. What have you been up to today?"

Cuinn tried to keep his tone casual. "I just got off the phone with Marius. He's trying to push his niece on me as an Adherent."

"You're talking about taking a new Adherent? That's big." She shut the oven and straightened.

"I'm not talking about it, he is. I'm not taking her. I told him no. Again."

Tierra rubbed her forehead and smudged more chocolate on her butterscotch skin. Cuinn suppressed a smile.

"Maybe it's time," she said. "It's been decades since ..."

He stopped smiling. "I know how long it's been. There are others who can help her. It doesn't need to be me."

She leaned one elbow on the counter, resting her chin in her palm. "Hmm. It doesn't have to be, but it could be. Have you talked to Adam about it?"

He shook his head. "I haven't heard from him for a few days."

Tierra sighed. "The last message he sent said his team took a contract hunting some Rogue in Russia, so he's probably off the grid. I hope he looks after himself. And you, too—how's your work going? Have you made much progress with your dreamwalks? Are the prophecies any clearer?"

"Yes, and no. They're blurry, much blurrier than my farsight is normally." He shook his head and realised he was grinding his teeth. He relaxed his jaw and circled his head. "All I can tell is, trouble's coming, and it's coming for all of us. The energetics. But I don't know how, who—even when. I have only fragments, not enough to piece together yet."

"When did you last get a full night's sleep?"

"I don't know. A while." *Weeks. But she doesn't need to know that.* "I'm spending all the time I can on this. When I'm dreamwalking, my physical body's lying down, so it's a sort of rest."

"It won't help your farsight if you don't stay healthy."

Cuinn gritted his teeth and tried to change the subject. "How's your work?"

Tierra wrote nationally syndicated gardening and agony aunt columns. "Good. I sent off both this week's columns early. Let's have a proper dinner tonight, at the table. I'll cook something you like. Stop working by six, and come help me set the table."

Tierra was always ahead of her deadlines, whereas Cuinn felt like he could never catch up with his. "I don't have time."

Tierra waved a hand. "You can stop for an evening. Another good reason to get an Adherent—an Ajna will make a perfect assistant—she can spend her time with all of those dusty books of yours."

Cuinn raised his eyebrows. "Those 'dusty books' are the history of our race. And probably the future too, if only I can decipher the farseeings of those who've gone before me."

"The books can wait for you to have a good meal and a proper night's sleep. You're too thin, you'll waste away."

"You've been saying that for decades, and I still eat twice as much as you. It's my metabolism. My energies. But," he put up a hand to forestall yet another argument, "I'll keep you company at supper. And I'll only do a couple of hours afterwards before I go to bed. How's that?"

"I'll take it. You can tell me all about this Adherent of yours when we eat."

"She's not …" Cuinn gave up as Tierra chuckled and pushed him out of the kitchen. He shook his head and gave a small smile, and as always, he felt lighter after spending time with his cousin, whose combination of earth and heart, Muladhara and Anahata, made her one of the most nurturing people he knew. He was lucky to have her in his life.

When Cuinn came back down again to dinner a couple of hours later, he was in a more relaxed mood. He'd found reference to a text that he thought might provide some suggestions about a way forward with the prophecies. He felt he had made some progress for the first time in days. He shut the door of his study area behind him for the night and took just the one book with him to read in the library after supper with Tierra.

As he walked towards the kitchen, he heard Tierra scolding someone who answered back in amused, lazy tones, "Don't pretend you're not pleased to see me, T."

Cuinn's eyebrows rose at the faint European accent that told him who she was scolding.

Cuinn came through the door and grinned. "Fintan! Why didn't you let me know you were coming?"

A tall, broad-shouldered, strawberry-blond man stood talking to Tierra's back. He turned. "What, and miss the opportunity to piss off your cousin here by adding an extra person to dinner?"

There was a 'hfft' from Tierra, who slapped at Fintan's hand, which was reaching for the spoon in her pot of sauce. It did smell great.

Cuinn walked to Fintan and they hugged like brothers—which was the way Cuinn felt about him. Fintan wasn't family, but after growing up in Scandinavia, he'd spent decades with Cuinn in Ireland when they were younger energetics, just as Marius had.

Marius. Of course. So that was why Fintan was here. He was backing up his phone pestering with a personal visit.

Frowning, Cuinn pushed away from Fintan.

"Marius sent you." Cuinn didn't have time for these games.

Fintan fidgeted and avoided his gaze. "What do you mean?"

"You know exactly what I mean, brother." He emphasised the last word. "Marius sent you, didn't he? Don't tell me he and Fai have gotten you involved?"

Fintan didn't meet his eyes, and shifted, moving over to where the crockery was waiting to be put on the table. "Let's have some of this delicious supper your cousin's cooked first, eh, Cuinn? Time enough to catch up about old friends afterwards. I hear there are brownies."

Cuinn could just hear the edge of Tierra's muttered "... brownies for Cuinn, not for thieving Scandinavians ..."

"Don't tell me you've already managed to upset Tierra? Watch how you go on this Maven issue, or you'll make it two for two." His tone was light, but Fintan's wince showed he knew Cuinn meant it.

"Come on, let's set the table and we'll talk after dinner. Surely there must be some gossip you've brought us back from the Guilds. That dreadful woman Maya, for example. What's she up to these days? You know Tierra loves her gossip."

At Tierra's huff he turned to her, giving her a gentle poke in the side. "I don't know what you're upset at, it's not your life he's come to turn upside down. I thought you wanted me to stop working? I'll never get anything done with this chatterbox around."

Tierra rolled her eyes but smiled, and some of the tension in Fintan's face disappeared. He put the crockery out and came back over to Cuinn, slapping him on the arm as he grabbed for the cutlery.

Cuinn put his unease and everything else that was on his mind aside for a couple of hours. "So, what did you bring us to drink? Something suitably expensive, I hope?"

CHAPTER
4

Blaize tried hard not to regret drinking the foul green liquid. She knelt on the sand, bowed over with pain and eyes squeezed shut, as she concentrated on chasing every last trace of poison from her system. She was close but was reaching the end of her energy reserves, and her limit on how much more she could pull from the ether.

It was a strong poison.

The pain in her arm was agonising. It burned as if acid was eating her from the inside out. She'd left it till last, had focused on her vital organs rather than her extremities. She swept her energies around her viscera again, before she breathed in and out once more and concentrated her attention on the pain and poison in her arm. *Don't think about what could happen.* She could lose the ability to hold, to touch, and feel in her arm.

She liked her arm.

But she was so tired. The fact that she'd had no food in the last 24 hours might be good for purification, but was less good for strength and energy. The last two trials had brought her close to exhaustion, and she'd struggled to bring herself back to full strength in between. She opened her connection to the ether wider. She needed to pull more energy to burn the final grains of poison out. Her head span.

A last burst of effort, and tiny threads of energy like the finest lace spread throughout the inside of her arm. *There. I'm done.*

With lead in her legs, she got back to her feet, determined to finish as she'd begun. She consciously slowed her breathing to pretend it hadn't been such a close call.

"It is done." She lifted her head to the Three, and again, met each of their eyes in turn, and if her gaze wasn't quite as steady as before, she didn't think anyone would blame her.

Once again, she met Fai's eyes last. Although Fai's face was still impassive under her cropped black hair, as Blaize watched, Fai's lips parted and she let out a soft, deliberate breath.

Blaize couldn't believe that just minutes had passed. She was drained.

"It is done." The Three intoned the phrase in unison.

How did they do that? Did they practise? Or did Huo mind speak to the other two so they knew when to say it? Who knew?

Huo spoke again. "We will confer. Remain in the circle until we return." They rose and walked out.

Blaize sank to the ground, all attempts at grace gone.

She gazed at the star-salted sky. *How insignificant we all are.* A million stars ... an infinite galaxy. Her efforts to pass the trial were pretty small stuff when compared to that.

Her eyes were as gritty as the sand beneath her, and she blinked away some of the tiredness before she closed them, and opened her energetic connection. She didn't pull any energy from the ether, but sent gratitude, and vowed once more to Source to be aware, conscious, and mindful in all her actions, whatever happened.

The link with Source calmed her. She hadn't even realised she was still anxious until her heartbeat slowed with the prayer and connection.

Blaize could sense the different energies as the Three filed into the circle once more. Their bare feet padded on the sand and stone—no one wore shoes in the temple—but Blaize continued to sit with her eyes closed until they were all settled. The evening sounds of the jungle grew, the noisy chorus of crickets a background of white noise.

She opened her eyes. The sun was going down and the night had cooled the air. Until now, Blaize hadn't felt the difference because of the energies she had raised. One of the benefits of fire energy. She didn't get too hot and she could keep herself warm when it was cold. Though she much preferred hot climates when she had a choice.

Once the temple was silent again, she shakily rose to her feet. She stood in front of the Mavens, unable to read their faces. They were as poker-faced as ever.

"Blaize Blackfire, we greet you." Serafina took the lead.

"We greet you." The others followed the ritual salutation.

"I greet you." She intoned the words back. This was the moment. She thought she had passed, but these trials were never predictable. But she was too tired to be anxious. She had given her best today, and it had nearly killed her. *What more could they ask?*

"You have purified body and mind, and passed the trials of Strength, Endurance and Finesse," Huo said. "You have completed the Manipura Trial in front of three Mavens. We, the Three, have weighed and judged you. Our opinion, representing the Manipura Guild, is that you are ready for the title of Practitioner."

Blaize's shoulders sagged. Something inside her opened up, and she looked down at the sand.

"We have a concern that we wish to share with you, however."

Blaize's stomach dropped, and her eyes snapped back up to meet Huo's dark stare. His gaze was unblinking and held her with an almost physical weight.

His voice was silky, but in the manner of liquid metal, his words capable of engulfing the listener and burning them up in an instant. "We rarely remove Practitioner status, but it is possible. This is a warning to you. Your anger, pride, your desire to be the best have the potential for harm as well as good. Practise safely. Do not take inappropriate risks, whatever the goal. Do not let others trigger you over things that are history. Be in the present where your actions count."

Blaize slowly nodded. *Not exactly rousing support. But I passed.* She knew she was proud, but she had her drive, her anger, under control. *And I'm only competitive about the important things.*

"Thank you for your faith in me, Mavens. I will do as you say. I hope to bring honour and pride to my Guild."

"Then kneel, Adherent. Take the Manipura oath," Huo said.

Blaize knelt in the hot sand. Her body felt as if it had been pelted with stones, her clothes were tattered and dirty, and she wasn't sure if she'd ever manage to get up again, but none of that mattered in this moment.

"I honour the power within me. The fire within me burns through all fears. I can do whatever I will to do. With these words I recommit myself to the Manipura Guild as a Practitioner. To uphold our precepts. To strive to conduct myself for the honour of Guild and energetics race."

She bowed her head and shuddered as the energy of all of the Three entered her. The heat was just the wrong side of painful, and she clenched her teeth. The fire had different undertones depending on their auxiliary energy, but it was still fire.

The skin on her arm burned, and she felt a new tattoo form on her left arm, the pain coalescing and hanging there for a white-hot moment, like the flick of a whip. As quickly as it had come, it was gone, adding a second band to the one she already had, a mark that couldn't be faked. Two bands was the mark of a Practitioner, and although for formal occasions she would wear a robe with the two red stripes on her left sleeve, from today she would bear the marks on her body as well.

The pain had gone, leaving a numb after-image like the negative from an old film camera, the lack of pain as surprising as the pain had been. She resisted the urge to rub the area to wake it up, her body and brain enlivened as the energy of the Three spun around her system.

"We use the energy of the Three to break the binding between you and your Maven, Fai," Huo said. "As a Practitioner, you are released from the need for a Maven in Manipura. You are independent, and the Guild treats you as such."

Another rush of energy and a sharp pain in her belly, the seat of Manipura Chakra, and the energetic bindings that tethered her to her Aunt were severed. She felt a wave of sadness along with the triumph. *Does Fai feel the same?* The pain faded though the absence of her bond with Fai remained.

"It is done," Huo said.

"It is done." Serafina's voice was lighter.

"It is done." Fai's voice held suppressed pride.

Blaize stood again, for the final time in the ritual. "It is done."

And if she never heard that phrase again, she'd be just fine.

She waited as the Three left. It was her job to clean up the temple. She blew out the candles and picked up fallen petals from the sand. She took the petals and threw them into the surrounding jungle, then found the broom in the cupboard. She felt her body, mind, and spirit settle as she erased the footprints and other evidence of the ritual, to leave the temple clean and ready for the next visitors.

Outside the temple, and alone, she pulled out a pair of shorts and a T-shirt from her scooter's storage compartment and swapped her once-white clothes for the new ones. She took a moment to stretch out the kinks in her neck and back before she swung a leg over the little scooter she used to get around the island. Since Fai would need to entertain the visiting Mavens a little longer, Blaize could deliver the good news to her cousin Nixie first.

The peace Blaize felt now might just be the calm after the storm, but she wouldn't analyse it too deeply. She'd done well today.

She had the right to be proud.

The elegant man, dressed, as ever, in a tailored suit, was visiting Indigo in the suburban house in Vancouver where she lived, and which he paid for. He sat on a hard chair in the basement but looked as relaxed and unruffled as usual. He was a man in total control of himself, his environment, and her.

Indigo felt a trickle of sweat down her back. Why had he come here today? She hadn't expected him till later in the week. She hadn't been ready. She liked to prepare. She wasn't prepared.

"Would you like a drink or something?" The words felt awkward in her mouth, but she knew it was what people did in this kind of situation.

He smiled at her, an indulgent smile, like a father whose child had done something clever. He had white hair, discerning grey eyes, and looked a well-preserved fifty, though Indigo knew he was many hundreds of years old.

"No. Sit," he said, and gestured to the concrete floor in front of him. There were cushions and even other chairs in the room, but she sat at his feet, and looked at his knees. She didn't want to meet his eyes.

He was her Maven, the man who'd seen something in the lost girl she'd been and moulded her into a woman. The first man who'd ever wanted her, though he'd never touched her sexually.

Their Maven-Adherent bond had never been broken despite the fact she had become a Practitioner many years ago. But although he did still—sometimes—use the bond to teach her, to protect her, usually he used it to control her.

"Things are coming to a head. An ancient prophecy has been set in motion. But as ever with these things, the prophecy can be changed at certain pivotal points. At this point, the prophecy is against us. But we have six chances to ensure it can never come true."

Indigo looked up at his serene face. "What happens if it doesn't?"

"Then, my dear Indigo, we have the chance for the kind of power you can't even dream of. Power that will mean we evolve past even the most powerful energetics you know. Power that will give us the opportunity to destroy our enemies and repay our friends. Power that will change our race forever."

She nodded, understanding now why he was here. He had a job for her. "What do you need me to do?"

"How's your energy?"

She licked her lips and tried not to glance behind her. "F-fine."

"It's time for you to branch out on your own. I've found an energetic match for you who just happens to be someone who has the potential to cause me a lot of problems. If you can take her, you can have her."

Indigo's foot started to twitch. "Who? Where?"

"I need you to move to a town called Merrow and wait. In the meantime, I'm going to share with you the prophecy I've seen so far."

She tried not to whine. "You can just tell me. I don't mind if you just want to tell me."

He smiled again and spoke gently. "It's better if I show you, my dear. You know that."

He beckoned her forward and she shuffled towards him and bowed her head. He put his hands on her hair, and she closed her eyes and braced.

Agonising pain shot through her head, as images were forced into her mind.

She saw twelve energetics shining in front of her, their faces as bright as the sun.

She saw a red-haired woman tied to a bed, an IV drip coming out of her arm.

She saw a tall, dark-haired man fall to his knees in a forest, his face agonised.

She saw, in her own Haven, her safe space on the etheric plane, the red-haired woman tied to a chair.

His hands left Indigo's head and she slumped down. Her head lolled and she felt something wet come out of her nose.

He clucked his tongue and put his right hand under her chin, lifting her head up. He put his left hand in his pocket and pulled out a pristine handkerchief, and wiped away the blood under her nose.

"The red-haired woman is your target. You're to move to Merrow, and to dreamwalk yourself to find what else you can of the prophecy. At the moment there is a possibility that the man and woman you saw may not even meet, in which case I will have other work for you. You will stay in touch." He let go of her head, which wobbled but she kept it upright. Her gaze was fixed on his knees again.

He picked up a black briefcase at his side, and pulled out a plastic wallet filled with papers. He leaned down and placed it by her side. "This is the information you need."

He stood up and looked down at her. "Now, get your mat. I'm going to make it so that no other energetic can recognise you with protection wardings. I don't want to spring the surprise early, after all."

She cringed, but got up and pulled her mat into position, and concentrated hard on ignoring the dead body that lay in the corner of the room. The blood from the corpse's nose had dripped past his chin and onto his chest but was now brown and dried.

"Lie down and relax," the man instructed. "You know it hurts more if you're tense."

She lay on the mat and screwed her eyes shut. This time, she tried to make her limbs slack as his energies—and the white hot pain—seared her every muscle and nerve.

It was for her own good, after all.

CHAPTER
5

"Must you ruin a pleasant evening?" Cuinn kept his voice amiable, but the warning was clear.

He and Fintan had retired to the living space, and as expected, Fintan had continued the argument on Marius's behalf.

But Cuinn had had enough.

"The answer is no, Fintan. I don't want another Adherent. I'm working on the prophecies. It's too important to be distracted by some inexperienced girl."

Fintan looked sombre, unlike his usual playful self. "I understand. Tierra tells me you've taken a sabbatical from the university to work on deciphering the prophecies you've seen. But it's time."

He sprawled in an armchair, his gaze on the fire that Cuinn had lit to warm the chilled room. Fintan raised and lowered the flames as rhythmically as some people stroked a cat.

Cuinn stood, his gaze on the fire, his posture stiff and unyielding.

Fintan's relaxed voice ignored Cuinn's reaction. "You're the right candidate. For her, and for you. The level of control that's needed to manage one's own energy plus an Adherent's is difficult, and you have the energy, the power, to manage someone who has strong potential but no training. It might be a hard experience at first, but you need it to heal. What happened to Sophea wasn't your fault."

Cuinn's fists balled, but the anger was drowned in a bleak guilt that lay like ice water inside his chest. "I don't want to talk about that."

"I know you don't. You never have. You've kept it inside you, where it's eaten away at your personality like a poison. You're becoming someone quite different from the Cuinn I knew of old. You were always serious, but at least then you had the capacity for a little spontaneity and play. That's been leached away by the burden you carry about Sophea. A new Adherent, and a more positive, successful relationship will heal you more than you know."

Cuinn was shocked by this speech though he tried not to let it show on his face. He took refuge in anger instead, sneering at Fintan. "If I'm not the person you want me to be, then piss off back to whoever's bed you're warming at the moment. I'm fine on my own. And anyway, I have Adam and Tierra keeping me company. I'm not alone."

Silence stretched between them.

Fintan played with the fire.

Cuinn crossed his arms over his chest. *This is none of his business. They should all just leave me alone.* He didn't want another Adherent, didn't deserve another chance. And the girl certainly didn't deserve him. She was better off somewhere else.

He closed his eyes and memories assaulted him. An ethereal woman, her face lit up as they discussed philosophy and literature. Watching her Ajna energies blossom and develop. Her Haven in the dreamscape a labyrinth of books. Keeping up with her as she switched languages depending on the topic, from English, to Latin, to Greek, to her native Italian when she was truly excited. The moment she had shown him the hidden room in her Haven, and his wretched handling of the situation.

He swallowed to reduce the thickness in his throat, and fought to keep the feelings off his face.

But Cuinn wasn't trapped yet, whatever Fintan thought. The cage door still had to close.

One word would determine whether it would.

He asked the question he had been dreading since Fintan came through the door. "Is Marius calling in my debt?"

Fintan looked grave. "Yes."

That's it. With that one word, the cage door slammed shut, and Cuinn felt light-headed.

"I need some time alone, Fin. We'll speak tomorrow." He spun around before Fintan could answer and left the room.

Marius calling in his debt was the last straw. Cuinn could no longer refuse.

He would have to become a Maven again.

CHAPTER

6

Cuinn walked through the door of his workroom and shut it behind him. He leaned against it, limbs heavy with fatigue. The idea of taking another Adherent made him feel sick to his stomach. His last experience had ended in horror, grief, and shame, and he couldn't face that again.

After the conversation he'd had with Fin, Cuinn's energy was unstable, and the room felt too dark. He pulled the armchair to the windows, which he opened as wide as they would go. The light of the moon relaxed him, and he added some candles to supplement its gentle light.

He pushed hair away from his face and sat in the worn and comfortable armchair. He leaned back and tilted his head towards the sky. With few artificial light sources such as street lamps or cars, there was little light pollution and it was easy to see the stars.

Ah, Tierra. He felt a stab of guilt. One of Fintan's best placed blows had been a claim that Tierra was lonely. Tierra was loving and sociable, and Cuinn had thought that with himself, Adam, and visits to and from her best friend Cara, who lived on an island off the west coast of British Columbia, Tierra had enough interaction to nurture her. And she seemed to enjoy looking after Adam's Husky, Argus, when Adam travelled to a country where foreign dogs weren't welcome.

But Fintan had told him the last time Tierra had seen Cara had been months ago. Adam seemed to be away more than usual at the moment, taking Argus with him, and Cuinn was locked in his rooms more often than not.

Tierra herself had never mentioned feeling lonely, though she wouldn't. She was kind, good-hearted, and meant the world to him. She was the sister he'd never had, and since his mother had died long ago, had been the main woman in his life for decades. Since ... the last one. Sophea.

His hand worried at the arm of the chair, at a worn patch his nervous gesture had created over years. The feel of the material under the pads of his fingers comforted him. Cuinn's gift sometimes meant he was ungrounded, and reconnecting with the environment around him brought him back to the physical world.

His energies also meant he spent a lot of time in his head. He blew out a breath, and closed his eyes.

Perhaps the girl wouldn't be too useless, and could help him. Dreamwalking and prophecy work was a critical part of mind training—it might be that he had to train her in a rather unusual order, but he could work it out.

He fell asleep in the chair minutes later, halfway through rearranging the typical Ajna training in his mind to suit his new purpose. But at the back of his mind, one thought kept intruding.

His world was about to change again.

CHAPTER

7

Blaize arrived at her family's cluster of traditional-style bungalows and parked underneath her own wooden-framed raised house. Instead of going inside, she walked across the hard-packed earth to Nixie's bungalow and shouted her name.

As Blaize started up the stairs, Nixie appeared on her balcony, wiping her hands on a towel. "Hey! How'd it go?"

Nixie's dominant energy was Svadisthana, or water, the energy of fantasy and imagination—and sexuality. Combined with her auxiliary energy of Vishudha, or ether, the energy of communication and creativity, it meant that Nixie tended towards sexy, a little spacey, and loved to chat.

A year or so younger than Blaize, Fai's daughter, Nixie had the petite frame, dark hair and eyes of many Thai women, combined with her father's Gaelic paler skin. Her looks were striking, and many men—and sometimes women—fell over themselves to talk to her.

Blaize, who saw Nixie as a sister, didn't notice her sexuality. In their teenage years, there'd been a time when Blaize had been unsure why the boys in their class flocked to Nixie, but seemed scared of Blaize. Nowadays, Blaize had her own share of attention, and just found men's regard amusing.

Blaize reached the top of the stairs and held out her arms to Nixie for a hug. "I passed! I'm officially a Practitioner of the Manipura Guild!"

She took Nixie in her arms and spun her light frame around.

"I knew you'd do it." As Nixie's feet touched the floor again, she stepped back and wrinkled her nose. "Put you through your paces did they? You need a shower."

"I haven't slept or eaten for nearly two days. A shower's on my list, but I want some food first. I feel too buzzed to sleep."

"Do you want a fruit shake? Or I could put a fruit salad together? You don't want to eat too much too quickly after a fast."

"A fruit salad would be great, thanks." Blaize eyed the light blue hammock hanging in the corner of the balcony. "Mind if I hang out here?"

"Of course. But you have to tell me all about it as you do—and don't fall asleep." Nixie went into the kitchen and asked over her shoulder, "Did Mom manage to keep a straight face?"

Blaize settled into the hammock. "Pretty much. She didn't change her expression even when I was almost poisoned to death."

"What?" Nixie ran back onto the balcony, a mango in one hand and a knife in the other.

Blaize laughed. "I'm fine. Now, anyway. It was harder than I thought it would be. I don't know what they used, but it was difficult to dig it all out of my system. I managed it, but it was closer than I would have liked."

"I don't know how Mom stayed impassive through that." Nixie shook her head.

"I don't think she'd have let me die ..." Blaize's brow wrinkled, "but it doesn't matter anyway. It's done."

Blaize rocked herself in the hammock, one foot out and balanced on the floor to give her a little momentum. She filled Nixie in on all the details while she worked her way through two bowls of fruit salad.

An hour or so later, when Blaize's eyes felt heavy and she and Nixie had hashed through every detail of the trial, Blaize heard the soft crunch of tires on sand. The car's headlights raked the balcony as it parked under a larger house nearby.

"Mom's back. Are you going to talk to her? It doesn't look as if she has anyone with her. She must have dropped the others off at their hotel after supper."

"I should probably have a shower before I speak to her."

Nixie shook her head vigorously, her silky black hair flying around her face. "Don't be silly! She's your Aunt as well as your Maven. She'll want to talk to you straight away to discuss how it went."

"And give me some feedback no doubt." Blaize winced. She loved her Aunt, but Fai didn't make any allowances in their Maven-Adherent relationship for their family connection.

"Off you go. Pop back later if you feel like it." Nixie poked Blaize in the side.

Blaize rolled out of the hammock and stretched. "Okay. I'll see how I feel once I've had a chat with her. I'm pretty desperate for a shower and some sleep."

Nixie put her hand out to squeeze Blaize's, but Blaize pulled her into another hug. Usually, Nixie was the demonstrative one. This time, Blaize was more than willing to share her happiness.

Blaize walked to the main house and caught sight of herself in the car's windows. She winced at her tangled hair and the crumpled clothes that had been stored in the scooter's seat compartment. But Nixie was right, Fai would want to see her as soon as possible. And Blaize wanted to see Fai and thank her again for the long years of training that had finally paid off.

Blaize rang the cowbell that served as a doorbell. Its resonant sound vibrated through her, and she took a deep breath, still a little spaced from the last couple of days.

When the door opened, Marius stood before her. He smiled and took her in strong arms. As he hugged her tight, he said, "Blaize, love, congratulations. I knew you could do it. Not an easy crowd to impress but you managed it."

He squeezed her again before he let her go.

A big man compared to Fai's slight build, he had several inches on Blaize, who at five feet ten inches wasn't small for a woman. He had a broad chest, with an imposing bulk when he chose to wield it that way. Which he rarely did. He was one of the kindest men Blaize had ever known—a man who had acted as a father to her since her own had died when she was nine.

She realised she was still standing there. "Sorry, Marius. I'm exhausted. I was miles away. Thank you."

He grinned and nodded. "After my first Chakra trial, I slept for two days straight. Of course, you're shattered—but I'm so glad you came over. Fai and I need to talk to you."

Blaize wasn't too tired to catch the seriousness in his tone. "What's the matter? Is everything alright?"

She hoped there wasn't a problem. She didn't have the energy for an important discussion.

"Everything's fine. Come through to the living room."

They moved into a spacious room on the right, with big open windows that let in the cool night air. Cushions were scattered across the floor, with low tables next to them. Fai sat near one of the windows but rose to her feet when they came in. She put her hands on Blaize's shoulders and looked into her eyes, examining her deeply. Blaize shuffled, and Fai sighed and opened her arms. Blaize stepped into them and put her arms around her aunt.

When she looked up at Blaize, tears shimmered in the corners of Fai's eyes.

Blaize's eyes widened. "Aunt Fai, what's the matter? I'm fine, I made it; you should be happy."

She put her hand up to the other woman's cheek and wiped away a tear.

Fai nodded. "Blaize, darling, I'm so proud of you."

Blaize's throat tightened. *Huh.* She wasn't sure she'd ever heard Fai say that before. Blaize drew away, and said, "Let me get you some water."

Marius, who'd watched till now in silence, shook his head. "Sit down, both of you. There are things to discuss. I'll get the water."

Blaize frowned. Something was going on. Fai returned to her seat and beckoned Blaize to follow. Blaize sank down onto a soft, flat floor cushion from India. On the walls were Chinese and Thai wall hangings, their only common ground bright colours and strong prints. As most energetics did, Fai and Marius had moved around in their long years together, and their house was a showcase of the best of all their travels.

What does Fai need to tell me? A small spike of anxiety hit Blaize, chasing away some of the grey fog in her brain.

"You did well," Fai said. "You worried me with the poison, but your finesse with the energy on the first task was beautiful."

"Thank you, Aunt Fai." Blaize's chest loosened.

"But your drive and competitive nature was noted by the judges. You must keep your ambition and anger under control. Your power is too strong to be combined with any kind of aggression. Huo was able to get under your skin too easily." Her voice was gentle, but the rebuke still stang.

"It's under control. I just wanted to pass the trial and make you proud."

Fai pursed her lips as Marius came back into the room with a jug of water and some glasses. He put them down on the table before he levered his body next to Fai. He leaned against the wall next to the window and put his arm around his wife. Her posture didn't change, but she inclined her head towards him a fraction.

"Fai, Blaize knows to be careful with her power—you trained her, after all. And her power can only help her in her journey," Marius said.

Blaize looked at him. "What journey?"

His face was innocent. "Your journey through life."

She narrowed her eyes. The spike of anxiety grew. There was no tiredness now. "What do you want to talk to me about?"

45

"Your Ajna Chakra training," said Fai.

Blaize frowned. *That has to be a joke.* She kept her tone light. "It's a bit soon for that isn't it? I've just passed Manipura."

Fai and Marius exchanged a glance. *Not a joke.* Blaize was confused now, as well as anxious. Energetics always had a break between their dominant and auxiliary training. She'd been looking forward to spending time on the island, and then working as a Warrior, capturing Rogues.

"You can have a month off to relax and recharge," Fai said. "But we want you to continue with your training soon."

"A month? After five years of training? You want me to have a month off and then spend another five years training? I want—I need—more." Blaize's voice rose. She took a breath and closed her eyes. "Maybe this isn't a good time to talk about it. I'm really tired."

She could barely think straight. She wouldn't win an argument with Fai feeling like this.

"The decision is made." Again that soft tone, with undertones of steel. "You're a strong energetic, and your control is good, as you've shown in the last twenty-four hours. But you're still ruled by the emotions of Manipura—and yet you have access to Ajna. When you harness the power of your mind, you could be one of the greatest leaders we've ever seen. Perhaps even a Circle member one day."

Blaize blinked. "There's no rush for that. Grandmother's tough. She won't be going anywhere for years."

"Child, Grandmother is one of the older energetics. She's tired and ready to step back from her leadership role. There's no rush— for her, another ten, twenty, thirty years is nothing, but we need to push you along more quickly than we discussed when you were young. You are her chosen successor, and the family supports that choice—but only if you have the best possible grip on your power. Until now you have focused on your dominant Chakra, Manipura. Your personality and attitudes are shaped by this. You are passionate, vibrant, and powerful. But," she held up a hand to forestall any comment from Blaize, "you can also be quick to anger, volatile, stubborn, and you love to have the last word."

Blaize scowled, and then tried to wipe the scowl off her face as she registered the content of Fai's words. *Damn. Boxed in.*

"I've loved training with you, Aunt Fai. Well, mostly," she corrected herself and her lips quirked up. "I've learned so much from you. And I'm proud to be an energetic, a member of our family, and now a Practitioner member of Manipura Guild. But I wanted some time to do other things. To be out there, using the powers I've developed, without someone looking over my shoulder all the time."

Fai's face was impassive, Marius's sympathetic. Neither looked as though Blaize's arguments were changing their minds. She tried again.

"To go from you to another Maven means going from one person being responsible for me to another. Plus, who would it be?" She struggled to keep her voice even given what Fai had said to prompt it, but with those last words it rose and cracked a little. "It's not as if there are loads of Ajna Mavens. It's got to be a very short list. And none of them are based on the island, or even in Thailand. ... Are you sending me away?"

"Of course we're not sending you away, Blaize, my darling. But if you'd worked in the human world again, or as a Warrior, you would have left us," Marius said.

"I could have come back whenever I liked. If training for Ajna's anything like Manipura, I'll be too busy to come back for a while, won't I?" The idea hurt. The island was her home. And after so many years of intensive training, she'd looked forward to time to relax. Time to recharge.

Fai nodded.

"So it's like sending me away."

"A very old, good friend of mine has offered to train you," Marius said.

Fai seemed to wince at this, but Blaize wasn't sure why. Blaize's growing sense of confusion told her there was still more going on here than she was being told, but she didn't have the energy to think of the right questions to puzzle it out.

"His name is Cuinn. You met him when you were young. You may not remember. I grew up with him in Ireland when I was a young man. We had some good times together, he and I, and Fintan later on."

Fintan, she knew—first as an honorary Uncle, and then when she'd been training for her Manipura—as a colleague with whom she'd been on several Rogue runs. But she'd never heard of this other man.

"Quinn? With a Q?"

"It's spelled with a C. He was born in Ireland, same as me, a couple of hundred years ago," said Marius. "That's how we know each other."

"If you were so close, how come he hasn't visited for a decade?" demanded Blaize.

"He had some challenges in his personal life about fifty years ago, and he hasn't been very sociable since then. He's a powerful Ajna-Muladhara mix. He could have been Guild Leader if he'd wanted, and he's been a Master for many decades. He's been Maven to several energetics."

Blaize's lips flattened. He didn't sound like much fun. Powerful but uninterested in people. He was probably arrogant to boot. "But he's feeling sociable again now?"

"Something like that." Marius gave a slight cough. "He lives with his cousins, Tierra and Adam, a couple of hours outside Vancouver, Canada. Adam's not there much of the time, as he travels with his job, but Tierra keeps house and makes it a home. She's wonderful, Muladhara-Anahata, and loves to look after people. I think the two of you will get on."

Blaize was less sure. She was an action-taker. The things she enjoyed most in life were physical—sports, martial arts. She loved setting goals and challenges. She didn't think that she'd have much in common with a homebody like that.

"So it's already been decided? And everyone knows but me?" Blaize struggled to hide her hurt feelings and got to her feet.

"Blaize. We're trying to give you the best possible chance to develop your energies, and evolve and grow to be a truly great energetic. To fulfill your potential as a leader. You'll be part of safeguarding the future of our race, and you owe it to yourself as well as everyone else to take every opportunity to harness your powers." Fai spoke from the floor, but Marius got up as Blaize had. He leaned down and stroked a hand over Fai's dark hair as he stood beside her still, seated form.

"And I will ... but I thought I had more time," Blaize said. "More time to spend growing in other areas before I committed to the intensity of training again." She wasn't going to win this argument. She saw no cracks in either Fai's determination, or more unusually, in Marius's. Usually, she was able to persuade Marius to her point of view, but he appeared just as committed to this future as Fai.

"Go back to your bungalow, take a shower, and get some rest." Marius moved over to her and took her hand. "Have you eaten anything yet?"

"Some fruit, with Nixie. Wait. Does Nixie know?"

Marius shook his head. "No. Do you want to tell her, or do you want us to tell her while you're sleeping?"

Blaize closed her eyes briefly. "You can tell her. I'll speak to her when I wake up. I'm so tired."

She got to her feet and headed out of the door, too tired for further conversation. *More training. Another Maven.* Her throat ached, and her eyes were damp. If she stayed in the room with her Aunt and Uncle, she might cry.

She really hated to cry.

Cuinn came to, cold and stiff, on the floor of his workroom. He'd decided to try a quick dreamwalk, and had lain on his ritual mat, and sunk into the light trance that enabled him to go to the etheric plane.

He'd been out all night.

His body cramping, he sat up and stretched out to grab the nearest paper and pencil. He needed to capture every possible detail of what he'd discovered.

As always, the details were sketchy. In previous dreamwalks he'd seen various shadowy figures, and he wasn't sure if they were humans or energetics.

They were accompanied by a sense of foreboding, of something off, something beautiful and good perverted for illicit ends. This dreamwalk had been the same as all the others—the presences were taunting him as he stood in front of the race of energetics, knowing he was all that stood between this evil and his race, his people.

As before, there were five male energetics to his right, and six female energetics to his left. He usually couldn't make out much about any of them apart from their genders, and some kind of coloured bracelets on each wrist—the right wrist for men, the left for women.

But in this dreamwalk he'd gathered some new details.

One of the females had stepped forward in front of the other energetics—and in front of him. She'd raised a sword of fire, and run towards the shadowy figures. Watching, he hadn't been able to move, shout, or do anything to stop her from sacrificing herself. And it had been agony to watch. Her energies shone, but the figures soon surrounded her, and their darkness absorbed her light like blotting paper.

He came out of the trance with a queasy feeling in his stomach, and a deep sense of unease. The female figure was important, as were the line of females and males he stood with in the dream in front of those shadowy figures. And he also had a role. He just didn't know how, or against what. The frustration made him feel scratchy and irritable.

He sighed, noted the date and time, and put the pencil and paper down. He would file it with the others later.

CHAPTER

8

"Did Fai talk to you?"

Nixie bit her lip. Her eyes welled up and tears overflowed as she sank into a cross-legged position next to the hammock where Blaize was lying, and rested her head on Blaize's leg.

Blaize had slipped home the night before without calling on Nixie, but Nixie had shown up on Blaize's balcony soon after she was up and about.

Blaize's anger and upset of the night before had turned into sadness and resignation this morning. She'd go to Vancouver. And if she was honest with herself, a part of her loved the idea that she would get to push on with her training this fast. Most energetics would need a year or more between trainings to let one side of themselves settle before they started working with the next. Fai must be very confident of her abilities to ask her to start training in her auxiliary this quickly. But Blaize had been looking forward to more of a break from learning, and time to actually use her abilities as a Warrior.

"I'm the one going, Nix, not you." Blaize bent and touched Nixie's cheek. "It'll be fine. We'll call; you'll visit."

Nixie nodded. "I know. But … I'll miss you."

"You managed when we were at university, and then when I lived in Singapore and you were doing your Chakra training."

Nixie had taken a different path. She had started as an Adherent directly after leaving university at twenty-one, so she'd completed her training in her dominant Chakra, Svadisthana, the water element, a while ago. She'd decided to take a break before starting her next Chakra training—just as Blaize had intended to do.

"Yeah, but it's been a good few years since we've both been back here and able to hang out together. I like it. Friends and family close by." Tears leaked onto Blaize's leg. As a water element, Nixie had a tendency to express herself with tears—happy and sad—a lot more frequently than Blaize, but Blaize was used to it, and just ran a hand over Nixie's glossy hair.

"How do you feel?" Nixie said.

Blaize lay back and looked up at the sky. "Like I'm not just tired today, but tired more generally. The Manipura training was tough, and I so wanted to do well. I feel like I did, but I also made mistakes. I'd have liked a break before I start studying something new."

She paused, looking out at the dense green jungle at the edges of the large plot their houses stood on.

"I love it here too. I love you, Fai, Marius, the people we know, our friends. The energetics community here and the humans. I love the pace of life, being able to go out trekking in the jungle or lie on the beach. Singapore was so built up, so many people, so many buildings, vehicles. I don't want to go back to a place where there are that many people."

"Cuinn doesn't live in a busy place; he practically lives out in the wilderness, way outside Vancouver towards the Rockies. It's pretty beautiful, but the sea is hours away." Nixie shivered in mock disgust.

Great. He lives in some country backwater. Not much chance of using her Warrior training, or helping out on Rogue runs there.

"You know him?"

"Yeah. He's a Professor at Vancouver University in the human world, and super smart. Some kind of brain science, which helps with his energetic work around the mind. I guess all Ajnas are pretty clever—apart from you, of course."

Blaize smacked Nixie gently on the top of her head.

"Ouch. Yeah, bright, a thinker. He does a lot of dreamwalks and prophecy work for the Major and the Minor Circle. He's maybe two hundred? Two twenty? He grew up with Dad. Not married or anything though. Which is not because of what he looks like—he's pretty hot." Nixie pretended to swoon. "And Maven-Adherent pairings often become romantic; it's part of working closely with someone for so long."

"Not a factor. You know my views on relationships."

"Well, it doesn't hurt if the face you have to look at every day is attractive, right? And anyway, you don't have to marry him, just, you know, have a little fun."

Blaize rolled her eyes but smiled. "Do you ever think about anything apart from sex?"

"Love?"

The energy of Nixie's two Chakras meant she almost always had a boyfriend. And Nixie was quite happy to audition men for the part for as long as was needed, though she never settled for long, always looking for 'the one.' Blaize guessed Nixie's parents also influenced her view, as they were still a solid partnership after over a hundred years together.

Blaize had a direct approach to sex, like most Manipura energetics, but she didn't romanticise it. She didn't see the need. She'd seen what love could do, and it wasn't always hearts and flowers. She wasn't interested in a relationship.

"What's he like as a person?"

"Well … he can be a bit … stern. Focused. But because of his earth auxiliary he's very grounded, which makes a good contrast for his Ajna. Practical. Disciplined. Works hard."

"Hmmmm." Blaize wrinkled her nose. "Doesn't sound much fun."

Nixie shrugged. "He's fairly senior in the Ajna Guild, so should be a good teacher at least."

Just what I need. A strict, joyless Professor that I'll be stuck with for the next few years. Yay.

She shook her head and turned the conversation away from her departure. There was time enough for that.

Indigo lay on her mat and stared up at the water-damaged ceiling.

The prophecy was in motion. Blaize and Cuinn would meet soon. And Indigo would get her chance to repay her Maven for his teachings and support.

There was little furniture in the dark and dingy bedroom, and yet although she had the whole house to herself, the meagre possessions she'd brought with her from Vancouver were all contained in this room. She travelled light.

She got to her feet and took her cell phone out of her bag. She switched it on and dialled his number. The man she'd been with as an Adherent and beyond.

She walked to the window and looked out while she waited for him to answer. The property was at the end of a lane, a twenty-minute drive from Merrow. There would be no one to interfere when she had Blaize here.

A click at the end of the line. "Indigo."

"Another piece of prophecy is confirmed. She's coming. He's agreed," she said.

"Get a job in town. Get more information on Cuinn and the set up at their house. Keep seeking more of the prophecy." The man's warm tones were deceptive. Underneath the velvet, there was a dark brutality in the voice that expected her instant obedience.

"And she's mine?" Indigo tried to keep the need out of her voice.

The silence echoed down the line, and Indigo shifted, pressing her palm against the window. The cold bled into her bones.

"I'm sorry," she said.

She was left with silence as he hung up.

She felt jittery, wired. She strode over to the door and threw it open. She ran down the creaking stairs and went out the old house's back door without pausing to grab a jacket. She was burning up, her energy keeping her warm. Too warm.

She went to the back of the overgrown garden where she'd set up a rough area for energy practice and stood in the centre of the charred circle. She took a deep breath. She pulled energy and forged the hottest fire she could between her hands. She put all her hate and shame into the flames. Then she spun and threw the burning sphere as fast as she could at the metal target fifty yards away. Sparks flew as the fire engulfed the metal, and it glowed a dark, angry red.

Her body trembled like an addict's. She panted and her sides heaved as she sucked in deep breaths. She needed more energy, and these days, she struggled to draw on the ether without help. The impetuous burst had tired her out. The chill damp of the spring morning drained the heat from her, and the trembles in her limbs intensified. She trudged back towards the house.

She needed to conserve her energy, not waste it. Her Maven had promised her Blaize, which would solve a lot of Indigo's problems, but only if she was able to catch her, physically or energetically. If Indigo wasted her chance, he wouldn't forgive her. And he was unlikely to give her another opportunity. He'd punish her, or watch her suffer withdrawal symptoms.

Either of which could kill her.

CHAPTER

9

Five weeks after her Manipura trial Blaize found herself on a plane.

Time spent meditating in the energetics' temple had helped her process her feelings of being abandoned, or sent away, by her family. Exploring and examining them despite the 'ouch' feelings they brought her, she was able to realise that she had total confidence in Fai and Marius's love for her, and their attempts to do the right thing.

Now, on her way to her next Maven, she didn't feel exactly enthusiastic, but she managed acceptance. Her journey gave her more time to centre herself, with several flights and a bus that took her from the hustle and bustle of Vancouver airport to a bus station at the edge of a small town.

She hadn't spoken to Cuinn directly yet—they'd emailed a couple of times before Cuinn had directed her to Tierra, who'd helped Blaize with practicalities. Tierra had been friendly, and her emails managed a lively and welcoming tone.

Cuinn on the other hand ... he was a bit of a mystery. His communication was terse, signed 'C,' with no niceties, and always focused on the factual information. There were no questions about herself, which Blaize didn't mind. Well, OK, she did mind a bit, but then he hadn't responded to her probes about him either.

Maybe it was a guy thing. She'd been used to working with her aunt, a woman and a family member, on her dominant Chakra, and Blaize wasn't sure if working with a male Maven would be different. Or whether she would like it.

She sighed as she got down off the bus and stretched out the kinks, trying to shake off a sense of apprehension. She reminded herself of her promise to be positive—after all, she could be here for years.

She looked around the deserted bus station. A lone woman stood waiting at the exit gate, reading from a tablet. Given that no one else was in sight, Blaize assumed she must be Tierra. *Cuinn's delegated again.*

Cuinn certainly gave a good impression of someone uninterested in her. How would that work when he was her Maven? The bonding ritual would create a link between them that would be long-lasting. Perhaps he was giving her space until then, when there would be a lot less choice about the two of them interacting.

She walked to the petite, curvy woman, who looked up and smiled. She radiated an earthy femininity—warm and natural. Blaize faltered, intimidated by her despite the fact that Blaize could probably take her out in seconds. Blaize was good with violence. She was less good with unconditional acceptance.

Tierra was quick to close the gap between them, and Blaize's hands were already half-raised in a defensive gesture before Tierra had thrown her arms around her. Tierra was a good few inches shorter than Blaize, with a soft, long skirt the colour of pine needles, and a fitted white sweater.

Tierra stepped back and met Blaize's gaze with dark-chocolate coloured eyes.

"Pleased to meet you! I'm Tierra. Of course I am, who else would I be? It's so exciting you're here! Your boxes have already arrived;

I've put them in your cottage. You'll love it; it has privacy but is close enough to the main house that you can pop over whenever you need. And for meals! It will be great to have someone else to cook for. I just love cooking."

Blaize let the words stream over her, and considered interrupting but decided there was no need. Tierra kept up her chatter all the way to the car, and for most of the half-hour journey back to the house. She peppered Blaize with questions, but rarely gave her the opportunity to answer them, which was fine with the weary Blaize. Despite that, Tierra was extremely likeable, a nurturing and agreeable presence.

Eventually Tierra said, "Almost there. It's spring now—a few weeks ago we still had snow, but it's starting to warm up. I guess still a lot colder than you're used to."

Blaize nodded. She was wrapped up warm—a lot more warmly than Tierra, who'd thrown her jacket and scarf into the back of the car once they got in. Blaize had taken her scarf off, and put it on her lap, tucking her hands snugly into it, but was still wearing her jacket, and even so was cold enough to consider using a little energy to warm herself up.

They pulled off the main street onto a route that was little more than a dirt track. Setting aside the vegetation and the weather, it was the kind of road Blaize was at home with, the kind she used to speed along on the island on her scooter.

The rough road continued for a couple of miles. They crested the gently rolling terrain, which revealed an elegant slate-and-stone house that fit into the green bowl of the landscape as if it had grown there.

Blaize stared. She'd never seen anything like it.

Tierra laughed. "Yeah, that view used to get me like that too. Still does sometimes, especially if I've been away. Welcome to Cathair Cuinn. Cuinn designed most of it himself, using Irish stone and working with the architect. And when Adam, that's my brother, and I moved in later, Cuinn had additions built for us. Plus, of course, there're a few cottages, bungalows, in the grounds for visitors. You'll have one of those for privacy."

Tierra spoke so quickly it was hard for Blaize to keep up after what felt like weeks of travelling. She was jet-lagged and dropping with fatigue. She focused on one thing. "What does the name mean?"

Tierra laughed. "It's a joke. Cathair means castle in Gaelic. Fintan—he's a friend of ours, I think you know him—named it as a joke when Cuinn had it built, and it stuck."

They parked on the drive, and got out of the car, and Tierra helped Blaize bring her luggage in. Blaize thought Tierra might ring the bell to bring Blaize's new Maven down, but Tierra unlocked the sturdy wooden door instead and pushed it open, gesturing with her head for Blaize to come on in, as her arms were full of Blaize's things.

Blaize followed Tierra through the door into an imposing hallway. A large wooden staircase led up to the left, and she counted at least seven different doors off the hallway.

Tierra put Blaize's belongings in the hall.

"You'll be in Garden Cottage. Your boxes are already there, but let's get you some food first, then you can settle in and sleep." Tierra looked at her watch. "If you can give it another hour or so, then you should sleep through the night and reset your internal clock."

Blaize nodded. She was almost too tired to sleep, and she wasn't sure she wanted to eat anything. She followed Tierra through a corridor to a huge room split into a kitchen and an eating area. The latter had a big farmhouse-style table and chairs, and huge windows looking out onto the lawn.

"This is the kitchen. We eat most of our informal meals in here. We only eat in the dining room when we have guests."

Tierra pulled out a chair and steered Blaize into it. Blaize's head was fuzzy, and she heard Tierra's words without really taking them in. Tierra talked as she poured Blaize water, and then brought over fresh bread, cheese, butter and some ripe tomatoes to put together a snack.

Blaize tried to nod and smile in the right places, but she knew she was being unresponsive. She drank the water, which helped wake her up a little, and then her stomach growled, telling her she was hungrier than she thought. She murmured a quiet "thank you" as Tierra pushed the food towards her, and ate.

It didn't take her long to demolish the sandwich. "That was amazing, thanks. I will have another glass of water, if that's okay. I think I got a bit dehydrated on the plane."

"Of course." Tierra jumped up, took Blaize's glass, and refilled it. "I'll take you to the cottage now, and you can get some sleep."

Blaize frowned. "What about Cuinn? Is he here? I'd like to meet him."

Tierra looked away, her usually constant smile wavering for a second. "He had to go away for some Circle business. He'll be back in the next couple of days. Sorry, I'm sure he wanted to see you. He gets called away sometimes. In the meantime you can hang out with me and get settled. Come on. Let's take you over."

Blaize felt a stab of disappointment. She hadn't even met the man yet, and he was annoying her.

Tierra cleared the table while Blaize fetched her luggage from the hall. Tierra led her to a back door, and they headed into the gardens.

The weather was sharp, cold and biting. Blaize was glad of the token warmth from the scarf she'd thrown back on. They walked a short way before a small cottage appeared out of the falling dusk. It was next to the woods, but the other three sides looked out onto the main house and the view respectively. Not that there was much of a view at this time of night, but she could see the lights of the big house from here, which was comforting in this foreign place.

Tierra pushed open the door and tugged in Blaize's big suitcase. Blaize trailed in behind her, laden with everything else. The cottage had a small hallway, and Blaize was surprised to see that it was a proper self-contained house. It had one large room downstairs, with a toasty looking fire—lit and smouldering, the fire guard up—a comfy sofa, and a table with a couple of chairs. The front window even had a window seat, which Blaize immediately fell in love with.

At the back of the big room was a galley kitchen. A microwave, a small oven, a hob with two rings, and a tiny fridge.

Tierra went ahead of her up the steep stairs. The doors of the two rooms on the first floor were directly off the stairs, opposite each other with barely a square yard between them.

Tierra plumped up the cushions on the bed, brushing imaginary fluff off the duvet.

"It's small but it's cosy, and it means you can have privacy when you need it. But I hope you'll join us for meals whenever you like— I'm so excited to have someone else here to chat to and spend time with." Her tone was a little wistful.

Is she lonely? Tierra was a gentle, warm person, with a curvy but strong body—she'd managed to lift Blaize's suitcase after all. Earth energetics needed people around them to nurture and look after. "Does Cuinn often go away?"

"Sometimes. He's been here a lot more recently. He's a good man. But he gets rather caught up. And his work is important."

Blaize nodded. She built a picture of Cuinn in her mind. Stern, cold and aloof, indifferent to his cousin's problems. And most probably indifferent to Blaize as well. After all, he wasn't here to meet her, so she couldn't be that big a priority for him. Thank Source for Tierra.

Cuinn was in Athens, sitting in front of Minh, the head of Cuinn's Minor Guild, Ajna-Muladhara Guild, and two of the other Ajna Minor Guild Leaders.

These energetics together were highly skilled in understanding and predicting prophecies, these were the farseers of Ajna: Past, Present and Future.

Three of the most powerful energetics alive.

"Minh, I'm concerned," Cuinn said. "These prophecies feel unlike any I've come across before. They have a sick, twisted quality to them. There's danger coming for all of us, and I can't tell what it is."

Minh's dark eyes appraised him. "At the moment you are the only one receiving such prophecies, and you know we have our eyes open in many areas. We have spoken to all the strong Ajna dreamwalkers, and nothing has struck us as unusual. We three, also, have tried specific dreamwalks to see if we can pick up any of the strands of the prophecy. We have found nothing that matches what you say you have seen."

Cuinn was frustrated. He and Minh had a difficult relationship because Minh couldn't understand why anyone with Cuinn's power—which both of them suspected was stronger than Minh's—wouldn't want to be Guild Leader. Cuinn had the power, but no desire. It made for an uneasy tension between them, and Cuinn tended to avoid him if he could. But this prophecy was too important to involve personal issues. He needed to make Minh understand. Believe.

"It's not a full prophecy at the moment, not while I can barely put words to half of it. But it is a warning of some kind." Cuinn leaned forward in his chair.

"Continue your dreamwalks, your research into the area. See if you can link what you've seen to anything we know. Take more books from the library." There was a hint of impatience in Minh's tone. "When do you start working with Marius's girl? I heard she did well in her Manipura trial."

He leaned back in a wide, high-backed chair, and tapped his fingers on the formal wooden table they sat around.

"She'll be there when I get back. Although I don't really have time for it. I'll start her on theory first, and reading, while I carry on with this task." Cuinn shrugged.

Damanea, the Ajna leader representing the future, whose gaze had been turned inwards until this point, appeared to refocus on the others in the room, and shook her head. Her eyes met Cuinn's with a surprising intensity. "Blaize Blackfire's destiny is bound up with yours, Cuinn. This I have seen. You must train her quickly. Troubles come before we ask for them. Have you looked into her future?"

Cuinn shifted in his chair. "I tried, but it's hazy, blurry. I thought that might be because she wouldn't stay long with me ..."

He felt a trickle of power in the room, like static along his arms, where it raised the hairs to attention.

"You're too close to her to see," Damanea continued, her voice low and forceful. "And there are many possibilities. But in all of those that turn out well, you need her. She is the female Warrior. You are the male Sage. You will also need the Protector, Creator, Healer, and Communicator. Male and Female elements. You have seen the troubles coming, and you are correct. They are not what they seem. Six smaller challenges will come, and be overcome, before the final battle is faced. The success of the small challenges will determine the last. Balance and harmony may depend on all."

She closed her eyes and bowed her head for a moment, taking a breath. "Work wisely and well with Blaize, Cuinn. You must lead, connect, unite."

Cuinn felt prickles of ice down his spine, and he shivered. He hadn't been involved personally in many others' prophecies. He'd seen his own, which had had implications for others, and sometimes implications for himself. But for him to be mentioned in this way in a prophecy—for that's clearly what this was—by Damanea, of all people, was disturbing.

Minh raised his eyebrows. "This is a personal prophecy, Cuinn. We will scribe it for you and you can review it to see if any of the elements resonate with your own dreamwalks and prophecies. Perhaps there is something to your own dreamwalks after all. For now we support you taking the girl as an Adherent. But be careful. You must provide stability. An anchor to her pride. Come to us again if you think you have more dreams of note. We will discuss this further between ourselves."

Minh stood up, as did Damanea.

Kenji, the past farseer rose more slowly. "Your history is weighing you down. It is a millstone around your neck. Be confident now that you have come through that experience wisely. There is no need for the past to be repeated in the future."

CHAPTER

10

Cuinn arrived home after a long night of travelling and very little sleep. He'd stocked up on coffee at the airport, knowing he would drive home tired. When he arrived at Cathair Cuinn, he wanted nothing more than a shower and bed. But before he could head upstairs to his rooms, Tierra appeared from the direction of the kitchen. She gave him a warm hug, then took his hand and led him back to the kitchen. "You need food. Sit there, and I'll get you something. Toast okay?"

Cuinn nodded and sat on one of the stools at the breakfast bar. There was an easy silence between them for a couple of minutes before Tierra asked sympathetically, "How'd it go?"

"It's been worse, and it's been better." Cuinn's tone was bleak, and he glanced over at Tierra's back, hesitating before telling her. "They gave me a prophecy. About me."

"What?" Tierra turned with a mug dangling from one hand.

"I know, I know. It didn't make much sense, but it was official. They want me to see if I can reference it with any of my prophecies. The small but nasty set of puzzle pieces I'm unable to work out."

"You'll figure it out." She put a plate and a mug of tea in front of him and went to tidy up. "And Blaize arrived yesterday, so you'll have some help. She seems smart."

"I tried to get rid of her again with Minh and the others." He spoke around a mouthful of toast. "It's the last thing I need right now. I'm exhausted and I'm not in the right space for teaching, but even the farseers seem to think it's important I take her. I don't want to risk it again, but I don't have any choice. I owe Marius for his help with the Sophea situation. And the worst of it is he thinks it's for my own good. They have no idea what we're messing with."

She coughed but he ignored her, ploughing on, "It's such a bad idea. For all I know she's not even capable of using Ajna energies anyway. What a waste of time."

"Cuinn. Please." She motioned urgently to something behind him.

He swivelled in his seat.

Blaize stood in the doorway, mouth open.

None of them spoke.

An eternity of seconds of tense stand-off passed as their eyes—his appalled, hers mortified—connected across the cheery kitchen.

Blaize shook her head, colour in her cheeks, pivoted on her heel and left the kitchen.

Cuinn put his head in his hands.

"Shit."

Blaize didn't quite run back to her cottage, but it was close.

Her brain felt muddled from jet lag and tiredness, but her cheeks burned. *How dare he?*

She reached her front door, threw it open and headed up the stairs in a few bounds. She pulled her case out from under the bed where she'd stashed it neatly just hours ago, and gathered her clothes, scooping them from drawers and dragging them off hangers. She heaped them into the case, dumping socks, underwear, pants, dresses, and shirts in together. Her eyes darted around the room, trying to remember everything she had tidied away into cupboards and drawers earlier, but she couldn't focus.

The noise as the front door opened and shut made her screw her eyes closed and wince. She pressed her hands to her cheeks to cool them down, and shook her head, trying to clear it.

Measured footsteps sounded on the stairs. Her face hot and her pulse hammering, she stepped from her bedroom door across the square yard of hall at the top of the staircase to grab more of her stuff from the bathroom. Her throat felt thick and it was hard to swallow.

She gathered her possessions from the bathroom and spun back around to the door. Exiting, she flew across the narrow space at the top of the stairs back to the bedroom, her arms full.

And slammed into a wall.

She had a split second to see that she'd run directly into Cuinn's back as he faced into the bedroom, his tall frame taking up most of the small space between the rooms, and then, thrown off balance, she toppled backwards and down the stairs.

The shampoo, soap, toothbrush, and everything else she was carrying fell as she threw her arms out to catch herself. Her stomach hitched in a burst of adrenaline as she pitched into empty space, managing only to slow her progress by grabbing the rail. But her head still slammed into a step, her feet ending up towards the top of the stairs and her head closer to the bottom.

"Blaize!" The voice seemed to come from a long way away. "Blaize, talk to me. Please!" But before she could answer, the dizziness took her, and she heard no more.

CHAPTER
11

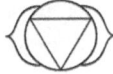

Cuinn scooped Blaize into his arms, and twisted his body to get them both down the slender staircase without bumping her again.

As he sped out of her front door, he kept up a constant stream of pleas and questions, his insides clenching at her lack of response. Energetics were usually pretty hardy, and long-lived, but it wasn't impossible for them to be hurt, injured, or even killed. He might not have wanted to be her Maven, but it was nothing personal.

His guts roiled as he carried Blaize to the main house.

As he went in through the kitchen door, he shouted for Tierra who ran in and quickly assessed the situation, then directed him to the living room.

Once there, he lay Blaize down on a sofa. Moments later, Tierra hustled through the door with a damp cloth.

"Did you need to move her?" Tierra leaned over the sofa to take Blaize's pulse.

"She was lying upside down on the stairs." Cuinn fidgeted in place.

Tierra's eyebrows rose. "What happened?"

"She walked into me at the top of those stairs, fell, and hit her head. I didn't push her if that's what you're thinking."

"Don't be silly." Tierra examined Blaize as she spoke. "Where did she hit her head, do you know? In one place, or more?"

"Where it's bleeding. Only once." Cuinn stood a few feet from the sofa, clenching and unclenching his hands, while Tierra used the cloth to gently wipe the blood and inspect the injury.

"It's probably not as serious as it looks. Head injuries always bleed more than they should," said Tierra, absently.

"What if there's internal damage? It was a pretty hard knock on the head."

Tierra didn't answer immediately. She lifted up the girl's eyelids to assess her pupils, and did some other fast checks.

"I'll look energetically to see if there's any damage to her brain. If there is, the nearest energetic facility is Victoria Island, so we'd need the chopper to get her there or maybe Cara here, but I don't want to do that unless I have to. Can you get me some ice and a clean dish towel?"

Cuinn nodded. He bolted out of the room and barrelled back through the door moments later, coming up short as he saw Tierra on the floor next to the sofa where Blaize lay. Tierra was massaging her own forehead. She used the chair to pull herself up and rubbed her wrist.

His heart jumped in his chest. *What the hell ...*

"What happened? Are you okay? Is she?" His gaze flickered wildly between the two of them.

"Calm down, Cuinn." Tierra sent out a calming thread of safety, security, and comfort from her earth energy towards him though it lacked her usual strength.

"She was protecting herself, and managed to kick me just as I was withdrawing. If that was Blaize harnessing Ajna energies without training, she'll be a force to be reckoned with when she's trained."

"But is she okay?" Cuinn persisted.

"I've checked her, and I think she's fine. I couldn't see any energetic or physical disturbances in her energy. There's some swelling; she'll have a killer headache and a bump. And we should keep an eye out that there's no concussion. There's no need for the chopper."

Cuinn's shoulders dropped from where they'd been up next to his ears and he let out a long breath. He sank to the floor near the sofa. Tierra touched Blaize's pale skin and did another fast scan, and then leaned back, nodding, her own body seeming to lose some of the tension of the last few minutes. "We need her to wake up now and keep her awake for a while. I'll bring her round, and you can sit with her for the day. It might be an opportunity for you to talk."

Cuinn hunched his shoulders. "Sure." He had an unpleasant cocktail of emotions inside him—shame, guilt, and mortification. And he didn't think it was going to get any better for a while. Tierra wasn't someone who shouted or got angry, but her disapproval of his actions was clear.

His cheeks burned. Blaize's body lay on the sofa like a reproach. He hadn't given her a chance. It might not have been personal to him, but it was to her.

Tierra placed some of the ice in a tea towel and held it against Blaize's injury. "Can you hold this while I wake her up?"

Cuinn shuffled over and put a hand out to hold the makeshift ice pack in place. Tierra dipped one of the other tea towels into water and wiped it around Blaize's face. Tierra closed her eyes, and Cuinn felt a shimmer at the edge of his consciousness as she sent a little soft energy into Blaize to gently bring her back to wakefulness.

After another minute, Blaize groaned.

"Owww. What the hell happened?" She didn't open her eyes. "Can someone turn the lights off in here? My head feels like a nuclear device went off."

Cuinn watched her, more relief pouring into him, along with more guilt at how pale she was, and at the shadows under her eyes.

Tierra walked to the curtains and closed them, blanketing the room in an artificial dusk. "Blaize, it's Tierra. You fell and hit your head. I've checked and you're going to be fine apart from a nasty headache. But we also need to make sure you don't have a concussion, so Cuinn will stay with you for the day to make sure you don't fall asleep again."

"Cuinn? Awesome." Blaize mumbled it, but her meaning was clear enough.

Cuinn took a breath to speak, to apologise, but Tierra held up a hand to stop him. Blaize still hadn't opened her eyes.

"Blaize, I'm going to put a cool cloth on your forehead and eyes, which should help with the headache and the light. You need to just stay where you are. I don't think you're going to want to eat for a while, but you only need to let Cuinn know when you do."

Tierra moved Cuinn's hands away from Blaize, and put a fresh cloth over her eyes and forehead. "Cuinn, move one of the armchairs over to the sofa. You should stay close."

Cuinn did as he was told, and then slumped down into the chair.

"You can't go to sleep, either," said Tierra, as she turned to Cuinn. "I'll pop in and see you both once an hour or so, but I think you should use this time to get to know each other a little better."

Blaize heard Tierra's footsteps leave the room. There was silence. Blaize stayed still, the pain in her head immense, an inflating balloon squashing her brain against the walls of her skull.

"Blaize?" Cuinn spoke softly, in a deep baritone.

"Cuinn." Her answer didn't invite further conversation. She had no wish to speak with him at all, and especially not with this pain in her head.

"I'm sorry," he said. "I just came back from seeing the Ajna Guild Leaders. It was a rough and tiring trip. I shouldn't have said what I said, and I'm sorry you overheard it."

She kept silent. The pain and anger mixed inside her skull in an ugly headache. She hated feeling like this, and she especially hated the fact he had created the situation. She wanted to curl into a ball on the sofa, but she knew if she moved her head at all, the pain would just increase. She was grateful for the cool, wet cloth across her eyes and forehead, which provided some measure of relief.

"I know you're angry with me. But I don't want you to leave." Cuinn said, his voice low but persistent.

"You don't want me to leave? Or you can't get rid of me?"

Blaize's eyes were still closed, and it took some effort of will to string that many words together, but her anger cut through the pain like a laser, forcing the words out with a deadly precision. *I won't stay where I'm not wanted.*

Of course, when she was no longer focused on talking, the pain rushed back. She gingerly put her hand up to her head to feel the damage. There was a bump the size of a robin's egg on the back of her head, and her hair was matted with water from the melting ice and something stickier, which she assumed was blood.

"Ouch." She tried to keep her exclamation under her breath, but Cuinn responded immediately.

"Can I get you anything? Let me know when you're ready to sit up."

Blaize kept silent because of the pain that had pulsed through her skull like thunder when she'd touched the bump.

Stupid. Never press a bruise.

"Blaize?"

Maybe if she ignored him, he'd get bored and read a book or something. Although his voice was nice to listen to and didn't increase the pain in her head too much. Though the fact it didn't hurt just irritated her more. *Gah.* She gritted her teeth and resolved to wait him out.

She didn't have to wait long.

"I think you can help me." He was hesitant.

"Really? You want my help? After the morning we've had?" Her mouth dropped, and she pried her eyes open only to find the cloth blocking her view. She put a hand up and pushed it to one side, blinking in the gloom. She saw Cuinn's silhouette next to her. What in Source's name made him think she'd help him now?

"Let me tell you what's going on." He spoke haltingly at first but gained strength as he gathered pace.

He finished, "Something's coming, something very bad, that threatens the whole of the energetic race. And right now, I don't know enough to stop it. Yet I'm somehow involved. And honestly, I'm conflicted about you."

Blaize snorted. Softly so her head didn't move too much.

He scrubbed a hand over his face. "I don't have a lot of time right now, and I hadn't planned to take on an Adherent. But I'd be a fool not to take all the help I can get."

His head dropped and he gazed at the space between his feet. "This is a challenging project, with far-reaching consequences if the prophecies are right."

Oh shit. She hated it when she had to feel sorry for her enemies.

"How do you think I can help?" She really hoped she couldn't. Cuinn was a rude idiot, but he clearly had a lot on his plate, and she could see that adding a new Adherent to the mix might be a bit much for him. *But then why did he agree? He should have just said no and we could have avoided all this.*

"If I'm training you in Ajna, then you'd have to understand dreamwalking and how prophecies work. It would include prophecy research. We could work together and you could help review previous prophecies for relevant information." Cuinn's head came up and his eyes brightened as he outlined the possibilities.

"Grunt work, you mean?" She was better than that. He didn't need an Adherent; he needed a servant.

"No," Cuinn sounded surprised. "You'd be doing this anyway. At the moment I'm doing it, which would probably continue, so I'm not asking you to do anything I wouldn't be doing myself. And maybe, if you show some talent for working with Ajna energy, you can support in dreamwalking too."

He told her about the personal prophecy he'd received from the Ajna farseers.

She listened, feeling her stomach squeeze at his mention of a personal prophecy. She'd only heard about one of those, and it had turned out badly for all involved. She put a hand up to her eyes and rubbed them, trying to clear the cobwebs so she could think as he talked.

When Cuinn finally went quiet, he sat in the armchair next to Blaize's head, his body rigid and still.

She considered his words. It sounded as if the problems he was dealing with were greater than him. And he was pretty senior in his Guild if he could get in to see the Guild Leaders. *I really need to find out more about him.* She hadn't been in the mood to discover much about him before she came.

And if she was honest with herself, she was intrigued by his story. Some kind of threat that affected everyone she knew and was close to? The Warrior in her, her Manipura energy, rose up ready to protect.

"What do you think?" he asked.

How bad could it be?

"I think … it sounds interesting. Now, for Source's sake, let me rest."

CHAPTER
12

But Cuinn couldn't let Blaize rest.

Instead, he talked at her for what felt like hours, but she wasn't listening. She was too tired.

Tierra came in to relieve Cuinn. She brought hot tea and freshly baked muffins. They smelled pretty good. For the first time in hours, Blaize turned her face away from the sofa cushions and back into the room.

Tierra put the food down and bustled around the room adjusting cushions and straightening things as she went. Although as far as Blaize could see, the cosy room was already spotless.

Blaize cautiously raised her upper body until she was leaning back with her head upright. Tierra made a pleased noise when she turned and saw Blaize's efforts.

"Well done. I think you should get some food into you as you didn't have breakfast," Tierra said. "I've sent Cuinn off to do whatever he needs to do. And I'll try not to babble at you like I did last night. I'm glad you and Cuinn have sorted out your differences and you'll be staying with us. It's a pleasure to have you here."

Blaize managed a weak, but genuine, smile. Tierra was easy to be around. She gave off a sense of strength and solidity, comfort and care. And the muffins smelled good. Blaize took one and asked, "What are they?"

"Ginger and chocolate chip." Tierra placed a muffin on her own plate on a small table between them. She poured the tea.

"I'm sorry that your introduction to Cuinn went so badly," Tierra said. "He's avoided meeting new people for a long time. Usually it's just myself, Adam, and him here."

"Adam's your brother?" asked Blaize. *Anything not to talk about Cuinn.*

Tierra beamed. "Yes. He heads up a security team that hunts down difficult Rogues."

Blaize raised her eyebrows. *Now that sounded like a man she could talk to.* "Sounds interesting. When's he back next?"

Tierra deflated a little. "I'm not sure. He comes and goes depending on how the hunt goes. You'll like him. He's quiet but thoughtful."

"Hmmm … a hunter and tracker, works in a Security team but thoughtful …related to you and Cuinn—I'm guessing Muladhara-Ajna? Muladhara for protecting others, and Ajna being where thoughtful comes from?"

Tierra's smile was back. "Yes. He's the reverse of Cuinn. Adam and I share Muladhara from our parents, and our mother and Cuinn's mother were sisters."

Tierra sighed and switched topics back to Cuinn. "Give Cuinn a chance. He's a good man, really. It's just he has a lot of balls in the air at the moment. It's not easy for him, having another Adherent. It's been a while. I hope he'll tell you about that sometime."

"What do you mean?" Blaize leaned forward slightly.

"It's not my story to tell. But, please, don't see this morning as typical behaviour. He can get very focused, that's true, but it comes from a good place."

Blaize had known Cuinn had had Adherents before, but no one had mentioned any problem with one in the past. She leaned her head back against the top of the sofa again and sighed. Was she involved with a Maven with a difficult past? When she was feeling better she was definitely going to ask more questions. And not only that, get answers.

Cuinn sat at his desk in his workroom. After Tierra's efforts over the last couple of weeks, the room was a lot tidier than before, with actual space on his desk and only a small number of books around the room—and most of those on shelves. He was still tired. He'd lain down after his first 'watch' over Blaize, but he hadn't been able to sleep.

Damn it, she infuriated him. He couldn't think about her without his jaw muscles clenching. Frustrated, he flipped through the pages of a book in his lap without taking any of the information in, realised, and went back to the start.

But his irritation was also laced with guilt, because although it was true he hadn't actually pushed her down the stairs, he had certainly been the cause of her fall. His heart had raced as he'd carried her downstairs, as he'd focused only on getting her to Tierra's sure and healing touch.

He hadn't noticed her thick red hair, soft and touchable against his chest, or her strong, spicy scent.

Except he did.

He shook his head and scowled. Where had that come from?

He hadn't had female company that wasn't related to him for a while. It was probably just a reaction to that.

He thought he'd persuaded her to stay, but he sensed it wasn't a given. He rested his head on the back of the chair and closed his eyes. Marius wouldn't be happy if Blaize returned home, whether Cuinn sent her, or Blaize went of her own accord. And Fai … well, he would have to avoid Fai for another fifty years if that happened.

The door creaked open, and his head snapped around. When he saw it was Tierra and not Blaize his face relaxed, and Tierra laughed. "It's only me—don't look so worried. I brought you some food. You need to eat. And something healthier than cake and muffins."

Cuinn looked at the plate and his stomach rumbled.

"Fine. Thanks." He put the unread book down and took the food.

Tierra angled a chair to face him at his desk and sat. "She's a nice person. And as I said earlier, smart."

He nodded, then slipped a forkful of pasta into his mouth.

"You need to get to know her. There's no way you can do any kind of binding ceremony right now. Neither of you trusts the other. You need to have a week or so where you just do stuff together— show her the grounds, take her to the sea, the mountains, anything. Just spend time together, talking and just being."

Cuinn stopped eating and stared at her. "But what about my work? The prophecies?"

"You need some time off too. Let the dreams and the information that the Ajna Circle members gave you percolate in your brain. Some of the best connections between ideas come when you're not trying."

Cuinn frowned but went back to the food. He speared a baby tomato on his fork, then pointed it at her. "You just want me to get out more."

Tierra smiled. "Of course I do. And in the company of an intelligent, strong woman—what could be better?"

Cuinn was horrified. "She's here to learn, nothing else."

But damned if he couldn't get that spicy fragrance out of his nose.

CHAPTER
13

Cuinn woke early. Much too early. He was finding it harder and harder to sleep even when he wasn't working. It was taking a toll on him. Wearing him down.

He decided he might as well use the time productively. Given his half-awake, half-asleep state, he decided to dreamwalk.

But it was a short and discouraging excursion into the ether. The only new scrap of prophecy he'd seen was a woman in trouble. He couldn't tell who she was, or what the danger was, but he hadn't been able to do anything about it, and he'd woken with a dry mouth and a neck like a block of wood.

Brow creased, he went down to the kitchen. Time to address the next problem.

"I'm going to apologise to her," he said, as he came through the door.

Tierra looked up from the sleek silver laptop she was using. "Good. I'm just working on a column about spring plantings for next week's newspaper, but I'll be done in about twenty minutes.

Ask her to breakfast, but don't push it. She might want some time alone."

She cocked her head as she examined him, then jumped up and went over to where more muffins were cooling on the side. "Take her a muffin. A peace offering. Oh, and Cuinn?"

He nodded, waiting.

"Smile."

He rolled his eyes and went out the back door, walking over to Blaize's cottage. He would wait to tell her about the getting-to-know-you week when Tierra was there to chaperone them. He and Blaize seemed to get on a lot better when Tierra was there.

He knocked on the door of the cottage. No answer. He stepped back and looked through the downstairs windows. No one.

He tried the door, but it was locked. He went round the back. That door was also locked, and pressing his face to the glass of the back window didn't show him any signs of life there either. The cottage was dark and empty.

He pushed a hand through his hair. Surely she couldn't have gone home already? Left under her own steam?

Or was the head injury worse than it seemed—was she wandering outside, hurt or in pain? The memory of his dreamwalk, still fresh in his mind, came back to him, and he ran back to the house.

"She's gone," he panted.

"What do you mean?" Tierra raised an eyebrow as she looked at him.

"She's not in her cottage. I'm worried. Can you track her?"

Tierra nodded, and closed her eyes. He felt the ripple of her earth energy as she connected to the grounds.

After what seemed like forever, Tierra spoke. "She's in the woods. She's using Manipura energy."

"What? Why's she doing that?" He didn't wait for an answer, but pelted out of the door into the forest. His heart beat erratically, and his stomach churned. What if she was in trouble? What if the woman in the dreamwalk had been Blaize, now?

The run to the woods took forever, and images played out in his mind as he pounded through the trees. He saw Blaize as she'd looked yesterday, pale-faced and crumpled at the bottom of the stairs. He imagined her now, lying on the floor of the woods, injured and signalling to them with her Manipura energy, trying to get their attention.

How long has she been out here?

Blaize missed using her fire energy. She'd woken very early, her body still not adjusted to the new time zone. She had first used the opportunity to place a video call to Nixie in Thailand, for whom it was late in the day. They caught up about Fai and Marius, and then Nixie asked about Cuinn.

"What's he like?"

"He pushed me down the stairs." At Nixie's horrified look, Blaize relented and told her the whole story.

"Hmm. Doesn't sound very promising." Nixie frowned. "What do you think of him?"

Blaize shrugged. "He's annoying."

"Does he have any redeeming features?"

Blaize thought for a moment. "He has a nice enough voice."

"And?" Nixie pressed.

"And he does seem to be dealing with a lot." Blaize hesitated. She wasn't sure if the prophecies were common knowledge. She guessed not. "He's working on a project for the Ajna Guild, which seems important."

"What kind of person is he?" Nixie was more interested in the person than the project.

"Arrogant. Proud. Works hard."

Nixie smiled and raised her eyebrows. "Huh. Do we know anyone else like that?"

Blaize scowled. "He's also conflicted. One minute he doesn't want me to work with him, the next minute he does."

"What do you want?"

"I want to help. And I want to learn about Ajna from an expert, which he does seem to be. But I hate the idea that I'm not wanted." She looked away from Nixie's picture as she said this last. It burned to admit it.

"He'll soon see you for who you are," Nixie said firmly.

"Who's that then?" said Blaize, amused.

"A confident, competent energetic who's going to learn fast and be of help in no time."

Blaize shook her head and laughed, and turned the talk to other things.

The conversation lasted another thirty minutes, and refreshed, Blaize went outside in the cool Canadian morning. She walked into the dense and damp woods, and played with a fire droplet, scattering it into many tiny drops that looked like a burst of fireflies around her head.

She started working—or playing—in earnest.

Strings of light dipped and twisted like thread, creating a fabulous pattern, the lightest and most delicate of lacework in fire in the sky. She played like this for another hour or two, and the day gradually got brighter and her creations more complex. She experimented both with power and delicacy. She revelled in playing with the energy in a way she hadn't done for years. For the last few years, it had been all about work, work, work as she practised for the Manipura trial.

She tried to hold a creation that involved several different aspects, a tableau of her aunt, uncle, and Nixie.

"What are you doing?" a male voice asked from behind her.

The voice startled her, and her creations wavered and disappeared as she turned in his direction. She groaned. It was Cuinn.

"I wanted to connect with fire again after my accident yesterday." She kept her tone level.

Something flashed across Cuinn's face and he scowled. "Anyone could have seen you."

"Anyone who, exactly? You live in the middle of nowhere. There's no one for miles." Blaize put her hands on her hips.

"You should have left a note to tell us you'd be outside."

"Why? Are you my keeper? I thought I'd be back before you were up." She flicked a glance at her watch and looked away from his glare. It was much later than she'd meant to be out. But she wasn't going to apologise to this idiot.

She passed by Cuinn as she walked towards the house. He caught her arm and turned her none too gently to face him.

I don't think so.

She travelled with the movement, deftly ducking under his arm and breaking his hold. She grabbed his arm and put it in a lock, forcing him to his knees.

"Don't touch me like that again." She looked at him flatly.

He stared up at her, eyes wide, but said nothing.

She released the lock on his arm with a little push and stalked back to her cottage.

Cuinn stayed on his knees in shock while moisture seeped into his pants.

When he'd come close enough to Blaize to see her playing games, he'd lost it. He'd been worried she had been using her energy to call for help, and instead, she'd been messing about like a child.

He hadn't meant to reach for her like that, but he'd just wanted her to stay in one place so he could tell her off. The feeling of relief he'd felt on seeing her had made him want to touch her, a feeling he'd shaken off even as he had made contact.

And then suddenly, he had been on his knees, and all the light and laughter had left her face, revealing the fire Warrior she was. He'd forgotten the physical training that went into Manipura, the many hours of martial arts practice. He'd forgotten that Manipura energetics were often—to the extent any were ever needed—the 'soldiers' of their race, the enforcers, those who captured Rogues and returned them to the Healers for rehabilitation.

And on his knees, he had looked up and into her cold eyes, eyes that so far he'd only seen run hot. This blank face, empty of emotion

85

but with a terrible strength behind it, had been disturbing in the extreme.

He wanted to run after her and apologise, and felt confused about the emotions she'd stirred in him. The muffin he'd brought as a peace offering lay in the dirt next to him.

It had been many years since he'd encountered physical violence. As a dominant Ajna, he solved his problems with words, with logic, with argument.

Not violence. Never violence.

His mother had been far too close to the fighting in World War II because of her healing gifts. She'd been working with her sister, Adam and Tierra's mother, also a strong Anahata, in a Polish hospital when she'd been killed. Her death—and the violence of it—had driven him and his father apart. Despite the fact he and his father shared Ajna energies, his father had refused to talk to him about it and had blamed Cuinn for supporting his mother's decision to help in the war. Of course, when Cuinn had supported her, he hadn't really understood what it might mean.

He blamed himself too.

He walked to the house and into the kitchen to see Tierra. She sat at the table drinking a cup of tea. When she saw him, she raised an eyebrow. "What happened? And where's Blaize?"

He looked down at himself, mud and grass stains on the knees of his stone-coloured pants. "She's gone back to her cottage."

"Why? I thought you were going to ask her to breakfast."

"I didn't get around to it. I was too busy getting up from the ground where she tossed me."

"What are you talking about?"

He reluctantly explained.

She sighed. "Cuinn, you need to get a grip on yourself."

"Me? I'm the one she pushed over." But he avoided her eyes as he said it.

"You grabbed her. That's both inappropriate and out of character. What's going on with you? I thought you'd feel a bit more stable after a good night's sleep, but you still seem all over the place. What happened to the new plan of getting to know her?"

"I'd say I got to know a different side of her, that's for sure." He shrugged.

"Of course she'd react like that. She's a Manipura energetic. And remember what happened to her parents."

Cuinn's body felt heavy, and he sat down at the table with a thud. Tierra shook her head and poured him a cup of tea.

"Do you think that me grabbing her reminded her of her parents?" he asked, the weariness seeping deep into his bones.

"There's a chance. Plus, she only came out of her training a month ago. There's a lot of fire there. And you say she was playing with her element when you went out? If she was deep in fire, then it's no wonder it turned to anger when you touched her—you were lucky she had such strong self-control."

When any energetic used their element, the qualities of that energy were likely to be more potent within them. Manipura was dominant, proud, and controlling. There was a reason why Manipura was the energy of the Warriors of the energetics race. He rubbed the heel of his hand on the table, using the smooth wood to ground himself. He was reasonably sure he could have controlled her if she'd attacked him. Assuming he'd been conscious. Mentally, she was no match for him. Physically, he was no match for her.

"I have to apologise again, don't I?" Cuinn kept his gaze on the table, misery in his voice.

"Yes. But this time I'll facilitate it. She'll never trust you if you behave like this. Cuinn, words are your gift. I'm not sure why this situation is making you lose your balance like this, but you've got to focus. Maybe you should go up to your room and meditate for a while? Find your centre? I'll talk to Blaize. Come back down for lunch and be prepared to grovel."

He grimaced. "I told you all I couldn't be a Maven again. Looks as if I was right."

"Don't be silly." Tierra's voice was brisk. "You just need to get over these initial … bumps in the road, and you'll be fine."

"Bumps? They feel like mountains to me."

CHAPTER

14

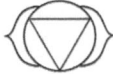

When Cuinn came back down to the kitchen a few hours later, he felt refreshed and considerably calmer.

Tierra and Blaize sat at the table, Blaize leaning her head in her hands and Tierra with a hand placed comfortingly on the other woman's shoulder.

Cuinn winced.

The two women looked up at him as he stood in the doorframe. There was a moment of silence and then Tierra twitched an encouraging eyebrow.

"Hi." Cuinn, for all his power with language, was feeling a bit lost. This was a different type of woman than he'd been used to—more volatile than the steady and peaceable Tierra. There had been no fire in either his own parents or Adam and Tierra's parents, so it was an element he wasn't used to. Perhaps he could appeal to her underdeveloped Ajna instead.

"Blaize, I apologise for my behaviour." His tone was formal, clipped.

Her eyes were a bright, hard jade and he had to steel himself not to flinch under their stare. He had no desire to end up on the floor again. But, he reminded himself, she was both fire and mind. He needed to engage with the latter.

"Let me give you some background." He talked her through his most recent prophecy image, and why he'd reacted as he had. With Tierra's encouragement, he managed a reasonably eloquent apology. The fire in Blaize's eyes dimmed.

He offered her the opportunity to get to know him outside the Maven-Adherent relationship, and showed her the itinerary he'd put together. A very logical itinerary.

And they agreed to start now.

CHAPTER
15

They started with a picnic, which was … okay. He couldn't really say much more about it than that. She'd told him about her education in the UK, and later working in the human business world in Hong Kong and Singapore, and, as part of her training, as a Manipura Warrior all over Southeast Asia. She'd certainly travelled a great deal in her short life.

All while he'd locked himself up in Cathair Cuinn for the last fifty years.

The girl seemed smart enough, but she had no concept of Ajna Chakra and the energies it contained. She was too steeped in her fire energies. Not unusual considering the short time between training in the two Chakras, but it might make things harder if she wasn't a fast learner.

Cuinn was back in his rooms now, still unsettled after their tempestuous morning. It was rare he had to apologise, and yet he felt as if that was all he'd done since she arrived.

He decided to try another dreamwalk. He'd use the energy of the morning to encourage more of the prophecy to emerge.

He made his preparations. He lit a candle at each corner of his mat and eased his long body down onto it. His body supine and still, he faced the white ceiling and took some deep breaths, clearing his mind.

He had to let go of the anxiety he felt about the prophecy. To forget Blaize, their arguments, and the fact she was now a millstone around his neck for the next however many years.

He had to be totally focused on the present moment. Mindful only of his breathing. To let everything around him fade away. He took another deep breath, and his body relaxed, some of the tension leaving him.

There was a rap at the door.

The noise jerked him back from the calm, empty state he'd been in, and confused, it took him a moment to place the noise.

There was another sharp crack, knuckles on wood.

He rose from the mat and went over to pull the door open. Blaize stood in front of him.

What is she doing here? "Yes?"

"You said to pop up later and you'd show me around the house. And your working area. It's late afternoon now." A slight crinkle appeared on her forehead, and she tilted her head a fraction.

Cuinn looked at his wrist, at what turned out to be a non-existent watch. "Oh."

He didn't remember saying he'd take her around the house. It didn't seem like him. And he really needed to get back to the dreamwalk. It felt as if she was at the end of a long tunnel, and half of him was with her, and the other half was still preparing for the ritual. He couldn't concentrate on what she wanted.

There was a beat while they looked at each other, her expectant, him unsure.

"So ... can you show me around now?" She spoke slowly.

"Oh." He paused, processing what she'd asked. "No, not now. I'm in the middle of something. Maybe tomorrow."

"Right. Of course. I'll ask Tierra then, shall I?"

"Fine." Cuinn was distracted. The meditative state was fading fast. He'd have to start again. He frowned.

"Right. So ... see you at dinner?" Blaize was backing away from the door and shaking her head.

"Fine." He shut the door and she was gone; he could get back to the ritual.

He lay back down, the girl disappearing from his mind, and breathed deeply until his body felt weighted and heavy. He relaxed more, his breathing slowed, his body still as death.

After some minutes, his body no longer felt heavy, but like nothing at all, as if he was no longer tethered to it. This wasn't literally true—some Ajna Masters could project their spirit, their energetic body, out of their physical body and move to other places on the Earth, but his movement today was all in the energetic world, and not on the physical plane.

He was now in a sleep state of sorts. But a lucid, conscious sleep state, where he knew he was dreaming and could act in the dream. He was on the energetic, the etheric, plane.

But his actions could have consequences for the real world.

He opened his eyes and looked around. The energetic plane was a wondrous one, where the mind could create a different reality—the energy that the energetics were able to pull through into the physical plane was all around here, and could be shaped and moulded as long as they knew how. There was some danger—unprepared energetics could kill themselves with the almost unlimited energy here.

When he visited this plane, he always began in his Haven, the name Ajnas used for their 'safe place' on the energetic plane. His Haven was a tower of thick stone walls, stretching up several stories, with one good-sized room on each floor.

To get into Cuinn's Haven would take an energetic of enormous strength if they could even find it in the first place, which was doubtful without an invitation or a previous visit.

Though much of his work on the etheric plane could be done from his Haven, for his dreamwalk today he needed to go to one of the unclaimed places in the energetics world. One of the places that was unshaped by energetics, full of untamed energy that might show him a glimpse of the future. It was dangerous because of who or what he might meet, and because the energy itself was so wild it could almost be said to have a mind of its own.

But that itself was a risky thought. Sometimes in the dreamscape, the energy reacted to your thoughts—good and bad—and created a reality from your mind. Which, given how jumbled and confused most people's minds were, could go very badly indeed.

His Ajna training had taught him how to keep a clear mind, how to focus, and how to be in the wild energy but keep his mind on the question he wanted answered. And sometimes, just sometimes, the wild energy would bring him answers.

The first inklings of this prophecy had been six months ago, and had been strange. He hadn't sought out the prophecy but been drawn by a feeling to one of the places of wild energy, where he had been gifted with a confusing jumble of images and feelings.

The few images made little sense, but the feelings that came with them hit home.

Despair, loss, destruction, emptiness—he'd woken up pale and sweating in his workroom at home, thrown from the dreamwalk without the usual decompression in his tower, and had staggered to the bathroom to throw up. He'd shared the images with Adam and Tierra, and later with Minh.

Since then, the prophecies had continued to come—some, unasked for like the first, powerful and exhausting in their intensity, and some, actively sought, usually clearer, but also much lighter in detail. These latter were like tiny shards of glass—whatever you could see in them was crystal clear, but only a very small part of the whole. The unasked-for visions were like opaque windows—a much bigger picture could be seen, but at the cost of clarity.

Both had an impact on him. Sometimes he woke up utterly drained. Tierra, Fintan and Adam all knew about his dreamwalks in search of more information on the prophecy, but as none of them were farseers, none of them knew quite the toll each dreamwalk took on him.

A dreamwalk involved not just a visit to the etheric plane – which could be taxing at the best of times, even when he stayed in his

Haven, his safe place – but once there, a trip out into the wild energy on the etheric plane, a world that would react to his very thoughts. That he could shape to his will—if he was powerful enough. 'Thoughts become things' wasn't just an inspirational saying in the dreamscape.

But the effort, the control needed, could be exhausting and dangerous. He'd been hiding the impact on his mental and physical condition as much as possible, fearing that Tierra, in particular, might try to stop him. And he knew he couldn't let her do that.

His health was nothing compared to the survival of his race.

Today, emerging on the energetic plane in his Haven, he walked downstairs and to the heavy wooden door that provided access to the etheric plane outside the tower. He breathed in and out, using the familiar energy of the tower to create a shield to protect himself as much as possible outside his own Haven. Some of the grounds were warded – energetically guarded by him – too, but his strongest protections were in the tower itself.

With the door open, he stared out onto the flat grassland that he'd surrounded his tower with and was his preferred terrain—all the better to see something coming. Everything within his boundaries he had created, by drawing on the energies of the etheric plane. Beyond his boundaries all he could see was what looked like mist, fundamentally grey, with the occasional spark of colour.

Pure potential.

He strode to the edge of his Haven's limits, where he paused for a moment to take a deep breath – and then stepped into the mist.

He experienced weightlessness, vertigo, claustrophobia, and agoraphobia all at once. His energetic essence on this plane was untethered, and he needed to ground it or he'd never manage to focus enough to gather more shards of prophecy.

He reached for the energy, which responded to him like a very sticky, resistant toffee. It took great amounts of effort to shape his own body and some of the environment around him. Eventually, after much work, he found himself standing on a barren, rocky plain with little but scrub in either direction. The horizon was formless, and even the sky was an unrelenting grey, with no sign of the sun. There was no life to be seen.

Now came the dangerous part. He'd managed to define a small slice of reality, and he needed to let some of the wild energies back in, but in a controlled, focused fashion, that might help answer his question.

He opened himself very slightly to the wild energy. He focused his mind on the image of the twelve energetics facing the threat. He wanted to know who they were, and the part they would play.

Holding his focus, as well as holding the environment steady took huge amounts of mental and energetic effort. He breathed deeply.

The image blurred, shifted, changed. Eleven of the energetics disappeared, till just one woman, the one who had been standing closest to him, was left.

Blaize.

The picture of her shifted. Her eyes, a dull olive, looked at him from a face that was bruised, with a smear of dried blood under her nose. She was tied to something underneath her, and her energy was fading, though he wasn't sure why or how.

As always with a dreamwalk, he couldn't alter the vision, just watch in despair as her energy drained, and her green eyes turned glassy.

As the life left her face, the image of the twelve energetics came back to his mind.

But even as he watched, the vision changed. In it, Blaize turned to meet his gaze, smiled sadly, and faded from the vision.

This change was accompanied by a desperate sadness, a longing, and a deep emotional pain. The wrench of her disappearance shocked him like a sudden blow, and he felt himself thrown back into his body in the physical plane.

He barely had the energy to open his eyes, let alone the energy to sit up on the mat. His eyes and cheeks were wet, and he realised he was crying.

He lay like that, empty, silent, tears falling, until dawn.

CHAPTER
16

Blaize had an unsettled night. Dreams came and went, slipping though her mind like stagnant water down a drain, leaving anxiety behind like a bad smell. But she couldn't catch any details as she swam in and out of consciousness, and when she finally woke, she felt as tired as she'd been the night before.

She put it behind her, as today Cuinn was taking her to the local town. He was already belting up as she opened the passenger door and got in beside him.

Blaize admitted to herself she'd been a little disappointed at Cuinn's choice of car for their trip, a tricked out charcoal Land Rover Discovery. He'd told her, uninterested, that Adam chose their cars, though they did have several in their garage. Given Adam was a Muladhara energetic, it was unsurprising that the cars turned out to be brutes, built more for safety than for speed. And logical, she supposed, given the terrain. But her own penchant was for sleeker cars, cars that were powerful and fast. *At least he didn't choose the pickup.*

She belted up as he put on some kind of highbrow classical music. Very Ajna, she thought. Not much rhythm in this. But she settled back in her comfortable seat and watched the scenery pass by, as it was clear that Cuinn wasn't—yet—in the mood to talk.

The landscape passing by was, like Cathair Cuinn, showing signs of spring. Trees had some pink or white blossoms, still tightly in bud, but there. There was plenty of mud in the fields around them, but also green peeking through at the sides of the roads.

Cuinn's hands were neatly in the ten and two positions on the wheel, and he drove with minimal effort and movement, his eyes more blue than grey in the morning light. From the side she could see his eyes were fringed by thick lashes that made her a little jealous.

"So, assuming we agree to work together, and be joined as Maven and Adherent, how do you like to work? How have you worked with Adherents in the past?" As the words came out of her mouth she saw his lips tighten, and felt the car jerk, presumably in reaction to him pressing a little harder on the accelerator. She could have kicked herself. Tierra had told her there had been an issue with a previous Adherent. She needed a fast change of subject.

"Me, I like room for spontaneity. Some structure, some goals, but also the possibility to read about a topic and explore anything that's interesting. Sometimes I can get really involved and consumed by an idea if I get really into it." She gabbled out the words, trying to make sure he didn't clam up again.

There was a pause. Blaize sipped the coffee she'd brought with her and looked fixedly out of the window, pretending that this kind of long gap between contributions was completely normal.

She turned back to him when he finally spoke. His face hadn't lost the pinched look. In profile he had a strong face with an aquiline nose and a firm chin. His skin was pale—*presumably because he never leaves the house.* "With Ajna there must be some planning, some looking ahead. We'll start out with a plan for what we do with our time. But I'll try and ensure you have time to explore your own interests within the topic. Over time you'll need to find your own speciality areas. Your own specific talents within the mind."

Intrigued, she asked, "What are your talents?"

There was another pause, smaller this time. His mouth relaxed a little. He was a lot more attractive when he wasn't annoyed with her. Which so far was about one percent of the time.

"I have a talent for prophecy. And I'm strong. I can dreamwalk, and work on the astral plane as well as the physical."

Blaize raised her eyebrows. "What's your Muladhara energy like?"

"These days I don't use it as much as Ajna, but it's helpful. It … grounds me. It helps keep the lighter energies of Ajna stable. We'll need to be careful of your own fire energies. Fire combined with the mind can mean speed of thought, burning curiosity, laser-like focus—or it can mean being consumed by your own power, being possessed by intellectual pursuits above emotions or relationships with others, or even being burnt out too soon." His glance flickered over to her, and she met his eyes, now as opaque as fog, before he turned back to the road.

She shivered. You really didn't want to hear someone with the gift of prophecy say something like that.

The powerful vehicle ate up the miles to the town, and after passing only a handful of other cars, with about the same number of words between them, they arrived.

Driving into the small town, he told her a little about it. "There's not too much in Merrow—officially it's called Merrow Mount, but everyone just calls it Merrow—but it's the biggest town around. There are a couple of guest houses, a handful of places to eat, some grocery stores."

He pulled into a space on what seemed to be a reasonably busy street, and Blaize watched as a passerby waved at Cuinn, who lifted a hand and returned the greeting. Blaize's eyebrows rose. *Interesting.*

"Shall we go and get a cup of coffee?" he asked.

They were both out of the car by now, and this time Cuinn caught her raised eyebrow.

"I thought you might want a drink, and I can introduce you to the best coffee shop in town." He remained polite.

"Of course," Blaize murmured, proud of her own restraint in not mentioning she'd just finished a cup of coffee. She caught up with his long strides as he made his way across the road, watching him wave to two more people. She was fascinated by how different he seemed away from Cathair Cuinn.

Entering the warmth of the coffee shop, Blaize inhaled the aroma of fresh pastries and coffee. The café and shop, 'Sugar and Spice,' was doing a roaring trade. As she and Cuinn approached the counter to order, the motherly woman behind it caught sight of Cuinn and made a pleased sound. "Cuinn, how lovely to see you. It's been a while. Working hard again?"

Cuinn smiled at her. "A little. This is a family friend who's moved here to help me with some research. Blaize, meet Rosa, who makes the best cakes and coffee in Merrow."

Rosa dipped her head in acknowledgement and thanks, and said "Coffee for you, Cuinn? With a little sugar? And a scone? It looks like you could use a few more calories in you again—does Tierra know you've been starving yourself?"

"I'm fine, Rosa, and Tierra does her best to feed me. You're lucky she doesn't set up a bakery in town—she's one of the few people who might be real competition." Cuinn smiled at her again, and Rosa laughed.

The woman was human, but she appeared to have an activated Muladhara Chakra, very unusual in a human. She, and those around her, would be unaware of it, but the energy and her natural warmth would draw others to her. Humans and energetics were different races, but every living being had Chakras within them. The energies were the foundation of all life on the planet.

"Hi," Blaize offered. "Can I get a cappuccino?"

"No problem, lovie. What would you like to eat? No, let me guess." She narrowed her eyes in thought. "Hmmm. I know. I just made some chocolate chili cupcakes. They're mainly chocolate, but have a little kick to them."

Blaize's eyebrows rose again, and she was starting to feel they might as well stay up near her hairline given the surprising turns the morning kept taking. "That sounds perfect."

"I'll send Indigo over with it all in a minute. Take a seat. And Cuinn, don't stay away so long next time."

He smiled back at her, and led the way to one of the smaller tables with two comfortable armchairs on either side.

"I can see why you like it here." It was interesting to see Cuinn in this new light. Perhaps he wasn't so bad if someone as warm as Rosa was fond of him. He folded his lean, rangy form into the soft and well-used cushions as she watched. She sat opposite him, perching herself on the edge of her chair rather than sinking into a soft, sagging seat.

He nodded. "Rosa's like a mother hen. Although what she doesn't know is that I'm nearly two centuries older than her."

He leaned back in the chair, his knees close to the table. "I like this town. We've managed to live harmoniously here for a long time. Not too much mixing with the town, some judicious ageing, and a little reincarnation. When I arrived here I wasn't feeling too friendly anyway, so that made 'coming back' a second time easier. Adam's been through several incarnations, partly because he enjoys it, I think. Anyway, it works."

Blaize nodded, and then shivered. *What the...?* She felt a trickle down her back, and turned, craning her neck to look around the coffee shop. She sensed a threat. But there was nothing in the scene before her that matched the menace that flooded her body with unease.

Mothers and their children, and students with books and laptops sat around them in the cosy space, knees against tables in squashy armchairs in reds, oranges and browns. Those rushing in and out to get their mid-morning coffee were dressed in work clothes. More often than not, Rosa would suggest to them a pastry or piece of cake, and though some managed to resist, the majority walked out with baked goods as well as their drink.

But there was something off here. Something wrong.

The twisted energy she normally associated with a Rogue.

Indigo put the grey-haired woman's order gracelessly on the table, baring her teeth at the two elderly ladies having tea and sandwiches. They didn't notice. She was invisible to them, just another service industry drone.

For a moment, her hate turned towards them and she narrowed her eyes, imagining pulling the hair of one and exposing her neck so she could slash it with a knife. She'd watch the blood pour out, covering the table and those repulsive sandwiches. The other woman would look at her in fear, and she'd know who was in control. Who had the power.

The woman looked up at her. "That's all, thanks." She smiled and turned back to her companion.

A hiss came out of Indigo's mouth. The woman looked back, confused, and Indigo pressed her lips tightly together and turned away.

She walked to the other side of the café to take the order of two irritating students so she wouldn't launch herself at Blaize, just yards away.

She'd been working at the café for over a month, to try and pick up town gossip about the reclusive family who lived just outside Merrow.

She'd chosen the café because Quinn and Tierra seemed to have a relationship with the over-friendly proprietor though Rosa had been annoyingly silent on the subject so far.

Indigo refocused on the students in front of her and took their order on autopilot, uninterested in their cake and coffee. Indigo didn't eat much these days. She took the details back to Rosa, forcing a smile as she handed the bit of paper over.

"Everything okay, love?" Rosa asked.

"Fine thanks, Rosa. Just a bit tired. I was up late studying last night," Indigo lied. In fact, she'd spent her two days off in Vancouver, with *him*, and driven back the night before. She shuddered slightly.

She went back to the kitchen to take another order out and passed scant feet from Blaize's back. Indigo's eyes filled with anger.

It would be so easy to set this whole place alight. To watch them all burn.

She and Blaize were an energetic match. Indigo was a Manipura-Ajna energetic, just like Blaize. But that was the only place where their lives matched.

Indigo hadn't had Blaize's opportunities. Her chances. No fancy university for Indigo. No family and friends who'd support her choices.

And now, Blaize and Cuinn were sitting in the café in a window seat watching the world go by.

They hadn't seemed to notice Indigo's energies. Indigo's Maven had both energetically warded her and given her his protection, and taught her to keep her energies hidden. In addition, Rosa herself was a human with some natural energies. Earth energies, which Indigo had little interest in, but energy nonetheless that masked Indigo's own power.

Indigo went back to the kitchen. She knew she couldn't attack them here, in public. Her role was to watch, and to gather information only. Her fists clenched. But she really, really wanted to.

"Table three," said Rosa, placing a cup of coffee on a tray that already held a chocolate chili cupcake, scone and cappuccino. "They're friends of mine. Introduce yourself."

"What's the matter?" Cuinn said.

Blaize didn't reply, still scanning the room. A waitress approached them with their order.

"Coffee and cake." The waitress put their order down and looked into Blaize's eyes.

Is she the threat? Their gazes locked. The waitress was very thin, with jet black hair and dark eyes. There was a hum in the air. The woman had energy, but Blaize couldn't tell if she was a human like Rosa, or an energetic. Either way, she didn't seem friendly.

All Blaize's instincts were on alert now, and Cuinn was looking at them. He half rose, but Blaize waved a hand at him.

If the woman was an energetic, she would surely indicate it. *And what would an energetic be doing waitressing in a town like Merrow?* But there was nothing. Blaize addressed the waitress. "Is everything okay?"

"Of course," said the waitress. "Enjoy your cake."

She strolled away, confident, and still Blaize wasn't sure. The sense of threat remained. The waitress paused a moment to chat with Rosa, who smiled at her.

Blaize frowned and pursed her lips. There was something here, tickling her consciousness. Her Manipura instincts had flared, and she just needed to concentrate enough to find out what it was. She closed her eyes and drew a little power. *Focus.*

She felt a warm pressure on her arm. "What's the matter?"

Her concentration broke and the trace of threat dropped away. She opened her eyes again and pulled her arm away from Cuinn's hand, irritated. *I nearly had it.*

"I don't know. Something's not right here."

Cuinn sat back and looked around. "Are you sure? I don't sense anything."

Her lips thinned into a line. "Yes, I'm sure. But it's gone."

She tapped her fingers onto the table. The waitress had disappeared back into the kitchen.

"Do you know that waitress? The one who brought us the coffee?" Blaize was looking past the counter of the café into the kitchen, straining to see the woman.

"Indigo? I've met her once or twice. She's new."

"Do you get a sense of energy from her?"

Now Cuinn frowned. "Energy? No."

"Nothing?"

He shook his head. "From Rosa, yes. Maybe you're feeling energy from her?"

Blaize pushed a hand through her hair. "It doesn't feel like Muladhara. I'm not even sure what energy it is. But it was a threat."

"There are no other energetics who live here," said Cuinn. He picked up his coffee and sipped it, leaning back in his armchair. "You're jumping at shadows."

Blaize stayed on alert. "I'm just going to use the bathroom."

She got up, movements abrupt, and stalked towards the door in the back. She'd touch the waitress and read what she could. If there was a threat, she needed to know.

But when she reached the back, sticking her head into the small kitchen, there was no one there but a young man with blond hair putting a sandwich together. "Can I help you?"

"Is Indigo here? I just wanted to ask her a quick question," said Blaize.

He shook his head. "She's stepped out for a minute as it's her break. Sorry. Do you want me to pass a message on?"

"No. Thanks." Blaize went back to their table, disappointed. The uncomfortable feeling had gone. *Am I imagining things?* Then a thought struck her. *What if the threat was from Cuinn?* Her stomach lurched.

She sat down opposite Cuinn, assessing him as a threat. He was strong, she knew that, despite having shown her nothing of his power. And strong Ajnas could project thoughts into others' heads, like Huo had at the trial. He hadn't mentioned that gift, but she knew very little about him.

She shrugged. *It's not like I've got anything to lose by asking him.* "Are you threatening me?"

CHAPTER 17

"Are you serious?" Cuinn put his coffee down. If there had been anything unusual in the coffee shop he'd have known it, and he sensed nothing. *Now she's accusing me?*

He didn't have the patience for this. He hadn't told Tierra or Blaize about his vision of the night before. He was convinced he'd interpreted it wrongly. The idea of this irritating, possibly crazy girl as a part of the prophecy disturbed him.

The vision had affected him too deeply. He'd known her less than a week, and he'd shed tears after seeing her disappear from the vision. *Dammit.* He was losing it.

And now this.

"I'm not threatening you, Blaize. Far from it." He pushed his chair out from the table and stood up. "Let's go back to the house. It sounds like we could both do with some space."

"It's fine. I'm sorry." Her cheeks were flushed. "Whatever it was has gone."

"Maybe it was the sugar or the caffeine going to your head. Or jet lag. Or you're oversensitive to Rosa's energy."

Her lips flattened and her eyes sparked. "No. I sensed something, and it felt like Manipura."

Unlikely. The nearest energetic was in Vancouver as far as he knew. Energetics weren't territorial, but in an area with a population as small as this, they tended to ask permission before settling in.

Was she getting confused about her own energy? Either way, they needed to head home. Perhaps he'd start her off on some grounding meditation exercises.

She could do those in her own cottage, and he could get back to work.

Blaize walked along Merrow's Main Street filled with shoppers, mothers and babies, and even the odd tourist, and felt a shiver run across her back. Cuinn was back in the café paying, and Blaize had come out for some air, regretting the impulse that had caused her to accuse Cuinn.

She stopped and turned around, surveying her surroundings, but saw nothing out of the ordinary. She frowned and was moving on again when someone shouldered her out of the way, knocking her off balance. She staggered and span around, tensed, looking for who'd bumped her.

The most likely culprit was a dark head moving quickly away from her. A dark head that looked familiar. Blaize began to jog after the figure, who she was almost certain was the waitress from the coffee shop. *What was her name?*

"Indigo? Indigo. Wait, I want to talk to you." Blaize pitched her voice to carry to the woman, ignoring the glances from those around them.

The other woman glanced back and started to run in earnest. That only made Blaize more certain that she was right. All her instincts were screaming at her to catch the woman, human or energetic. Just because Cuinn didn't believe Blaize's gut about the woman being dangerous didn't mean Blaize shouldn't check for herself. He wasn't her Maven yet. And the woman had been stick thin. No match for Blaize's own training and honed muscle.

She would find out what was going on without any help from Cuinn.

Blaize sprinted down the street, dodging strollers, and small dogs being towed behind smaller children. The gap between her and the figure was closing. It might have been a week since Blaize had last trained, but she was fit, agile, and very motivated.

A ripple in the air, and Blaize sensed energy being used. *Shit.* She didn't know what energies the other woman had, but at least now she knew she was dealing with an energetic and not a human. Though she must be a well-shielded energetic not to have triggered Cuinn's nose for power, and to have set off Blaize's own instincts only a little.

Blaize span around a corner and came up sharp. She was in an alley between shops that was sheltered from the street. There was nothing in the alley but garbage cans—and the energetic.

"What do you want?" Blaize said. She put her arms up in front of her in a defensive crouch, and pulled a little energy from the ether, spooling it inside. She was as able to defend herself physically as energetically. And she was ready for either.

The woman didn't speak, but closed her eyes for a second before bringing up her arms fast and shooting a stream of fire at Blaize.

Blaize staggered back, throwing up her own defensive shields to protect herself. She hadn't expected the other woman to attack so quickly, especially so close to humans.

"What do you want?" Blaize said again. She wasn't ready to make a move, though at this point, if she saw an opportunity to restrain Indigo, she would. She'd dump her in Cuinn's lap and not say "I told you so." *Well, maybe just a little.*

It was against all energetic laws to use energy close to humans, so Blaize had reason enough to hold the woman. But Blaize needed to keep Indigo in this alley until she could either calm her down enough to have a rational conversation or she could take her down.

"Indigo, is it? What are you doing in Merrow?" Blaize kept her tone reasonable though the fire in her blood was itching to get out. She tried another tack. "What's your auxiliary Chakra?"

It was obvious enough that the woman's dominant was Manipura, just like Blaize's.

Indigo's eyes were hard and burned with emotion. She still said nothing. She was angry. Not just angry, raging. But Blaize had no idea why, which meant she wasn't sure how to address it.

Blaize took a step closer. "Why don't you come with me back to my home? There are several energetics there, and we can help you if you're down on your luck."

Energetics were rarely on their own. The family and Guild structure meant that energetics were linked like the warp and the weft of cloth. And energetics always, always offered hospitality to each other. It was a fundamental part of their culture. If Indigo turned it down, it would be an insult unless there was a very good reason. Which she would need to provide.

Not that Blaize expected her to accept given Indigo had just thrown a fireball at her. You didn't get much ruder than that. But you never knew.

If anything, Indigo's eyes went harder. The rage in them burned, and power shimmered in the air around her. If Blaize hadn't been sure in the coffee shop, she'd have needed only a second of seeing Indigo like this to know she was an energetic, and a powerful one. A Practitioner like Blaize, or maybe even a Master.

This time, when Indigo threw the fireball, Blaize was ready for her. She caught it with her own energy and absorbed it, ensuring it didn't get loose into Main Street behind her. But even as she did, she ducked and crossed the few feet between them. She kept her head down and propelled herself into Indigo's stomach. The air went out of the other woman in an 'ouf,' and she fell backwards, thumping into a large trash receptacle.

Blaize grabbed the woman to keep her upright, and put her right arm like a bar across her windpipe. The other woman clawed at Blaize's arm, clutching it to bring it away from her air supply.

"Really," said Blaize. "Why are you here?"

Blaize was aiming for cool and composed, but her blood was up. A week at Cuinn's without proper physical or Manipura training and no way to take out her frustrations with him, Blaize was left with a lot of pent up energy, despite regular sessions of meditation.

"Now's not the time for this," said Indigo. She was holding onto Blaize's arm, pulling on it to keep the pressure off her throat. She was starting to go red.

"Are you ready to come with me? You know you can't use power like that in public."

"I couldn't help myself. You're just so … irritating." The woman rasped the words out through a constricted throat.

"What?" Blaize loosened her arm very slightly in surprise. Indigo took the opportunity to wrench Blaize's wrist away from Indigo's neck and down. Indigo, still holding the wrist, stepped forwards, which broke the arm lock so Indigo ended up behind Blaize. Indigo had now reversed the situation so Blaize's arm stretched out painfully, Indigo's hands on her wrist in a lock that held Blaize in place.

Blaize could no longer see Indigo. She craned her neck to see what Indigo was doing, but Indigo jabbed her arm down, pulling at the shoulder joint. Blaize winced. *Ouch.*

"Much as I would love to spend more quality time with you," Indigo spat, "now's not the time for us to meet properly."

She bent Blaize's arm and forced her against the wall, using her other hand to push Blaize's neck into the rough surface. It was a classic control arm lock.

But Blaize knew Indigo would have to break the hold at some point unless she had an accomplice or some kind of restraints.

Blaize was ready for the transition. She just needed a little movement to get out of this. She kept her head twisted to make eye contact with Indigo.

"There's no need for this. Please. Let's talk. I have no idea what your issue is with me. I don't know who you are or what you want. Tell me. Maybe I can help."

Indigo snorted and just pushed Blaize's cheek harder into the wall. The irregular surface grazed Blaize's face, stinging like a thousand tiny whips.

Indigo leaned closer to Blaize, still shoving her into the wall. Blaize was trapped, her arm held tightly up and out behind her back.

"You can still walk away from this, Indigo," Blaize tried. "Don't let it become more than it is, or you know I'll have to report it to the Guild."

It was likely both of them knew that she'd be telling the Guild anyway, just as soon as she could, but there was no need to escalate things further. Blaize drew power to build defensive shields. She would have to work fast against another Manipura, but it could be done. She could heat her way out of the situation. She drew in a breath.

Indigo leaned her weight on Blaize's arm, and bent her head forward so her obsidian eyes looked into Blaize's. They were magnetic. Blaize couldn't look away.

"I'd love to leave you something to remember me by, but I'll get in trouble if I damage you this early in the game." Indigo's tone was conversational, but the hate was still there.

"So relax. Take a breath." Indigo's voice softened, and she almost crooned the words.

Blaize felt her muscles go lax, and she stopped drawing power. She felt … odd. The alley blurred a little and she blinked.

Indigo stood, sparks flying from her hands and hair. She drew Blaize upright as she did, easing the pressure on Blaize's shoulder.

Blaize came to a standing position. Her head felt fuzzy. Confused. *There's something I'm supposed to be doing. What is it?*

She looked around. Indigo was watching her, a smirk on her face. Indigo stepped back towards the entrance to the alley, Blaize staring at her. *Why can't I remember what I'm supposed to be doing?*

"Okay. Maybe just a little something." Indigo's smirk grew wider.

Blaize felt as if her brain was full of fog. She shook her head, trying to clear it.

"Blaize bitch?" Indigo waggled her fingers.

Blaize turned her head slowly back towards the voice. Indigo's voice. There was a haze in the alley and it was hard to make out the details of what she was seeing. Was Indigo an enemy? *No. Yes. What?*

Indigo whirled towards Blaize, snapping her foot out and into Blaize's stomach. Pain blossomed in her abdomen, and she crumpled forward.

"Teach me," Blaize demanded of Cuinn. "I need to learn what she knows. She took me by surprise today. It won't happen again."

They were home in the kitchen. Cuinn had insisted they report the incident to the police and to Rosa, who had been shocked to hear her waitress had attacked Blaize. Neither report to the humans had involved any mention of energy, and it had gone down as an attempted robbery. Cuinn had asked Rosa to let him know if Indigo returned but had made her promise to call the police first.

Cuinn stood leaning against the wall while Tierra dabbed at the scratches on Blaize's cheek. Blaize held ice to her stomach to bring the bruising down. She'd refused Tierra's healing Anahata energy, saying she wanted to feel the pain so she'd be prepared next time.

"You think she was an Ajna. That she controlled your mind," Cuinn stated. He hadn't believed it at first. How could the woman, someone he'd met two or three times, be an Ajna strong enough for mind control? *How didn't I sense her?* The vision of Blaize, beaten and tied up, was still fresh. Seeing her bruised and scratched wasn't helping him stay calm.

"Of course she was. How else do you think I got these?" Blaize waved at herself.

"Perhaps she was just faster than you. Better trained." Cuinn kept his voice mild.

Blaize growled. "She was better trained. In Ajna. There's no way she was better trained than me in fighting physically. She had no muscle tone. And I'm pretty sure I was the stronger in Manipura. No. She did something to me. Held me in position. I got confused during the fight. I didn't know what was happening, whether she was a friend or an enemy. Everything went foggy like there was some kind of mist in the alley. She kicked me in the stomach while she was controlling me with her mind."

Blaize gestured sharply, still clutching the ice pack. Tierra put her own hand on Blaize's arm and gently pushed it back down. "Keep holding the ice, love."

Blaize was confident, he'd give her that. But today, it seemed, overconfident. He couldn't afford that. She couldn't afford that. She needed to be more careful. He needed to remind her that she wasn't as good as she thought she was. "Then how did you get the scratches on your face?" Cuinn asked.

There was a pause.

"She had some training," Blaize admitted sullenly, "but not enough, and not to take me down with a kick in the stomach. I was ready to break her arm lock. All she needed to do was transition out of it and I would have had the upper hand again. But she did something—"

She broke off in frustration.

Cuinn walked deliberately over to the sink and poured himself another cup of coffee. He set the full cup on the side and gripped the sides of the sink for a moment, looking out of the window, his gaze on the gardens outside. He took a few deep breaths. It had been decades since he'd felt the kind of anger and frustration that Blaize managed to bring out in him. She was so unbelievably stubborn. She'd been in a fight with an unknown energetic who was potentially an Ajna and/or a Manipura Master, and here she was, raging to go another round. *Does she have no fear?* Tension contracted his back muscles and he put a hand up to rub his jaw, to release some of the tightness there.

When he walked back to the table, his tone was still calm. "I didn't say I didn't believe you. I just wanted to explore all the possibilities."

"So we can begin training?"

Cuinn sighed. *This is a bad idea.* "Be at my room at 9.30 a.m."

CHAPTER
18

Cuinn was ready and waiting for the sound of knuckles on the wooden door at 9.30 a.m sharp. He trudged to the door and opened it. She stood in front of him radiating a strange mix of eagerness and distrust.

"This is the room where I work." He gestured around him.

Blaize nodded. The room was less clear and tidy than it had been after Tierra's efforts a couple of weeks before, but he'd managed not to completely fill it with books again. There were only a few on the floor. A few piles, that is. He coughed and her attention came back to him.

"I bought you something."

Her lips flattened, the eagerness leaving her face, leaving only distrust behind. "What?"

He reached behind his desk and brought out a large cloth bag, handing it to her. She opened it and pulled out some heavy fabric.

"What is it?"

"It's a meditation mat. We're going to ward it, energetically guard it, so that you can use it to dreamwalk. It's easier to have something familiar that you use every time. That way your energies seep into it—it's like seasoning a wok."

She blinked and he hastened on, sensing the example hadn't worked that well.

"When we dreamwalk, we're open and unprotected in a way we're not on the physical plane. We need to protect ourselves. Most Ajna energetics, rather than drawing chalk circles all the time, use a warded rug or mat that they can carry with them. It doesn't have the drama of a physical circle, but it's a lot more comfortable when you're lying on it." He tried a smile.

She stood back to shake open the rug. As the folds fell out and it hung in the air from her outstretched arms, she looked at it with a smile, pleased. "It's lovely, Cuinn, thank you."

Cuinn relaxed, and his own smile became less tentative. He'd picked the rug up in Merrow, before the incident with Indigo, when Blaize had been in the small sporting goods shop. He'd chosen it carefully.

He felt something shift inside him as she touched the finely woven strands with unreserved happiness, her face soft. Perhaps he didn't give enough gifts, if generosity could feel as good as this.

"I want us to spend some time meditating together. To get a feel for each other's energy. Before we can even think about dreamwalking, we need to become used to each other."

"I'm a fast learner." Blaize took her gaze off her rug for a second to meet his.

He kept his sigh internal. "I know. But this isn't about intelligence. It's about getting a 'feel' for each other. It's nothing intellectual, or cognitive."

She nodded slowly. "How will we know when we've got this 'feel' for each other?"

"We'll know." He walked to the large windows, throwing them open, letting cold, damp air flood the room, along with the low morning light.

Blaize wrapped her arms around her. "Is that really necessary?"

"You'll get used to it. Be grateful. When I did my Ajna training, my Maven made us do all our work outside. He said it was more conducive to the energy of the mind."

"And when was that?" Blaize asked, her eyebrows raised, her head cocked.

"It was ... some time ago." *Okay, two hundred years ago.* "I don't think we need to go that far, but I do think fresh air helps clarity of mind and meditation. You can set up."

Cuinn cleared some of the piles of books to the sides of the room to make space for her mat. Blaize leaned down to help and he stopped her. "I know what's in each of the piles. It's better if you don't touch anything."

Blaize's face tightened. Cuinn looked away and moved some of the piles closer to each other, keeping the books in the right order.

He cleared enough of the smooth blond wood floor so that she could put her mat down next to his, still out from the night before. When the two rugs were laid out lengthwise next to each other, he gestured to Blaize to sit on hers. She frowned.

"What's the matter?"

She hesitated for a moment. "I don't like sitting with my back to the exit. No Warrior would."

He forced himself not to shake his head in frustration. "You're in my heavily warded rooms, in a heavily warded house, on a heavily warded property. Any danger you encounter isn't going to come through that door. It's what's in your head that you need to worry about today."

He continued, trying to relax his jaw. *Why can't she just do what she's told?* "As Adherent, and student in the process, you sit with your left side—your receptive side—towards the window, the light, and the air. As Maven and teacher, I sit with my right side, my emissive side to the window."

She pursed her lips, but dropped into a crossed-legged position facing his rug, her left side to the window—her back to the door. His back was to his desk as he sank down in front of her.

He held his hands out, palms up. "Rest your palms face down on mine, parallel to the floor. Then our little fingers and thumbs slot into each other."

"I know how to behave in a meditation like this. I've just come from my last Maven, remember?" Blaize's tone was polite, but her words had an edge of irritation to them.

"It's better if we start from scratch. There'll be some things your aunt and I might do in the same way, but given the very different energies we're focusing on, I'm sure there will be things we do differently too. And when the consequences of a mistake can be madness for one or both of us, it's worth being certain."

Blaize's eyes narrowed, and she gave a grudging nod.

I guess working with a fire energetic's never going to be easy.

They joined hands. Hers were warm and dry against his own cooler fingers. There was a curious sense of rightness as her hands fit into his, smaller than his own, but equally slender and fine. Neither of them had hands that had seen much manual labor. Despite his affinity with earth, it had been a long time since he'd tilled the land.

"I'm going to take us through a guided meditation. As you get more experienced, you'll need less ritual and preparation, but for now I want you to close your eyes, listen to my voice and follow my instructions. We'll keep it simple, and get a sense of each other."

"A feel."

"That's right. You'll see what I mean. It will be different from working with your aunt, someone you've known for a long time, and both of you having the same dominant energy. For you, Ajna is your auxiliary energy, and not strongly developed."

Again she took a breath, leaning towards him, and he added, "I didn't say not strong. You may have a great deal of potential; I don't know. Just not strongly developed."

She settled back.

The cool spring air had refreshed the room, airing it out as they'd settled on their mats. The room smelled of new growth and the earth after rain. The sun, still gentle at this time of the day and year, touched Blaize's hair, giving it natural highlights of burnished fire.

She shook her head to remove a strand that had fallen too close to her eyes, and he was distracted as sun and strands danced.

He rarely got distracted. He was more tired than he thought. Her small but pert chest rose and fell, unconsciously echoing his own deep inhalations, and he realised he was staring when he caught the slight crease between her eyebrows.

Damn.

He needed to begin.

"Close your eyes." His voice was soft, persuasive, and her eyelids fell obediently.

His own breath was rhythmic, and he consciously deepened it, making his exhalation a fraction longer than his inhale. After a few of these, his thoughts steadied.

"Breathe, Blaize. Relax your shoulders, your neck. Your jaw, and all the tiny muscles in your face." Her breathing slowed. Her hands relaxed in his.

He lowered his voice further, keen not to disturb her as she focused. His aim was to put her into a very light trance state, a practise session for later dreamwalks. He expected she'd need to practise many times before they got anywhere near that. Today was just about relaxing and seeing if she could feel his energy. He could already feel hers.

He wanted her to use a little of her energy so he could see how visible it was to him when he made a conscious effort, but didn't want to tip his hand. So instead he pulled some of his own energy and sent a tiny and delicate tendril to touch Blaize's aura, the natural energy that every energetic, and in fact, every life on the planet had around them.

Whilst the auras of most life on earth were faint even to the eyes of energetics, the auras of energetics—at least to other energetics—were palpable. His energy brushed lightly against hers, and she shivered.

He pulled back quickly, stunned at her receptiveness and the sensation the touch had created within him. The heat of the contact seared him and he tried to keep his breathing steady as the hair on his arms stood on end.

Hmm. Perhaps more caution was warranted.

CHAPTER
19

What was that?

It was several hours later and they were still working.

Whatever it was, Blaize couldn't hold onto the vision. She fell out of the light trance and her eyes snapped open as the images slipped away from her. When she focused her eyes she found Cuinn staring into them. She flushed. What had just happened? She wasn't sure if she wanted to ask, but Cuinn spoke before she had a chance.

"Good. You created a safe space in the dreamscape, a Haven, which for you was a garden. Your energy, which was all fire at first, was able to brush against mine and shift to a more Ajna energy. Did the smell, taste, or even 'feel' change? What could you see?"

He'd had her imagine herself in a place of positive memories, and to imagine him there with her. They'd no longer been in his Haven. He'd had her interact with his energy. "It changed colour. Well, sort of. It kept flicking between red and blue, with purple and all the colours in between. It was intense. ..."

She hadn't been able to hold on to the feeling. It had been too much.

"That's good. Did you see my energy as blue?"

She nodded. She didn't want to tell him what a beautiful blue it had been. She'd been drawn to it, and to him, and when she'd reached out with her own energy to touch his, she'd only been able to do it for seconds before the delicious intensity had slipped away.

"Your energy adapted to the touch of mine, and it brought out some of your own dormant Ajna energy. Great start. Let's break for lunch."

"But we've only just started," Blaize protested. She was here to work. And she had been surprised to find she'd been enjoying it. Even enjoying spending time with Cuinn. He was a good teacher, calm and helpful, providing useful feedback but letting her find her own way.

"It's one p.m.; Tierra will kill me if I keep you up here and we miss lunch."

Blaize shifted and felt the fatigue in her body, her limbs stiff. Several hours had passed. Where had the time gone?

Several sessions later, Blaize was still trying to trust the process.

"Try to call your own Ajna energy. Use the sensations you felt when you touched mine to guide you."

They were back in her Haven and she felt clumsy, with no idea of what she was doing. She'd forgotten what it was like to be such a beginner and she found herself wanting to impress Cuinn.

I can do this.

She opened herself up wider than normal to see what else was out there that might be different from fire energy. What else could she draw on? She reached out, seeking the blue energy that had surrounded Cuinn to see if she could call up her own.

Instead, she touched something very different.

A dirty, oily blue energy that came into the garden fast and began to attach itself to her.

Suddenly, Cuinn wasn't just watching her. He shouted and moved towards her, his face filled with fear.

But it was as if he was moving in slow motion.

She turned to him, puzzled, as the oily blue began to replace her own red fire energies, turning them a dull brown. She felt heavy, her heartbeat loud in her ears. Her hands shook, and her eyelids fluttered. She wanted to ask Cuinn what was happening, but she couldn't form a single word.

This was not going as planned.

Something … else, something more, had come through. Cuinn had leapt to protect them both against it, trusting his own defences would hold against whatever was intruding where it didn't belong. But before he'd managed to get to Blaize, she'd fallen unconscious, and he'd found himself thrown out of her garden and back in his Haven.

He'd jumped out of the etheric plane and back into his own body as quickly as he could, wincing as he moved between planes too fast, only to find her lying on her mat in his study, a trickle of blood under one nostril in a hideous echo of the prophecy.

He slid from his mat to hers and shouted for Tierra. Then he turned back to Blaize. "Blaize? Blaize. Wake up. Wake up, now!"

As Tierra rushed through the door, she appraised the situation and gestured to him to move aside as she knelt down beside Blaize. "What happened?"

"I'm not sure. Something tried to get through and I was kicked out of her dreamscape and into my own. When I got back, she was like this."

"I don't like the blood." Tierra checked Blaize's pulse and felt her forehead.

Cuinn rubbed the back of his neck, all traces of the relaxation he'd felt in the dreamscape gone. *What the hell had happened?* Was Blaize alright? Was he responsible for this?

Tierra sat back on her heels and closed her eyes to examine Blaize energetically.

Blaize was horribly pale as if the red smear under her nostril was the only blood left in her lean body. Tierra was motionless, hands in her lap, but he had no doubt her mind and her energy were working furiously. Cuinn wiped away the blood on Blaize's face, at a loss as to what else to do while his cousin worked.

He waited a few more seconds before he broke. "Tierra. What's going …"

She shushed him. A few more minutes passed. Cuinn's neck muscles got tighter, and he rubbed the heel of his palm in a repetitive motion on his thigh. He was considering calling an ambulance and involving the human medics when Tierra finally opened her eyes. "She's okay."

His body sagged a little and he pressed his palms into his eyes for a moment. "Why hasn't she woken up then?"

"She will in a minute. She seems to have had the energetic equivalent of a knock on the head. Another one."

A sound came from Blaize. Not loud enough to be classed as a moan, it was definitely a sound of pain. Blaize's hands flexed, and her head lolled a little to one side.

"Cuinn?" Her voice was soft, not at all what he'd been used to hearing over the last few days.

"Blaize." He put his hand out and when they touched, her hand closed around his like a drowning woman holding a life preserver. "Blaize, you're fine. Tierra and I are here."

"Where are we?"

"In my study again. Something happened and you were knocked unconscious and back into this plane."

Blaize's free hand came up to her face, which started to get some colour back. He stared into the now murky-green depths of her eyes and saw confusion, mixed with a little fear. He was sure his eyes held the same emotions—though with a lot more fear.

Seeing her like this brought back a lot of memories he'd tried to forget. It was one more reminder of the reasons he hadn't wanted to take on another Adherent from the start. He rolled his head, stretching out his neck, still almost unbearably tight. Tierra looked at him, concern in her eyes. She knew what he was thinking. He couldn't deal with that now. He shook his head before turning back to Blaize.

"Blaize, you're okay, you just need to rest. Tierra, can I sit her up?"

Tierra nodded. "Carefully. Blaize, sit up slowly. I've checked you over, and you don't have any lasting damage."

"Just another bump on my head," Blaize muttered the words, but Cuinn caught what she said, and looked away.

"There won't be a physical bump this time." His words were sharper than he'd meant them to be, and Tierra frowned at him.

He moved behind Blaize, and with Tierra's help lifted her so that her head was propped up on his lap. Blaize's eyes were open, but unfocused. She winced as she put her hand up to her head and rubbed her forehead. "Ouch."

Tierra moved and left Blaize's weight solely supported by Cuinn.

"I'll make you something warm to drink. Cuinn will look after you." Tierra shot Cuinn a warning look. "Help her into the chair when she's ready. And remember, slowly."

She put her hand over Blaize's and gave it a short squeeze. "You're going to be fine, I promise."

"Yeah, until the third time." The words were quiet but stopped Tierra as she was getting to her feet.

"What?" Cuinn wasn't sure he'd heard correctly.

"The third time. When you knock me unconscious a third time. Three's the charm, so they say."

Tierra smiled and walked out. Cuinn moved Blaize up his body so she rested in his arms. Her body was as supple as it looked, and he could feel the toned muscle under her clothes.

"Umph." Blaize scowled. "No big moves yet. Please."

"Sorry." He shifted his weight so his position was more comfortable, and sat back with his legs outstretched, Blaize resting warm against his chest. "I'm sorry. There won't be a third time. Really. And this time it wasn't me."

Blaize's eyes had closed again. "Whose fault was it then? Was it mine? Something I did?"

He had to lean down to hear her voice, which faded as she spoke the words. As he did, he could smell her fragrance, light and exotic, a hint of jasmine and something else.

His breath quickened, and his arms tightened around her. Blood flooded his groin and he almost dropped her in his haste to hide his body's betrayal.

What the...?

It had been a long time since he'd touched a woman he wasn't related to. He obviously needed to get out more if he was aroused by a woman with whom he did nothing but argue. *Focus, idiot.*

"You didn't do anything. Well, you did, but nothing you shouldn't have. You started to pull energy a little strongly, and something happened. Something tried to piggy-back on the energy you were pulling through. I don't know what. We were both kicked out of the etheric plane before I could discover what it was. You were doing well—some people take weeks to create their Haven, their safe place. You did it in a day."

"It wasn't that safe." Blaize's hands came up to rub her face again and she opened her eyes.

Her face flushed and she grimaced, as she realised she was leaning against Cuinn. She placed her palm flat on his chest as if to push herself away.

He put a hand over hers. *She mustn't get up too quickly.*

"Just rest for a while. Tierra will be back with a drink in a minute. There's no rush." He tried for soothing in his own voice, but could hear a rough edge in it from the arousal he was still fighting.

"There's no need to sound so cross about it."

He cleared his throat.

"I'm not cross. Not with you, anyway. I don't know what happened, and given how much in the dreamscape I'm unable to explain right now, it makes me edgy."

"Crabby."

He smothered a smile. "Maybe."

"You're always crabby with me. Except when you're not."

"I'm sorry for that." His voice was gentler now, and he gave the hand under his a little squeeze. Her hand was over his heart, and he tried not to consider whether she could feel his heart rate pick up the longer it stayed there. He shifted again, restless, and when his hand let go of hers to cradle her body, the simple movement put her hand on his face. He looked at her.

As his face tilted down, hers turned up.

"You could be kinder," she whispered. He felt her warm breath on his lips.

It seemed the most natural thing in the world to close the gap between them and brush a careful, gentle kiss over her lips.

Her mouth opened with an "Oh," and as it did so, his tongue slipped inside as if someone else was directing it. She tasted sweet and tangy, and as enticing as her perfume. Her tongue curved over and around his, matching his soft exploration.

He smothered the sound of desire that the kiss drew from him against her lips, his arms going around her as if he did it every day.

And that movement, that movement, which had happened without a thought, without a decision, stopped him dead.

He never, ever, went with instinct alone.

CHAPTER

20

Several hours later, Blaize lay on the sofa in her living room, a blanket draped over her, and everything she needed within reach. The spring rain had returned, and she was glad she had made it back to the cosy cottage before it had started or she felt sure Tierra would have kept her in the main house overnight. As it was, Blaize had strict instructions to call if she felt unwell in any way.

She wasn't certain if she felt unwell exactly, but she certainly didn't feel like herself. In fact, all aspects of her were tired—mental, physical, energetic, and emotional. Her hand strayed to her mouth, touching her lips gently. As gently as Cuinn's kiss had begun.

Why had he stopped? He'd moved his hand to cradle her skull and pressed her closer to him. She had felt as if she might combust at any moment, the adrenaline melting the headache she'd been fighting. But she'd felt him falter. He'd rested her head back on his chest.

Tierra had found them soon after when she returned with a cup of spicy herbal tea sweetened with honey, and, Blaize suspected, brandy and healing energy.

Tierra had looked at them with her head tilted and her eyes narrowed. She'd tapped her bottom lip with her fingers. Blaize felt her cheeks heat as she wondered if Tierra had realised what they had been doing moments before she returned.

Blaize really hoped not.

Cuinn wouldn't think about Blaize.

He'd gone with instinct, something he never, ever did. He was a thinker—a decision-making style perfectly aligned with his energy. Every choice he made, every action he took, was planned and considered. And that kiss had definitely not been in the plan. Any plan.

It had been a bad idea to agree to another Adherent. Today was a reminder of the terrible events that had happened last time he took on an Adherent.

He went to the library and pulled out a heap of books that might have references to something trying to come through when an energetic pulled energy. What had it been? And had it been connected either to his farseeing of Blaize dying, or to the prophecies in general? So many questions and so few answers.

He worked late into the evening, sorting his way through books with very little to show for it. He needed to go back into the dreamscape himself to see if he could find any trace of the presence that had tried to invade Blaize's dreamscape. But if he was going to track it, he needed access to Blaize's Haven, and he needed her for that.

It was already late, and she needed the rest. He'd put it off until tomorrow. He sat in his chair by the window, and looked out into the dark, wet night. He needed the time too.

He needed to distance himself from that damn kiss.

CHAPTER

21

Indigo hummed as she walked around her Haven. A fairy-tale castle, it glittered and shone. Her Haven was her most precious, safe place. A place where she could have whatever she wanted, and do whatever she wanted. Where she was free. A huge four-poster bed sat in one corner, a dressing table fit for a princess against a wall. She had a closet full of clothes, and more possessions here than any girl could need. Not to mention the room full of weapons.

She curled up on a window seat in the castle and played with the crystals hanging down from one of the lamps. She watched the light dance as it hit each individual drop. It had been satisfying to attack Blaize in the ether. She'd been waiting for days for Cuinn to take that bitch into the dreamscape. She couldn't understand why he'd waited so long. But her own slivers of the prophecy had told her that a chance would come if she was patient, so she'd waited.

And Indigo had nearly had her. She wasn't sure why she hadn't been able to destroy Blaize. Take her. The bitch was untrained and shouldn't have been able to fight Indigo off. Twice now, once on the human plane, and now on the etheric plane.

I'm a Practitioner. She's not even an Adherent. She shrugged the thought off. She'd get her eventually. She'd seen it. She'd have her here, in this very room. Indigo looked across the wide expanse of the main room of her Haven. At the heart of her castle a chair sat in the middle of the space, chains neatly stacked underneath it. Ready.

There was a brief ripple in the energy of her Haven, and she looked up, her muscles tensing. There was only one person who could get in here without Indigo providing a bridge. Only one person she'd introduced to her safe space. She cowered in the window. She pressed herself into the cushion, pulled her legs into her body and hugged them tight.

The energetic locks and chains that Indigo had created fell away from the door and the tall, elegant man came through.

"Indigo, my dear. How are you?" His voice was a pleasant baritone that caused shivers down her spine.

"Fine. Just fine." She didn't want to upset him. Say the wrong thing. But it was so easy to say the wrong thing with him. In fact, it was hard to say the right thing.

"You failed to capture Blaize."

She stifled a whimper. "Yes. But I will. The prophecies say I will. It's just a matter of time."

She wanted his approval. Wanted him to think she'd done well.

"Indigo, didn't I train you better than that? You learned that the future is fluid, pliable, in your Adherent training. A prophecy is seen, the most likely of futures, but not the only possible future." He walked closer, his steps light. "We must do everything we can to ensure that our version of the future wins out. I want Blaize here in your Haven before the month is out. She must be destroyed; Cuinn damaged."

She nodded. Her back was against the window now. There was nowhere to go. He was still coming closer. He was unpredictable. Would he hurt her? Or help her? She was tired. Energy low. He could help with that. *But will he?*

The sparkles in the room had dimmed. Her beautiful knickknacks dulled and discoloured in his wake. It amused him to tarnish some of her glitters when he came in. It always took her days to clean them again.

He was standing in front of her now. She looked up at his clean-cut jaw, his kind face. Should she stand up? She couldn't. He was blocking her way.

"We will. I will. She'll be here before the month is out," said Indigo, the words falling from her lips like a mouthful of bad food.

"Hmm," said the man. "Because bad girls get punished, but good girls get rewarded. Don't they, Indigo?"

She nodded.

"Should you be rewarded or punished, I wonder?" His hand rubbed his chin.

She closed her eyes. It was a trick. It was always a trick. Whichever she said, he'd punish her. *I don't want to be punished.* She hunched down, trying to make herself as small as possible.

He put his hand out, and she reared back. She hit the window behind her hard, and it cracked with a loud bang. She pulled energy without thinking, repairing the damage. But she was weak and didn't have much energy to spare. Her head ached. She attempted to pull some energy from the ether. The headache grew worse.

He watched her, his mouth twitching in a smirk. "I can help."

She shook her head. *No.* His help always came at a price.

But his hand reached out, and clamped down on her shoulder. His grip bit tight, his fingers grinding against the bones. She suppressed a cry.

Energy bled from his fingers into her body. At first, it was blissful. A cooling balm. It replenished her energy and soothed the headache.

But he pushed too hard. Too much. His energy was so powerful. So strong. It began to burn. She moaned aloud. "Enough. Please."

He laughed. "Until you have Blaize here, you need this."

His energy invaded hers. She fell to the side, her body tightening into the fetal position. She looked up at him, eyes pleading for him to stop. A tear fell onto the cushions underneath her. He looked down, dispassionate.

Eons later, the pain stopped. He stepped back. She looked up at him through bleary eyes.

"That was necessary. I want you to search in the dreamscape for more of the prophecy. We need to increase what we know." He walked back towards the door.

She couldn't speak, though as the pain faded her body rallied, electrified by the energy he'd shared with her. She began to shake.

He opened the door to exit. "And you're done with the waitressing job now. Burn those bridges."

"What happened between you and Blaize yesterday when I was out of the room?" Tierra asked Cuinn as he joined her for breakfast.

He shrank down in his seat and huddled over his coffee. "Nothing."

"Ha! Don't be ridiculous. I know something happened, I just don't know what. It looked to me like you smooched. Am I right?"

Cuinn was amused enough at the word 'smooched' to sit up. "We didn't smooch. Whatever that even means. We might have … touched lips. Briefly. Accidentally. It won't happen again."

Tierra came round the table and sat next to him. She placed her hand over his hand, which was still clutching the coffee as if his life depended on it.

"She's not Sophea, Cuinn. Sophea's gone. Blaize is strong in body and mind. And this time, the attraction isn't one-way."

"There's no attraction. And I know she's not Sophea." His words were flat, and he ignored her hand on his. "I'll give Blaize another opportunity to back out today. But if she doesn't, I'll do the binding ritual this week."

Tierra's eyebrows rose. "Really? So soon?"

"I need access to her Haven in order to find out what happened yesterday."

"Cuinn! You can't do a binding that could last for years just for research! You know this is a lasting commitment—you can't go into it half-heartedly."

"I know." He sighed. "It's not that. I can protect her better if we're bound. And I'm not half-hearted. I've spent most of the night thinking about it. I can see she's strong, Tierra. But the energy that knocked her out yesterday, it was … malevolent. Nasty. And I have no idea what it was. If we perform the binding, we'll have access to each other's Havens, and I can protect hers with wards as strong as mine. Nothing will be able to touch her."

"But you're going to give her the chance to back out."

He nodded.

"You know she won't. She's too proud. She doesn't have that aspect of Manipura fully under control yet."

He shrugged. "I can't force her either way. It will be her decision. But our energy recognised each other yesterday. And I have a … feeling about this. I'm worried about her now, as well as the prophecy."

Tierra flinched. "What do you mean? Have you seen Blaize in your dreamscape? Is she involved in the prophecy?"

He still didn't want to tell her. He might have made a mistake. Tierra would only worry. He hedged. "Maybe. I don't know. I still don't have enough information. But it's hard to believe that whatever happened yesterday isn't connected in some way."

"I agree. But Blaize doesn't understand what she's signing up for. You need to tell her more about what's going on. All the details." She rose. "I'll check on her. I'm not sure she'll be up to lessons today."

"That's fine. I need to do more research anyway. I just wish I had more to go on."

"Is there anything else I can do?"

"I don't think so." He stood and engulfed his cousin in a long hug. "Thanks. I'll let you know if you can do more. For now, looking after Blaize helps."

She hugged him back. "I love you, cuz."

I'm lucky. Even with all that's going on, I am lucky.

And I'd do well to remember that.

Blaize had woken several times in the night, each time coming to from some kind of weird dream. In every one, there was some reason to pull energy, to pull power, and each time, she had resisted—but then the dream ended badly for her. She fell from great heights, was hit by cars, drowned, and had been bitten by a poisonous snake. When she woke up at dawn, she felt just as tired as when she'd gone to bed.

An hour or two later, Tierra knocked on the front door and came in. She put her hands on Blaize's shoulders and assessed her. "Did you sleep?"

Blaize nodded.

"Just not very well. A lot of bad dreams." Blaize tried to shrug it off. "Want some tea?"

Tierra's mouth twisted in sympathy. "I'm sorry, love. What were they about?"

After a long exhalation, Blaize said, "I think something is trying to get me to use my power. I keep being sent dreams where people I love are put in danger, and a voice I don't know tells me that all I need to do is use my power, my energy, to save them. And I feel if I draw on my energy, then something bad will happen. I don't know why I don't just use power to stop it—after all, it's not really pulling power in a dream, is it?"

Tierra was frowning and biting her lip. "Your auxiliary is Ajna, and sometimes those who have Ajna as one of their energies can make things happen in dreams. It's just another version of the dreamscape. We need to tell Cuinn about this urgently. It's bound to be connected to what happened between you yesterday."

For an embarrassing moment Blaize thought she meant Cuinn's kiss, which showed just how off her game she was. Heat touched her cheeks and she turned to the kettle to pour hot water over a tea bag.

She spoke over her shoulder. "You think? I just assumed that yesterday was because I wasn't very experienced."

"What did Cuinn tell you happened?" asked Tierra.

Blaize brought the cup of tea over to the sofa where Tierra was perched and sat at the opposite end, her legs curled under her, the tea on a table beside her.

"I'm not sure. Something about me pulling power too strongly? I don't really remember." She avoided Tierra's eyes as she said this last, her hands worrying at the edges of a cushion.

Tierra frowned. "The two of you need to have a proper conversation. Considering what's going on, there are some important gaps in your education."

Tierra leaned forward. "I understand why Cuinn's doing it this way, to help give you the choice about whether you want to enter into a Maven-Adherent relationship. But I don't think it's helping."

Blaize thought that the slow speed of their relationship was more a result of Cuinn's reluctance to take her on as an Adherent than him protecting her from making a bad choice.

"By taking you into the dreamscape yesterday without the two of you being bonded, he opened you up to danger. Did he tell you that?"

"No." There had been no suggestion of concern as they'd been working together. Had he really been trying to protect her? *I hate it when people do that.* A trickle of annoyance ran through her.

"The risk was low but still, as a beginner you had no idea how to ward yourself on that plane, and without being properly bound, it would have been harder for him to protect you. And as you saw, split seconds in the dreamscape can make a big difference."

Tierra got to her feet. "Leave the tea. I'll make you something in the main house, but you need to come with me. It's time for you and Cuinn to talk. Really talk."

CHAPTER

22

Cuinn was in the library, books strewn about him. He'd moved to the floor so he could spread the books out in a bigger space, and the room looked unlike its usual tidy self.

Tierra barged through the door. "You and Blaize need to have that talk earlier than planned. There've been some new developments."

Cuinn glanced at the door behind her, which had bounced on its hinges, and then looked up at Tierra's serious face. "What? Why? Is Blaize okay?"

"She's fine, for now. Come down to the kitchen, and the two of you can share your secrets." She started walking back down the hallway. "There's hot chocolate on the stove if you want some."

Cuinn scrambled to his feet, trying not to dislodge the piles of books with their many bookmarks. *What now?*

When he strode into the kitchen, Tierra was already at the stove stirring a fragrant liquid that he assumed was hot chocolate. But his attention was drawn to Blaize, who was sitting in a chair at the big wooden kitchen table, her gaze focused down, and her hands wrapped around a glass of water.

When her eyes rose to meet his, he saw that the green was faded, and the colour of her hair was in sharp contrast to her pale skin. She had been so vibrant when she'd arrived. She had still had some colour from the Thai sun, and her spirit had been so alive.

Now she looked drained.

"What's happened? What secrets do you need to tell me?"

"I think you should start with a few of yours first." Tierra's tone dripped disapproval as she brought mugs, the pan, and a ladle over to the table. "You should have been clearer with Blaize about what taking her into the dreamscape yesterday actually meant."

"I didn't want to inhibit her. She's a natural." Tierra's impassive face made him shift his weight on the chair. He stared down at the floor. "I wanted to see what we could do in that session. The danger was minimal."

"And yet," said Tierra.

Harder to argue against that. He met Blaize's gaze. "I'm sorry Blaize. I had no idea there would be any danger."

He couldn't tell what she was thinking and he didn't like it.

"She's right, you should have told me. I make my own decisions; I don't like to have those choices taken out of my hands." Her tone was even though dulled with fatigue. Had the experience the day before taken so much out of her?

"I wanted to see whether our energies were compatible before we did anything rash and went through a binding ceremony that's almost impossible to undo. It might have been years before your own energy was strong enough to release from mine."

"Don't make this about me, Cuinn." A little of the fire was back in Blaize's eyes, and he took a perverse pleasure in seeing it there, even at his expense. "You haven't wanted me here from the start, you've made that clear. I just wish I knew what I'd done to deserve that kind of reaction."

Cuinn stayed silent, not ready to give up all his secrets. But Tierra rapped his hand with a teaspoon. He jerked. "Ouch."

She stared at him, her usual good-natured gaze now a steely glare. *Damn.*

"It's not all about you, Blaize. I had a … bad experience with my last Adherent." The words were hard to say. What was she going to think of him when she knew the truth? He hadn't exactly made a sterling impression so far. This might be the last nail in the coffin.

Blaize's arms were crossed, and she leaned towards him, waiting.

"My last Adherent, Sophea, was a Vishudha-Ajna mix. She was a bit … um, otherworldly. I wasn't used to her combination of energies. My Muladhara keeps me grounded most of the time despite my Ajna. With her Vishudha, the element of ether, of space, combined with the Ajna, she was very abstract. She loved to talk about the concepts and ideas of energies. She loved learning, knowledge. We had some fascinating discussions."

He paused again, his throat congested as he forced the words out. "What I didn't realise was that she was falling in love with me."

Blaize was getting some colour back in her cheeks.

"Sophea had been here about a year. One night, we were alone in my rooms, which wasn't uncommon. We'd been discussing a particular aspect of the dreamscape, she wanted us to go there to experiment with the theory I'd been teaching her about. It was late, and we were both tired, but her enthusiasm was infectious." He rubbed his face with his hands, feeling that same tiredness now. He put his hands around the mug of hot chocolate that Tierra had passed to him, and gripped it as if it tethered him to the earth. "She'd been planning it for a long time. She'd created a special room within her own Haven, a bedroom I'd never seen. She'd scattered flowers and lit candles. When we reached her Haven, she took me there. And then she tried to seduce me."

Blaize held his eyes, but she was very still. He couldn't read her. *What is she thinking?* This was his darkest secret. It had coloured everything—everything—in the last fifty years of his life. He felt cold.

"I didn't react well. I hadn't seen it coming, I'd had no idea she felt that way. I didn't see her as a romantic or sexual partner. And she saw it on my face. She slammed her defences in place against me and took me enough by surprise that I was thrown back to the physical world."

Cuinn didn't look at Tierra, who knew this story as well as he did. Even after decades, her face would still show supportive sympathy. She'd been one of the rocks in his life since the tragedy of Sophea, and without her practical help, looking after him and forcing him to eat and live a normal life, he would also have been lost. But he didn't deserve her sympathy.

"I waited for her to come back. Our mats were side by side and hers was as powerfully warded as mine. She was a strong energetic and knew what she was doing."

He fell silent, unsure if he could bear to tell the story's ending.

Minutes passed like eons.

"What happened?" Blaize whispered.

"She lay on her mat, face peaceful, and I paced around my study, waiting. I was agitated and didn't want to go back to the astral world immediately in that mood." His fingers twining and untwining as he repeatedly rubbed his hands together, the agitation of that night echoed here.

"After an hour, I returned to the dreamscape to find her. I wanted to talk about what had happened. I went back to my own Haven and tried to get across to hers. When you complete an Ajna binding ritual, your Havens are linked and you can move between them." He shook his head. "She'd managed to block me. I don't know how—I'm very powerful. But I couldn't get to her. It was as if her Haven had become untethered from mine, lost."

"What do you mean?"

"She never returned. Her body remained as she had left it, essentially in a coma. But her mind was lost somewhere in the astral realm. Her mind had become untethered from her body, and she either couldn't, or wouldn't, return."

Blaize's eyes were wide, and she hugged herself tightly, her arms wrapped around her body. "That can happen?"

"Of course. It's one of the reasons why we spend so much time training and why the binding is so important, because even if your Haven becomes untethered from your own body, your Maven can find you and bring you back. She shouldn't have been able to sever the connection between our Havens. I still don't know how she did it."

"Where is she now?"

"She's in a Rogue rehabilitation centre on an island to the west of Canada. Tierra's friend Cara works there and gives me updates. And I go and see her when I can. I still hope ..."

"You think she might come back?"

"It's possible." He glanced away as he said it.

"Is it ... likely?"

"Possible is enough. And if she does come back, I'll be there. Sometimes I look for her in the dreamscape. Our paths might cross. It's feasible." His head dropped. He'd had hope at the beginning, fifty years ago, but while he said the words, he no longer felt them. But he couldn't let her go.

Her body, still youthful as energetics aged so slowly, lay as if in stasis in the rehabilitation facility, hooked up to machines to help her eat and expel waste. And she could stay like that for hundreds of years. It was a terrible fate for an energetic. His stomach curled inside him.

"So, now you know my darkest secret. I killed my last Adherent."

Blaize's fatigue had lessened as she'd heard Cuinn's tragic story. And her heart had wrenched for both Cuinn and for the young woman who had tried to give him her love.

Energetics lived a long time, but tended not to talk about their past, living with the mantra of 'live for the now.' It wasn't that the past was taboo, it just wasn't seen as relevant or necessary, and it helped to iron out sometimes huge age gaps between energetics, who lived, worked, and loved together.

Blaize, who'd studied psychology for her undergraduate degree, wasn't so sure that it was possible to always live in the now. Here was a case in point. In this case, Cuinn's past explained a lot of his reactions to her over the last week or so. Including why he'd pulled away from their kiss, and why he had seemed so against having her as an Adherent. It had nothing to do with her personally, and everything to do with him. And Sophea.

"You didn't kill her, Cuinn." Her voice was sharper than she meant it to be.

He took a small sip of his hot chocolate.

"What happened was terrible, but it wasn't your fault. Sophea made her own choices." Immature choices, from Blaize's point of view, but she knew love could affect people in different ways. Most of them bad. Another good reason to avoid it.

"I looked for her for months afterwards. I spent all the time I could in the dreamscape trying to find a trace of her. But it's an infinite place. I could look forever and not find her." She had to strain to hear him. "Your uncle, Marius, helped me keep my sanity when I thought I would go under. And Adam and Tierra's earth energy kept me grounded and made sure I didn't disappear. But I was tempted at times."

Tierra got up and stood behind him. She put her arms around him and rested her face on his shoulder. "Drink the hot chocolate."

Blaize shook her head. "I'm not her. Manipura energy is very different from Vishudha. The only similarity between us is that we're both your Adherents, and we both have Ajna as an auxiliary energy. That's it. Right?"

Blaize turned to include Tierra in her appeal.

"Yes, love. You're very different." Tierra lifted her head from Cuinn's shoulder and sat at the table between them. "And Cuinn, you think you're the same person as you were then, but you're different too. But you should have prepared Blaize better for the dreamwalk yesterday."

Cuinn half-shrugged, and he leaned heavily on the table.

"I told you both, I thought it would be easier if Blaize approached it naturally. She's powerful, and gifted. I didn't expect her to create her own Haven so easily. I'm sorry, Blaize. You don't want to be my Adherent. It's not safe. I'm not safe."

That was practically a compliment. Tied up in a rejection. "I can make my own decisions. But only when I'm given all the information."

She was almost too tired to be angry, but there was a spark to her words. She hated being kept in the dark.

Tierra nodded briskly. "I agree. And Blaize, you need to tell Cuinn about your dreams. No more secrets on either side."

"This wasn't a secret," Blaize protested. "It's only just happened."

"Tell me," commanded Cuinn, a touch of imperiousness back in his words.

The room was dark, and when Blaize glanced out the skies outside were overcast, heavy with the promise of rain. She got up and flicked the switch on the lamp in the corner of the room. It cast a gentle light over the three of them, and the room instantly became cosier.

She took a breath as she sat back down, waiting a beat before she launched into a fast and concise retelling of her dreams. Tierra listened more calmly this time, but Cuinn's face had the same look of concern Tierra had shown on the first telling.

"Why didn't you tell me earlier?" He was no longer slumped.

Her eyebrows rose. "Earlier when? In the middle of the night? Four a.m. when I woke up the second time? I thought they were just nightmares. I was hardly going to get you out of bed for a bad dream. When another one came this morning I told Tierra, and here we are." There was something going on here. *Why is he so bothered about a bad dream?*

"How do you feel now?" Cuinn's tone was gruff.

"Fine thanks." She crossed her arms over her chest again. "Apart from the lack of sleep and the sense of impending doom."

Tierra subdued a smile as she put a hand out to touch each of them. "Relax, both of you."

Blaize let out a shaky breath. "Okay, I'm sorry, Cuinn. Let's start again. For some reason, you wind me up the wrong way. But if you could try to remember that a) this isn't my fault as far as we know, and b) I'm doing my best here, I'd appreciate it."

She looked across the table into eyes that echoed the grey of the sky outside. They met hers, and for a moment, all three of them were still. Connected. Energy shivered through them, balm on physical and emotional hurts. Tierra removed her hand, and Cuinn moved his gaze to hers. "Thank you."

She nodded. "I know you don't love me using energy on you, but the two of you need to calm down. Neither of you has had much sleep recently, and as I've said, we all make bad decisions when we're sleep-deprived. You're on the same side. Really."

The energy Cuinn had shown as she'd told him about her dreams had gone. His usually upright spine was bent, and his gaze was on something unseen out of the window. He shook his head, and looked back at her. "I'm sorry, Blaize. There's so much going on here. And I need to tell you something else."

He described the newest slivers of prophecy he'd collected. About seeing her injured and restrained. How he'd recognised her in the group of energetics who stood with him in the first glimpses of the prophecy.

She couldn't believe this. She'd been there for days, and he'd said nothing. Her body felt as taut as a violin string. *How many more secrets were there?* "You should have told me earlier."

"I know."

"If you had told me before, I'd have come straight to you with the dreams. Source, I'd have woken you at four a.m."

"I know."

She stood and paced around the kitchen. She felt sick. He'd seen her brutally beaten, but perhaps also ready to save their world. How was she supposed to handle all that?

He sat quietly, watching her. After a few agitated minutes, she put her hands on the back of the wooden kitchen chair she'd been sitting on and stared into his eyes again. "No more secrets, Cuinn. Seriously. No more. You have to tell me everything. Is there anything else?"

Cuinn and Tierra exchanged a glance. Tierra's look seemed pointed.

"My Guild Leaders told me I needed to work with you. That my future and yours are bound up together. That I would need you."

Blaize felt overloaded by all the information. She wanted to stomp around, to smash things. More, she wanted to break something over his pigheaded skull. Some of the most powerful farseers in the energetics race had told him their futures were linked, and still he fought taking her as an Adherent?

Tierra rose and gave Blaize a quick hug. "That's everything. Why don't you help me prepare some lunch, and we can talk about it more when we've all had some food? You—both—need time to process this morning."

Blaize wasn't sure that preparing food was going to help in terms of saving the world, but she'd use the break and be grateful for it. She felt frazzled from the intensity of the emotions in the room. She put a hand up to rub her temples, to soothe the headache she could feel lurking.

"I agree." Cuinn pushed his own chair back from the table and got up.

Tierra stepped in front of him as he moved towards the door to the corridor. "I don't think you should go back to your room, Cuinn. You need to replenish your connection to the earth. Go outside and walk for an hour while Blaize and I cook."

He gave her a cool look, but he went to the utility room and grabbed his jacket. "Fine. But if it rains and I catch cold, I'm blaming you."

CHAPTER
23

"Talk to me," Tierra said to Blaize once Cuinn had left.

"I feel ... a bit blank. It's hard to imagine featuring in a prophecy. My only –" Blaize fumbled for the word "– experience with them has been negative."

Tierra tilted her head a fraction, eyebrows furrowed. "What do you mean?"

Blaize so did not want to go there. She was already raw from the last hour. She wondered whether she would get away with a diversion, but Tierra stayed silent. Expectant.

This was a dark part of Blaize's past, and one she rarely discussed. But she wanted to explain her strong reaction to Cuinn's latest information. She hadn't thought about the connection between Ajna and prophecy when she'd been told she was to start training, but it seemed there was no getting away from it as a part of the Ajna energies. She'd keep it brief.

"My parents were given a prophecy when they were married. It hinted at what eventually did happen. They ignored it. And they both died." Blaize kept a tight rein on the emotions that bringing the topic up raised. She was proud there was no break, no hitch in her voice. *It was a long time ago. I barely knew them.*

"I didn't realise." Tierra's voice held anguish. "You need to tell Cuinn that. This situation is bad enough, but both of you are carrying a lot of baggage from your past. You need to share everything and get past that."

Blaize nodded and let out a breath, trying to relax but stay in control.

"Is Sophea why I hadn't heard of Cuinn? Now I'm here, he seems as powerful as any of the Master energetics I've met, but I didn't know who he was before Fai told me about him. Yet I know all thirty of the Minor Circle's names, even if I haven't met them."

Blaize traced patterns on the table as she thought aloud. She had a lot of questions. "Is it because of what happened with his previous Adherent?"

"Yes, but not in the way you think." Tierra got up and went over to the kitchen island. She motioned for Blaize to follow her and sit at the breakfast bar. "Cuinn's always been involved in Circle business. He would have been a good choice for his Minor Guild's Circle seat when the last energetic who held it passed away. Many energetics in his Guild—and outside—were keen for him to take it, but since Sophea, he's resolutely refused any formal position. He'll help out based on his sense of duty, but he doesn't trust himself to be in a position of responsibility."

Tierra brought over a bag of potatoes and a peeler. "I hoped you could help him move past that. By taking on a new Adherent, a new responsibility, he would regain the confidence he lost. It was a big deal for him to agree to take a new Adherent, and to be honest, we—Adam and I, and some of his other friends—pushed him into it when the opportunity arose. He has so much to offer. And as I told you at the start, he's a good person who's lost his way."

Tierra hesitated for a moment. "And as you'll have understood from the story about Sophea, he's also not that great with women. Sometimes his book smarts get in the way of his people smarts."

Blaize rubbed her face to hide her blush. When she thought the colour had died down again, she took out a potato and began to peel it, concentrating on the task as if it was brain surgery. "Cuinn and I still have some talking to do, I guess. And we should perform the binding ritual as quickly as possible."

"Really?" Tierra looked surprised.

"Our energies work together, and there's danger ahead—not just for us, but for the whole energetic race. I've trained to be a Warrior, Tierra. It would go against everything I've trained for up to now to back off because of the personal consequences." And in saying that, Blaize felt a kind of peace settle over her. She was someone who liked to have a goal, and the more stretching the better. This definitely fitted the bill. Maybe she'd be able to use her Manipura training sooner than she'd thought. "But I need to start physical training again. Will you open up the gym for me after lunch?"

"Of course. But are you sure about the binding?"

"Yes." And the simple word resonated with the total confidence of a Manipura Warrior.

Cuinn spent an hour walking his land and renewing his connection with the earth. The day had remained dry despite the clouds above. He moved through the woods, smelling the damp, peaty earth, and paused in a clearing bathed in one of the few patches of sunshine he'd seen that day. He sat on a fallen log, closed his eyes and leaned back on his hands, the rough bark digging into his thighs, grounding him.

Tierra had been right, he'd come almost to the end of his resources. And while he could see that the secrets he'd been keeping from Blaize needed to be shared, exposing himself like that had been one of the hardest things he'd done in years. He couldn't bear to see the condemnation in her eyes. Or worse, pity.

But when he'd been brave enough to look at her, he hadn't seen either. He'd seen empathy. Compassion for the man he'd been, and acceptance of the man he was now.

Blaize was also unsettled, and he didn't blame her. Her dreams were worrying, along with her sense that she shouldn't draw on her power—which had persisted after the dreams had ended.

He had just told her about a prophecy where she was terribly injured. That tended to put a crimp on someone's day. He hadn't been able to bring himself to tell her he'd seen her die. That wasn't keeping a secret; it was holding a little something back. Something that might have pushed her past her reserves.

Should we go ahead with the binding? He wasn't right to be a Maven. His arrogance and ignorance had caused the last tragedy. And if he was honest with himself, really honest, his feelings for Blaize had become—complicated.

He hadn't allowed himself to think about the kiss until now. He'd taken advantage of her when she was barely in her right mind after being thrown from the etheric plane by Source knows what. He groaned. *What an idiot.*

He couldn't repeat the strange behaviour, the impulse that had overtaken him. She was desirable, an attractive woman, but he could control himself better than that.

Anyway, it had probably just been his own stress reaction to seeing her lying on the floor, bleeding. He'd been terrified. When she'd come around, his relief had been so great, it had translated into the kiss. In fact, when he thought of it like that it was almost as if he had hugged her. Sort of like a sister.

But he then thought, ashamed, of the reaction of his body. The lascivious heat that had spread through him like honey as he'd kissed her. Heat that was firmly centred around his groin. That hadn't been the way he reacted to female family members—in fact, it wasn't the way he reacted to women at all these days.

He wasn't a man who went in for brief, uncomplicated sexual relationships. But right now, he wished he did. A night of healthy sex with a woman who had the same understanding might have gotten rid of these complicated feelings he had for Blaize.

His body reacted to the thought of Blaize and sex in the same sentence with its own opinion, his cock throbbing, and he adjusted his pants. It seemed that some parts of him were quite strongly in favour of the concept.

He groaned again.

This wasn't helping. He and Blaize couldn't get involved sexually; it would just complicate things further. The feelings would probably fade as they got used to each other.

He'd just take plenty of cold showers until they did.

CHAPTER
24

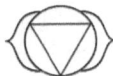

Blaize and Cuinn helped Tierra set the table, then sat to eat.

"I have one more secret. Well, not so much a secret, as something I didn't think was relevant." Blaize took some salad and passed the bowl to Cuinn. "But Tierra thinks I should lay out all the pieces for you."

He nodded and added a veggie burger to his plate.

"My parents." She stopped.

"I know what happened to your parents, Blaize." He bit into his burger.

"Yeah. I guess the story got around." She flared for a moment, angry. She gritted her teeth and stabbed at a potato. "There's more that not many people know. And I'd like to share the whole story with you."

"You don't have to. And I know because of my friendship with Marius, nothing more."

She shrugged. "If we're going to be bound, you need to know it all. It's the last secret. I think, anyway."

"And are we?" He'd stopped eating, his eyebrows high. Her anger died as she saw that he had been genuine about his offer to release her from their agreement to be Maven-Adherent.

"Yes. It's the right thing to do. If I—we—can help to protect our whole race, why wouldn't we?"

"You have the right to say no."

"I know. I'm making a choice, don't worry. But you'd better help me train as quickly as possible so I can protect myself. I'm a Warrior—I don't like it when others have to protect me." She really hadn't liked the experience in the alley. She was proud—justifiably— of her fighting abilities. To be beaten like that had been a difficult experience. She needed to know how to beat Indigo when she next came up against her. To bring her in so she couldn't do that to anyone else.

"You have a great deal of Ajna power. I could sense it when we were in your Haven. It won't be long before you're able to create barriers and protect yourself with energetic wardings." He leaned in towards her, sketching walls in the air with his hands. "But, you can still change your mind. We'll provisionally schedule the ritual for a couple of days' time. But promise me you'll sleep on it. You can still back out. It's not something to be taken lightly."

"Fine by me. But the answer will be the same." She took her own small forkful of food. Her stomach felt tight, knotted. She chewed. She would learn. And she would take Indigo down.

Tierra put another spoonful of fried potatoes on Cuinn's plate. "Eat."

He did so, digging into them. "This is great."

Tierra nodded. "Blaize, love, carry on."

Blaize drew in a deep breath and put her own knife and fork down. "My parents … my parents were Aria McCarthy and Aden Blackfire. A couple very much in love. Eyes only for each other, they were together many decades before they had me."

She shifted in her chair. "When I was nine, my mother went on retreat as she did most years. I was left with her brother, Marius, and my father. One night, I overheard them arguing, and my father stormed out. That was the last time I saw him."

These were her blackest memories. She'd had a good childhood, before and eventually after this. But this tragedy still incited her anger. She just didn't know how her father's energy could have twisted so badly. That he could have committed those terrible actions.

And whether that potential is in me, too.

"Later, Marius told me what happened," she said. "My father's jealousy had got out of control. He'd made up his mind that my mother wasn't on retreat, but with a lover. He left the house to find her and bring her back to where she belonged, with him."

Her pulse sped a little. *Breathe.*

"Without her Anahata energy to ground him, his energy overpowered him, and he went Rogue. He found her on her retreat, alone, as she'd said she would be." Another breath. "A few days later, Marius found the two of them, dead."

"I'm so sorry, Blaize," Tierra murmured.

"None of this is the point." Blaize pushed her chair out and stood, adrenaline washing around her body as if she was about to defend herself to the death. *I want to run. To move. Or to fight.* "I'm telling you this because before they were married, a Seer gave them a personal prophecy that not many people are aware of. The prophecy said their marriage was likely to be the source of both great good and great harm. That they would suffer, but that that suffering would bring about a greater positive change in the world. That they still had a choice as to whether or not they married, but the odds weren't in their personal favour. And that a man would come between them in some way.

"My Father, never that interested in Seers, ignored it, but my mother felt the greater good was worth her suffering, and felt her love for my father would be enough. But, as is often the way with prophecies, the seed planted by the Seer that a man would come between them stayed with my father. Eventually, it was what tipped him into a Rogue state. He was convinced that there was a man. But in fact, the words just meant that the idea of a man would come between them. There was no man."

She walked over to the back door and threw it open. She stood in the cold draft, breathing deeply.

"So I'm not sure how I feel about prophecies. They caused a lot of damage in my own life. And destroyed my parents. They're twisty things. Slippery, hard to pin down, and cause as much harm as good."

Silence.

"I'm sorry, Blaize. I had never heard about the prophecy." Cuinn looked at her with compassion. She rubbed her arms and blamed the cold air for the fact that her body was shaking. She held her elbows and looked away from the cosy scene inside the kitchen. She had a feeling none of them would eat much this evening.

"Thankfully, Marius and Fai adopted me into their family without question and always showed me just as much love as they showed Nixie, their own daughter, and my cousin. You'd love her, Tierra. A gorgeous spirit." She smiled briefly. "And so here we are. With me still wondering, thirty or so years later, what exactly the greater good was that came out of their deaths. Because it all seemed pretty senseless." She took one hand away from her body, and gestured, palm down. Tiny sparks flew from her hand, her energy making its presence known. She felt a sense of unease and spooled the power tightly inside her. She hadn't shaken off the dreams yet, and she wasn't ready to use her power.

"You can never know." Cuinn's words were quiet but gentle. "The butterfly effect is a simplistic idea that explains something very complicated—how one tiny action can leave traces on all kinds of other things. It's hard to know what the greater good might have been—it could have been something small that affected many people, or perhaps it's still to come."

He and Tierra exchanged a thoughtful look, which Blaize caught as she turned back into the kitchen, no longer shaking, some of her adrenaline burned away. "Yeah. Grandmother thought that I must be the greater good. It's one of the reasons she wanted me trained to be a Guild Leader. But it seems pretty unlikely to me."

CHAPTER

25

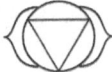

Later that afternoon Cuinn went down to the gym to see what Blaize was doing. She was trained as a Manipura Warrior, and he wanted to see her in action.

He told himself it was to see what her skills were like, and whether she might be able to translate some of them into the dreamscape. *Yeah, right.* The thought of that strong, toned body had intruded one too many times on his consciousness in the last few days.

He pushed the door to the gym and it opened smoothly, letting a little of the stale air-conditioned air out. He felt the temperature drop as he moved into the space. The sound changed too. The underground gym was soundproofed, and opening the door let out a blast of some kind of alternative rock, high energy and angry.

Blaize pounded on the heavy bag with a number of sharp elbow strikes and punches that looked like some kind of martial art.

Dressed in a black and red sports bra and some kind of tight workout pants that came half-way between her ankle and knee, she moved like danger. Her power was sleek and deadly, and she flew through the moves in a blur. It was a completely different side to her.

He thought she hadn't noticed him, but after a few minutes of watching her, fire in motion, she stopped. She wiped the sweat from her face with a small towel and turned to him. Her mouth moved, but he couldn't make out what she said over the music.

But even if he had, he wasn't sure if he'd have been able to answer. He'd only seen her back as she had been facing the bag up to now. Getting a front-view of her in her workout clothes had given him a punch that was just as effective as any she'd given the bag.

She dripped with sweat, her flame-red hair slicked back in a rough pony tail, and her workout gear showing off every curve on her lean body. He was transfixed. She stepped closer to him, and he wanted to pull her towards him by her hips and press her up against the door behind him.

He was still possessed by the idea when she waved a hand in front of his face in puzzlement. "Cuinn?"

He had an image of pushing the sports bra up and licking the sweat off her stomach and breasts. *Where the hell did that come from?* He shook his head and turned away from Blaize. He reached for the music volume knob on the wall behind him.

His cheeks hot, he turned back to her and pushed his hand through his hair.

"Is everything okay?" Blaize held the towel in one hand and her water bottle in the other. "Did you need something?"

"I just came ... to check that you were alright."

Blaize's frown deepened, and she touched the base of her neck. That drew Cuinn's eyes down again to the trickle of moisture running down from her neck until he realised and snapped his eyes back up again.

"Thanks. But Tierra showed me around when she turned everything on earlier." She took a drink from the bottle and wiped her face again. "Really, are you okay?"

"I'll leave you to it." He turned quickly—and walked into the door.

"Bollocks." Luckily he'd been leading with his shoulder, so the damage wasn't too bad. He checked his arm, but it all seemed fine. Apart from the bruise he'd probably have tomorrow, as well as the gaping wound in his pride.

A muffled laugh came from behind him. "Still okay?"

"I'll be fine." *Just as soon as I get out of here.*

"Maybe you should do some exercise. You seem to be a bit off. More grounding needed?"

"Thanks. I'm fine." He turned back to face her. She was much closer than she had been. So close, in fact that they were almost touching. He could smell her, very faintly, spicy with hints of sandalwood. He looked down at her, and she put one hand up to touch his face.

"Really? Because I have to say, Cuinn, you don't seem ... fine." That lilting laughter was still in her voice, and he closed his eyes for a second as skin met skin. As always, she was hot to the touch, and his whole being focused on that one spot on his cheek, his bruised shoulder forgotten.

When he opened his eyes again, her other hand moved up to his face, and before he could form any words, she'd drawn him down to her mouth.

And then, all thought vanished. There was just sensation. Her soft lips. Her mouth, sweet and spicy at the same time. Her scent, the sandalwood much stronger now.

At first he just dipped his head as her fingers guided him, and let her lead the kiss. And then her tongue flicked out, gently insistent, and he parted his lips to give her access. Their tongues danced, coiling around each other in a heated sensual tangle.

And he lost his mind again.

He brought his arms up swiftly and pulled her in towards him. She gasped, and he took the opportunity to explore her mouth more thoroughly.

She put one arm around his waist, and rested it just above the jut of his hip, and pressed their bodies close. His hands roamed around her back, especially the damp and naked skin between the waist of her workout pants and her top.

She moaned. The sound was erotic, and he wanted to worship her, to lay her down on the floor and praise every inch with his tongue and fingers. He wanted to hear her moan again, more frequently and with renewed volume.

And just as he was considering doing exactly that, her hands swept down his back, below his hips, and he lost his reason again. But as quickly as she'd shifted them down and brushed his ass, she moved her hands again, and pushed and spun him at the same time. It left him a few feet away, dazed and confused, with her now between him and the door.

This time she didn't stifle the laugh.

"I thought I'd better help ground you. I'm going to shower now. See you at dinner." And with a grin, she blew him a kiss and disappeared through the door, leaving him staring after her.

Perhaps Cuinn was right, and Blaize needed to think more about strategy. It probably hadn't been that clever to kiss him. She was starting to think she might be quite comfortable having a sexual relationship with him without any other complications, but somehow she doubted a casual relationship would be enough for him.

And then there was the issue of Sophea. She hadn't been thinking of Sophea when she'd kissed him, and Blaize was damn sure he hadn't been either. But he was certain to afterwards. It had been one of the reasons she'd decided to eat alone this evening. That, and she thought Tierra had some kind of radar for this kind of thing, and Blaize wasn't ready to discuss it.

There had been so many confessions between her and Cuinn today that she'd barely had a chance to think about the horrible dreams of the night before. She desperately needed a good night's sleep. Maybe she should have asked Tierra for something dosed with her earth energy to help her sleep.

As if she didn't already have enough on her plate, she still felt a lingering sense of worry about using her power. The dreams had unsettled her, and the discussion with Cuinn had only heightened her anxiety. She would keep her power controlled until she'd gone through the binding ritual with Cuinn. At that point, she'd have his protection in the astral world, which was where she felt the real danger was.

But all the emotions of the day had left the energy churning inside her, stirred up by the confessions and subsequent feelings. She wanted to use it, to let it loose. *But I have more control than that.* She was impulsive, sure, but not stupid.

So tomorrow she'd go over to the house for breakfast, confirm that she was going to take part in the binding ritual, and spend the day in meditation. She wasn't sure if there was any other preparation needed; she'd have to check with Cuinn. He'd continued to be close-mouthed about the ceremony itself, but she thought that was probably due to the fact he'd thought it would be way off in the future rather than because he was keeping more secrets from her. They were beyond that now. Weren't they?

Her Manipura ritual to bind herself to Fai had been a long time ago now but she remembered it clearly. Knowing Fai so well had helped. The element of fire was about change and transformation. Fai had given Blaize instructions to bring something dear to her, something she needed to let go.

She had chosen a toy that her mother had given her, which had grown moth-eaten and ragged. At nine years old, old enough to understand that her parents weren't coming back, the big-eared bunny had been the thing she'd clung to at night in the strange house, trying to fit into a family that wasn't her own.

But by the time she was ready for the Manipura binding, and truly a part of the very happy family that was Fai, Marius and Nixie, it was time to let go of the toy. And let go she did, because as part of the ceremony Fai had required her to sacrifice it to the flames, in order to help power the energy of the binding. It had been hard. But change, courage, transformation, were all part of what she was embracing.

She wondered what, exactly, she would be embracing with the power of the mind.

CHAPTER

26

Cuinn cleaned his rooms on the physical plane, and then needed to clean the energy of the room. The space was already protected because of his work there, but he still performed a short cleansing ritual to refresh the room itself. He drew a new sacred circle and placed his and Blaize's mats in the middle. They would draw the circle together later, over the top of the work he'd already put in, strengthening its protection still further.

He also redrew the protection symbols he had at the windows and both the door to his bedroom and the door to the hall. The symbols flared in the air each time before disappearing from normal vision, though if he drew on his Ajna energy he'd be able to see them there.

When finally satisfied with how everything looked, he sat down on his own mat, ready to move to the astral plane and begin again there.

He went directly to his own Haven, the tower. Though it was heavily protected by hundreds of years of his wardings, the last few weeks had made him wary and extremely cautious.

He went down the thick stone stairs of the tower to the heavy door, using energy to redraw the wardings on this as on every other opening of the tower before heading outside.

They would enter Blaize's Haven from his own. But before that he would construct a connection, a gate between their Havens that would ensure that as part of the binding he could extend some of his own wardings to her. He looked around, considering the landscape.

His tower was surrounded by open land and plains. It was the basic protection mechanism used by his ancestors in Ireland who built their houses and castles on them so that they could see enemies approaching. But it meant he wasn't sure where to create the connection to Blaize's Haven. This connection was important because it would be a weakness in his own defences—a place someone who wanted to get into his Haven would choose, rather than other much more heavily guarded areas.

He chose a piece of land near a small stream. Just because water wasn't part of his own mix of energies, didn't mean he didn't find the sound soothing. He sat on a boulder with his back to the water, and he drew power.

He wanted to create a doorway between parts of the astral world, but a doorway that wouldn't be activated until the ceremony with Blaize. He deliberated a minute, then concentrated. Something began to grow a few yards in front of him. Two things. Two shoots came out of the grass about a yard apart. They grew steadily and swiftly until they were about six feet high. Ash trees, supple and strong. The trees bent towards each other at an unnatural angle and grew. Their branches touched with a shudder, and tiny buds exploded into a riot of leaves.

He stood, pleased with his work.

He put his hands on the trees, connected with them, and thanked them. They shivered under his touch, responsive. He curled energy around them, the power of earth and of the mind.

His many years of experience meant that he was able to use the power of both of his energies on this plane, not something everyone could do. He didn't need earth energy to do what he had just done on the astral plane. The power of the mind was enough. But enhancing it with the energy of the elements made it somehow stronger, more real.

The door was now energetically warded, if not activated. No one could use it at the moment, and even when it was opened, only he and Blaize would be able to activate it. He would make sure of that.

Blaize had also spent the day preparing. A long yoga practice in the morning, stretching her body into impossible poses, had expanded her body and mind at the same time. She'd taken it slowly, holding the poses for a long time, sinking into each one to connect to the energies it aroused, working her way through the seven Chakra energies, at the end opening herself up to Source.

These seven energies enabled life; and each of the energies brought something different to the world. All energies were present in every living thing, though only energetics were blessed to have an 'activation' of two of their Chakras.

Yoga was one way in which energetics—and humans—could get in touch with their energies, balancing all of the energies that were present within them, even those that weren't 'active.' Yoga helped to ensure an energetic was in balance, harmonious.

But only six of the energies could be active in an energetic. The seventh, the energy of Sahasara, was the energy of Source. The Crown Chakra. It was the purest of all the energies, and could only be experienced through the Grace of Source, a Grace that few experienced. Source was the energetics' name for the creator, the divine, the supreme being. The other six energies were distributed among the energetics' race much as they were through the body.

Each energetic manifested the two energies that would become their 'active' energies in childhood, mostly during puberty. For Blaize that had meant some unfortunate fires and a strong ability with puzzles. But since then, it had been Manipura that Blaize had concentrated on. Immersed herself in.

She was about to change that.

She'd spent the day preparing herself, body and mind, and she felt as ready as she thought she'd manage. It was time to focus on her Ajna for a while. She wasn't as comfortable with it as she was with her Manipura. Well, of course. She'd spent years on her Manipura, her dominant Chakra, whereas Ajna was just her auxiliary.

She walked in bare feet across the grass between her cottage and the main house. The woods and plains around her seemed hushed, everything waiting for the ritual's start.

She paused at Cuinn's door, checking herself one more time. She loved the dress that had been a present from Tierra that morning. The material was soft and gauzy, and Blaize enjoyed the way it moved around her. With her height, Blaize rarely felt delicate, but the dress had done the trick.

She knocked on Cuinn's door, and took one more deep breath. When he opened the door, they both stopped. She took him in in a rush.

He wore loose white trousers that hung from his hips, and a classic fitted white shirt that emphasised his lean, compact frame. The shirt had the three indigo stripes across his right shoulder that showed he was a Master, and a tiny embroidered symbol of an owl in royal purple thread that indicated he was a Maven. He was freshly shaved and his hair was tied back neatly, and seemed darker than usual against all the white.

She dropped a curtsey to break the tension, her white dress pooling on the ground around her. She stood back up again with a mischievous smile. "I guess we both scrub up well then?"

"I guess so." He moved out of the way. "Come in."

His workroom had been transformed. He'd put up fairy lights, and the ritual sacred circle around their mats was beautiful. Something flickered at the corner of her eye. She squinted and caught a hint of purple at the windows. She stepped closer. "Are these warded?"

He smiled. "I strengthened the wardings today. It's a good sign that you can sense them. It means your Ajna is waking up."

He shut the door behind her, and she felt a tingle as he pulled a little more energy to protect and ward the door and seal them in. He turned back to her. "Are you ready?"

"As I'll ever be."

"Don't worry, I'll guide you through. Let's draw the circle."

He went to the small altar, took two candles, and gave one to Blaize. The room grew darker, the fairy lights growing more distinct.

"We're going to light the candles." He held up a hand as she took a breath. "Don't use your Manipura energy. Tonight you need to focus on Ajna alone."

They lit their candles from the candle he already had burning on the altar, and both blessed the ceremony in their own words, taking their time to connect to Source. They then moved to their mats, faced each other, and placed their candles in front and to the side—both the same side, his right and her left.

She was aware of her body, her every movement, her heartbeat. The anticipation was almost unbearable. There were no nerves now. Just excitement.

He took a canvas bag of rock salt that was next to the altar. "I've blessed this already. I'll cast the circle first, then you, then we'll draw it together, so we've cast it three times."

They cast the circle individually, then he took the bag of salt from her, and cupped her right hand in his. He poured salt into her hand, and steered her hand to drop salt around the circle for the third time. She shivered a little at his touch, feeling his breath on the back of her neck as they moved clockwise in the flickering candlelight.

He paused and she half turned in his arms, looking up at him. His gaze captured hers. His eyes changed from dove grey to almost charcoal, the iris blending with the pupils. She couldn't look away.

He broke her gaze and gestured down. "The mats."

She pulled away and sank down onto her mat, a puppet with the strings cut. She could still feel his arms around her, missing the feel of his skin against hers. The infuriating man really did have the strangest effect on her. She sat cross-legged, and closed her eyes. The air moved as he sat opposite.

"We have drawn the sacred circle and are protected for the night," he said formally. "Breathe deeply, and focus inside. Consider the infinite power of the mind. Centre yourself."

He fell silent, and they sat, immersing themselves in meditation. Blaize enjoyed meditating, but her mind—like most people's—had a tendency to wander. She focused as much as possible on the mind, using her breath to draw her back when she got distracted.

"Blaize Blackfire, you come to offer yourself as Adherent in the Guild of Ajna," Cuinn said in a lower tone. "Stand now as we offer our binding to the elements."

Blaize stood. His voice seemed different as it took on the power in the room. She opened her eyes. He almost seemed to shimmer in his white clothes, a commanding presence.

"Offer yourself to the North."

Blaize turned to the North. "I offer myself to the North."

"May you be blessed by the element of earth. Of strength, stability, and a strong sense of self."

At his instruction, she offered herself to each direction, and the circle itself, as he asked for a blessing from each of the elements: earth, water, fire, air, and ether.

"Thus we petition the elements to support our binding ritual." He drew in a deep breath, and there was another tingle, the air shimmering between them. "Hold out your hands."

Blaize did. They trembled ever so slightly. He took her hands and turned them over gently so both faced upwards, then crossed them so her right arm was on top of the underside of her left wrist. He turned his arms so that the palms faced down, crossed them, and grasped hers.

"Our hands join together in the sign of infinity, eternal renewal. We commit ourselves to be linked until Blaize Blackfire reaches the level of Practitioner in the Guild of Ajna."

He looked deeply into her eyes, unblinking. A heap of purple silk thread on the floor moved towards their wrists. Cuinn's gaze didn't waver from hers as he directed the thread with his energy to loop around their joined wrists, binding them. "We are bound in fact. Let us be bound in blood."

His grip on Blaize's hands tightened, and a sharp pain pricked her palms. Drops of blood fell from their joined hands.

"Our blood mingles; our energy mingles." A tingle started through her left palm, moved around her body and then through her right palm until her whole body was alive with energetic power. Goosebumps rose along her arms and she shuddered. The power was cool, and felt different from her Manipura energy.

Ajna energy.

Her left arm burned with a sudden, blinding pain. She turned her head to see an indigo Ajna mark, a band around the top of her arm, a little above her Manipura bands.

She was an Adherent on the physical plane.

"We stay bound as we move to the astral plane. Let's sit together."

They sat opposite but close to each other, their legs crossed and their hands now resting, joined, on their knees.

"Close your eyes, Blaize, and follow the sound of my voice."

She did. He talked her into the light trance she needed to get to the astral plane, taking her to his own Haven.

They stood in his tower.

"So this is your Haven?" Blaize, fascinated, drank in the scene. They were in a large airy room that, given the view out of the window, seemed to be fairly high up. "Lucky I'm not a psychologist, or the fact that your Haven is a great big tower might make me think—"

He shot her a look that was almost an eye roll, and she smiled.

"You did well to follow me here. Your Ajna energy is strong. Can you see my energy again?"

She tried to see the streams coming out of his body that she'd seen last time. It took her a little longer, as if they were at the edges of her vision, and she could only see them from the corner of her eye. But after a while, she caught the trick of it again and suddenly he was surrounded by purples. He shone with it. This was nothing like what she had seen in the village garden, in her own Haven. The streamers had become a mass.

She gasped. "Wow. There's a lot more than before."

He nodded. "Good. That's because this is my Haven—the place I created on the astral plane. It's the centre of my power on the astral plane. It's almost impossible for anyone to come here unless I want them to.

"We're going to build a connection from my Haven to yours, so you will be welcome here all the time we're bound. This will effectively be a binding on the astral plane."

"How?"

"No hesitation?"

"Once I'm in, I'm in."

"Good. The door we'll build is in the gardens of the tower. So you don't have to worry about being contaminated by any phallic symbolism." He laughed. "But first I want you to get used to this place. The more you can visualise it, the easier it will be to return. So, have a look around."

She raised her eyebrows. "You're giving me permission to poke around?"

"Well, I wouldn't put it like that exactly, but yes, I want you to get to know it. There are a few floors with different rooms. Be my guest." He sat on a chair, crossing his legs elegantly at the ankle.

She walked around the room they were in first, going out to the balcony to look out. "This is a wonderful view. But it's all from your head? How does it work? Is what I can see real?"

"Hmmm. Sort of. If you go closer it will probably become real. Although it could also change depending on what I wanted or needed it to be."

Blaize frowned. What he said didn't make sense.

"It's hard to explain, easier to show you."

CHAPTER

27

Cuinn hadn't realised that Blaize would be quite as interested in every nook and cranny as she was. He shook his head as she picked up every object and opened every door and cupboard.

He finally managed to draw her out of the room, and led her down the solid stone stairs to the heavy tower door. They went into the gardens and to the archway that Cuinn had created.

"That's beautiful." Blaize walked around it. "How does it work?"

"It doesn't—yet. We have to activate it together." He took her hands again in the same crossed-wrists position they'd held in Cuinn's physical rooms, and tugged her to stand so that the archway was in between them, hands directly under it.

"We're going to create the doorway to your Haven. This door will open if you need it." He changed his voice to the more ceremonial tone he'd used in his rooms in Cathair Cuinn. "Blaize Blackfire, do you agree to link your Haven with mine for the duration of our binding as Maven and Adherent?"

"I do."

"You're already on the astral plane this time. All you need to do is visualise your Haven, and will yourself there. This archway is a door designed to follow and capture the movement between spaces. Will your Haven to be the other side of the archway, and when we step through we will be in your Haven. Does that make sense?"

A small crease appeared between Blaize's eyes.

Cuinn smiled. "Don't worry, you have more than enough power. You just need to believe in it. Can you see your streams of power?"

Blaize looked down at herself, trying to see her own power in the way she had Cuinn's. Her eyes roamed the space around her body as she sought to do as he asked. After a moment, she shook her head and met his gaze, chewing her lip.

He tipped his head, asking her wordlessly to try again. She did, and he saw the moment when she caught sight of her energy. Her mouth fell open and her eyes grew huge, their green luminous.

Unlike last time, when it had been mainly Manipura she had been manifesting, this power was mainly Ajna. The purple was purer, less red, more blue. And it shone. She was powerful.

She blinked.

"Good. That will help. With Ajna, a major part of being able to use the energy involves believing you can."

Blaize shook her head. "I'm still not sure I understand."

"That's okay. You don't need to understand it to use it. Sometimes understanding comes through use. So, can you visualise your Haven again?"

"I think so." Her voice was anxious, and her breathing had speeded.

"There's no danger this time. Don't let go of my hands— physically in the 'real' world, here in my Haven, or when you visualise yourself in your own Haven. I'll come with you that way, and I am heavily warded." He didn't tell her he'd also done what he could to energetically protect, or ward her in each situation.

Her own Haven was the weakest spot at the moment, but there was nothing he could do until she took him there. As soon as they arrived, he would energetically protect the space until there was no possibility of anything getting in to hurt her, ever again.

"Okay."

"Trust me, Blaize."

"Do I need to close my eyes?"

"Whatever's easier. All you need to do is visualise your Haven. Think of the garden, the river. The flowers and the bees. It's a beautiful day. ..." He made his voice as hypnotic as possible and her eyes closed involuntarily.

A few minutes later, she opened her eyes again. And her grip on his hands loosened as she was distracted by the sight of her Haven. He tightened his, terrified she might slip out of his grasp at this crucial point. All the time they were joined, he could protect her. Shield her. Ward her. If she let go with the binding incomplete, her Haven unguarded, and her energy and magics unleashed and enhanced by his own, she would be a shining target for every malevolent being in the ether. As it was, it was still possible for anything to enter her Haven until the binding, and wardings, were complete. They needed to get this done.

"Ouch!"

"Sorry. But you can't let go until we've finished this." He kept his voice calm, though his mouth had gone dry.

"I wasn't going to let go," she grumbled. "I was just surprised, that's all." She glanced around her, and he did the same. The Haven was alive with tiny details—brightly coloured flowers, the buzz of bees, and the feel of the grass underneath their feet.

They stood under a mirror image of the arch that he'd created in his Haven, their hands still clasped in the middle of the arch, their bodies either side.

"We've made the link. Now watch me while I set some wardings up. I'm going to draw on the energy of the etheric plane and create shields that are anchored to the boundaries of your Haven. Eventually I'll teach you how to ward on this plane, but for now, I'm just going to secure the space as much as possible. You'll also grow and develop your Haven, just as I have. But that takes time."

He closed his eyes, and pulled more Ajna energy. He had been pooling it all day, carefully building his reserves, as well as building his strength in case he needed to pull more unexpectedly. This time, he would be prepared. Nothing was going to harm her. All he needed to do was finish the warding and complete the binding.

He opened his eyes and warded the area, creating more delicate trellis work around the pretty garden to set some boundaries, and using the river as another. Blaize watched. "They're beautiful."

"Hmmm?"

"The roses you just grew out of nowhere."

"I'm setting boundaries so you know not to go further than that in your Haven at the moment. Eventually, as your ability to pool Ajna energy grows, you'll expand your Haven, and move the boundaries back with your own power."

"How big can my piece of Haven real estate be?"

Cuinn frowned as he tried to focus on his task. "As big as you like. Although usually it's related to your power, as you need to be able to hold the territory with wardings, like this."

Blaize watched Cuinn, and each time he drew a new symbol with Ajna energy, she would lean a little more towards it, attempting to see exactly what he did. Each symbol would hover in the air for twenty seconds or so, glowing with power. They were mainly purple, but other colours came and went in ripples, creating a rainbow anchored by violet.

Finally, he finished and her Haven was as warded as he could make it. It was time to test the wardings and the link.

He caught her gaze again, and she stared back solemnly, unblinking.

"Blaize Blackfire. We are now bound, you and I, as Maven and Adherent. I pledge to protect and guide you, teaching you to harness the power of your Ajna energy for as long as it takes for you to be ready for the Ajna Practitioner trial.

"Do you agree to follow my teachings and guidance? To study until you are sufficiently proficient with Ajna to take the Ajna Practitioner trial?"

"I do." Her voice was firm.

"Then we start a new chapter, you and I, this night here in your Haven." He stepped through the archway, but she didn't move back, and he found himself inches away from her. He could feel the heat coming off her body. She tilted her head up, her breath feather-like on his neck.

He wanted to kiss her. For a moment, he couldn't think of anything apart from the shape of her mouth, the curve of her cheek.

"The first thing I'll do is teach you to move between our Havens. Watch."

With a grateful exhalation, he stepped backwards through the trellis, towards the spot he'd so recently vacated.

And disappeared.

CHAPTER
28

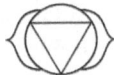

Blaize blinked. One minute, Cuinn stood in front of her, glowing with power, and the next minute he was gone.

Although given she'd had to prevent herself from kissing him again, perhaps a moment of space between them was for the best.

She examined the trellis door, which had a sort of shimmer effect inside it. She thought she could see his garden through it, but the image wasn't still. It was like the heat haze you sometimes got from hot sun on tarmac.

Should she step through? Would that take her to his Haven? She assumed so, but what if she needed to draw on her power to get through it? She hadn't used her power since the dreams had started and wasn't sure if now was the time to start.

She cautiously moved her leg forward when Cuinn popped back—and stumbled straight into her, knocking her to the ground.

Stunned, she lay beneath him.

"Third time's the charm," she mumbled, still dazed.

"What on earth were you doing standing there? Didn't you move at all?"

"No ... you didn't tell me to move."

"Oh, so now you're obedient?" He shifted his weight and put one hand on the ground to push himself up. She felt his muscles flex and the warmth of his breath on her cheek. There was a flash of heat in her groin.

He stopped pushing himself upright and put his hand under her head, cradling it. He raised and tilted her head until they were staring into each other's eyes, scant inches between them. "Are you okay? Blaize?"

She sighed, and gave in to the inevitable. She loved a man's hand on her neck. She snaked her arms around his neck and pulled. He fell to his elbows, one hand still supporting her head.

She closed the gap between them, and pressed her lips softly to his, her nerves overstimulated, on fire.

At first, he resisted, mumbling something against her lips, but she used the opportunity to bring him closer by slipping her tongue into his mouth, and opening her own to invite him to do the same. His mumbling turned into a moan that vibrated through her.

His body pressed tightly against hers, pushing her into the earth. She didn't mind the hard ground against her back, but they'd have to do this again in bed one day. Her body hummed, tingled with energy and power. She wasn't actively pulling power, but it was as if she was swimming in it.

She wrapped her legs around his hips and moved her hips to rub his hardness against her softness. He returned her kiss, and she sighed and poured passion and need into the kiss.

She shifted her hip and put her foot on the floor so her leg was bent. Then she pushed and used the force of the movement to flip them both over, so she was on top. As she did, she caught sight of something in the garden, something that hadn't been there a minute ago.

She sucked in a breath and stopped halfway back to Cuinn's mouth.

He was instantly alert. His eyes snapped open and he took her with him as he sat up, his arms encircling her so she sat in his lap. He had gone from lover to fighter in seconds. "What?"

She pointed a finger at the object that had appeared in the garden.

Cuinn followed the finger with his gaze, and the tension in his body flowed out of him. He laughed. Big belly laughs, coming from somewhere deep inside him. He hugged her to him, his body heaving with amusement.

"W-what the hell?"

"You must have created it. Because I know when I create something on the astral plane, and that wasn't me. We're definitely going to have to teach you how your Ajna works, or your subconscious is going to be stripping you bare all over the place."

"What?"

"You wanted a bed. Or some part of you wanted a bed. And so, your energy gave you—a bed." He gestured towards the object that had appeared out of nowhere as they'd been kissing. It was, indeed, a bed and a glorious one.

The bed of her dreams.

It was big, and both solid and delicate. Gothic-looking, black ornate iron scrollwork danced towards the sky in straight lines and curls. Two smooth, hard posts reached upwards from each side of the bed, joined by another black rod that went between them. The rod supported gauzy red curtains that looked like living flame. Serving no purpose other than decoration, the curtains dropped gracefully from the rod down past the headboard made from iron scrollwork to the floor.

"Wow," Blaize said.

"Yeah." Cuinn stood and took her with him, her legs around his hips, his hands cupping her buttocks. She wriggled with desire, trying to move her hands closer to the space between his legs. He hadn't stopped smiling.

He walked the few yards to the bed and released Blaize onto the soft red sheet that covered a firm surface. He drew his own shirt, pants, and boxers off before following her onto the bed, pinning her arms above her head with one hand. He used his other hand to shimmy her dress up over her head, leaving it between her head and her elbows to hold her still.

His heated gaze raked over her body, catching on her slight white underwear, and her nipples peaked in response. She shifted on the bed, urging him to touch her. His skin was pale and his hair fell scruffily around his face, the dark of it contrasting with his ivory skin. An indigo shimmer surrounded him, his Ajna aura flaring, pulsing in and out of existence. He was hard and ready. She wanted him inside her.

Cuinn kissed her again, licking the flesh surrounding her collarbone. She moved her hips restlessly, trying to get him to shift down on the bed and move against her. *Why doesn't he use his hands?* Her blood pumped hot around her body, pressure building between her legs. She jerked her wrists, meaning to take back control, to free herself from the dress. She needed to remove her underwear, and she urgently wanted to touch him. To take all that male firmness inside her body and pleasure them both.

She noticed too late the red silk that seemed to be growing from the ironwork at the top of the bed. He pulled the dress free as the silk flowed towards her and trapped her wrists in a strong hold that left Cuinn free to use his hands in other ways. Cuinn threw the dress out of harm's way, then dragged her underwear down her legs, and scraped his teeth and tongue after them. "You're out of your depth here, Blaize. I've been using Ajna for centuries." His grin was wicked now. "Play nicely or who knows what I'll conjure up."

Her eyebrows rose at this new side of Cuinn. *It was always the quiet ones.* But that was her last coherent thought for a while. She tugged against the bonds—bonds she could burn away in an instant—not because she didn't like them, but because she relished the unusual feeling of someone else being in control. It was a measure of how much she'd come to trust Cuinn, despite everything, that she found the silk wrapping her wrists added to her excitement rather than anything else.

Her body craved the pleasure that Cuinn was now bringing with mouth and hands. His skin was smooth on hers. Droplets of sweat from both their bodies mingled and minimised friction. His teeth were a dull rasp as he dragged his mouth down from her breasts, over her belly, and to the hot flesh between her legs.

Here was relief from her worry about how to find Indigo and how she was going to develop her Ajna quickly enough to beat her. Here was a beautiful distraction, strong and masculine. Here were cool hands that traced her curves and ran over her hips.

And here finally, *finally*, he drove two fingers inside her.

The shock of it sent adrenaline coursing through her body and she gasped, raising her hips higher, driving them against his fingers to push him deeper. Her breath came in short pants, her heart beating like a hummingbird's.

He slid his fingers out, and stroked her, urgency compelling them both. His shaft was taut, and she wanted all of him inside her, not just his fingers. She shifted her hips again, and he rolled eyes the colour of granite up to look at her, his gaze fierce and possessive.

He was magnificent.

When her orgasm crested, she grabbed the bonds and clenched her fists around them, her body bowing, as she pushed herself into Cuinn's palm, his fingers and tongue dancing in and on the hot flesh at her core.

Tension she hadn't even known she'd been holding onto released, and her body lay limp beneath his, endorphins chasing pleasantly around her body in the after-glow.

He paused a moment, eyes still locked on hers. The savage desire in his gaze made a shudder run through her. But he wasn't finished. He worked his fingers more deeply inside her, stroking the spot that made her cry out with the violence of the feeling. She made breathy sounds as she tried to relax into it, but her body instinctively twisted away from the intensity that hovered on the edge of too much.

"Blaize." His voice was a low rumble.

She could take more. She would take more.

He'd conjured a condom from somewhere, and she moaned a little as she watched him roll it over his impressive dick. He slid up her body so he lay on top of her, skin pressed together. He kissed her neck and replaced his fingers with his dick, thick, hard and ready.

He entered her liquid heat with a gentle push that quickly turned into something much more forceful.

She welcomed him in. Had she ever wanted anything so much?

"Oh." He drove the shocked noise out of her as he changed his angle and penetrated her more deeply. She made a long, low sound as the visceral feeling transformed again. It hurt a little, but it also felt good. Really good.

She felt a hot flush move across her chest and climb up her neck. He kept his movements rhythmic and constant, and she curled her legs around him, digging her heels into his buttocks to draw him in closer. They moved in time, and her head fell to the side. She wasn't sure how much longer she could straddle the fine line between ecstasy and too much. She paused and looked up at him.

"Relax, Blaize. Trust me and let go." He growled out the words, seeming to read her mind.

As their eyes met, some final barrier lifted, and their energies bled into each other's. His power raced through her, the light mystery of Ajna, and the heavy grounding of Muladhara. He captured her body and mind.

Her own energies smashed into him, the fire of Manipura dominating, but threads of Ajna woven through. She wanted to burn him up from the inside, to consume them both in an orgasmic fire. He was hers.

Stars formed and exploded inside her, and her whole body was suffused with energy and light.

Cuinn groaned. He held himself over her, one hand on the bed, and the other grasping her head and holding it firmly in place under his. He covered every inch of her with his body and kissed her again. Their mouths formed another conduit for the power that now span and mingled around their bodies.

Cuinn's long strokes deep within her continued, drawing out the experience, her core rhythmically clutching and squeezing him to his own explosion, causing her in turn to crest another peak.

The aftershocks rippled through her body as she shuddered beneath him, her body trembling, eyes closed, head lolling to the side.

Cuinn.

At some point, he'd released her arms from their silken shackles, and she brought them around him now to hug him as close to her as possible.

He relaxed against her, and burrowed his face, his hair hanging around it untidily, into her shoulder. He nipped at her neck, and she wriggled underneath him. "Cuinn! Enough! I've got nothing left."

His head came up, and he smiled at her again, his face relaxed and open in a way she hadn't seen before. It was as if all the troubles that were weighing on him had fallen away.

"I do." He raised his eyebrows. "And I'm sure I can re-energise you. …" He drew away from her and sat up, straddling her waist. As he did so, his attention focused on something behind the bed. He froze, and his jaw dropped. "Um … Blaize …? I think you need to see this."

29

Sex with Blaize hadn't just been amazing because it was Cuinn's first time in a while. There had been an … intensity in his connection with Blaize. Deeper than the physical.

And if he hadn't already thought that, the scene that greeted him when he raised his head would have been evidence enough. The previously simple space, the pretty English garden with grass, some wooden tables and chairs, and a few trees providing shade had blossomed.

If that was the word for it.

The warding boundaries were thickly covered by climbing roses, with pink, red, white, and yellow blooms in full flower.

Blaize propped herself up on one elbow and gazed at the garden around them. As well as the roses, the grass had also blossomed with wildflowers, a riot of colour with the bed at the centre.

Ajna energy responded to the creator's thoughts and desires. The bed had given him the confidence to respond to Blaize's kiss, a clear statement of what she wanted from him.

And this time, unlike Sophea, he wanted it too. They were equals. Blaize was strong. More than a match for him. He wasn't going to hurt her as he had hurt Sophea.

The explosion of flowers said that he wasn't alone in his feelings about the sex they'd just had. It also said that Blaize had a great deal of power waiting to be tapped. "I see you've started creating."

"I did this?" Blaize looked as though she'd been hit over the head. Again.

"Correct. Unconsciously, perhaps, but these are your creations. And you were certainly shining with energy at the, er, end there. The power needed an outlet, and it found it here." He gestured around them. He sat up next to Blaize and put an arm around her, drawing her into the crook of his shoulder. She complied, unresisting, and drew in a breath.

She frowned. "Why can't I smell the flowers?"

"Well noticed. That quirk is the way you can tell you're in the dreamscape. Nothing has a scent here. If you're ever unsure, all you need to do is sniff."

"Why?"

He smiled. Her curiosity was still present and correct, despite the slightly stunned look on her face. "I don't know. Just one of those things."

He glanced towards the garden, and closer to the river where what looked like a stone altar had appeared. There was something on it.

He raised his eyebrows. *Strange.* He got no sense of threat from the new addition, but he'd also never seen anything like it manifest in an individual's Haven though similar objects were in every energetic temple. He gently disentangled himself from Blaize, and got up and went to check it out. Blaize wasn't far behind.

They both stood, unselfconsciously naked, over the altar, which held two objects.

"What are they? And where did they come from?"

"Good questions." Cuinn put his hand out to touch the objects. They were similar: two tightly corded bands, one slightly larger than the other, made of purple, red, yellow, and white silks. The colours were interwoven. He considered them, and the context. "I think it's the colours of our Chakras. Purple for Ajna, red for Muladhara, yellow for Manipura. And white for the divine, for Sahasara, the crown Chakra. They're bracelets. Probably one for each of us."

He picked them up carefully, and measured one against his own wrist and the other against Blaize's. A perfect fit. Which didn't mean they should put them on. *I know these. I've seen them somewhere.* He searched his memory to find where it had been.

"Did I create these too?" Blaize's voice was soft and hesitant.

Cuinn shook his head slowly as he realised where he knew them from. "This is Source's altar. I think these are gifts from Source. And, Blaize—I've seen us wearing these."

She looked from the stone to him, tilting her head, confused. "What do you mean? I've never seen them before."

"In the prophecies. You, I, and the other five men and five women were wearing similar bracelets in the prophecies. And you were wearing it when …"

"When I was beaten." She looked away from him, and her hands curled into fists by her sides.

He nodded.

She snatched hers up. "Easy. I just won't wear it on the physical plane then. In fact, it probably won't even exist there. Will it?"

"I don't know. It's my first 'gift' in this way." He fingered the larger of the two. "There's energy here." Gifts from Source could grant the recipient power or other blessings, but they always came at a price.

She slipped hers over her left wrist. "It's lovely. But I'm going to leave it here."

As she said the words, the bracelet moved on her wrist, and she gasped. Before Cuinn could do anything, the bracelet wrapped tightly around her wrist, not so much that it would have hurt, but too tight to pull it off.

Cuinn didn't hesitate, and placed the other bracelet over his right wrist. It span and when it stopped, it rested in the same way on his wrist, snugly bound.

"What did you do that for?" Blaize had frozen in place, eyes locked on his wrist.

"I won't leave you alone in this." Even if it meant another snap decision. Another decision without thinking it through.

"In what? We don't even know what's going on. That was a stupid thing to do."

He hoped she wasn't right.

"Perhaps it's just another symbol that Source approves our binding. We just created powerful energy. Look around." He waved at the new additions to the garden. "And we added an extra layer to the binding by making love here."

Blaize put her arms over her chest and frowned. "Making love?"

"Would you call it something else?"

"Yes ... no ... maybe. I don't know. So we're bound even tighter now?" Blaize's voice was a little higher than usual.

"You agreed to the binding, Blaize. And you certainly seemed keen on making love. Where's the problem?" He put his hand out to cup her cheek, but she shifted out of reach, her eyes not meeting his.

"We had great sex, amazing sex, in fact. But it's not the start of some great love affair. Sex between consenting adults is a beautiful thing, but it doesn't need to mean they have to become attached. You don't know enough about me, Cuinn." She stalked to the bed and pulled her underwear up her long legs. Cuinn tried not to be distracted.

"I agree. And I want to know more. But I know enough to know I want to explore this relationship—"

Blaize's eyebrows shot up.

"This relationship," he emphasised the word, "with you properly. The binding's complete, anyway, so whatever happens we need to work through the sexual side as adults, because we're going to be spending a lot of time with each other in the coming years."

He walked to her, more quickly this time so she couldn't move away, and put his hands on her face, tilting it up to meet her eyes. He tried to imagine what Tierra would say. How she would empathise with Blaize. What was it that Blaize was worried about? He thought back to their conversation of the day before and thought he had it.

"You're not your father, if that's what you're worried about. Just because you have your dominant Chakra in common doesn't mean you're anything like him."

Blaize's chin went up, and her cheeks flushed an angry red. "Can we go home? Is the ritual done?" Her tone was empty.

Was that too close to home, or nowhere near? *Why was she so bloody stubborn?* Women, again a mystery to him. Cuinn sighed. "Yes, the ritual is done. More than done. I'd like to see what happens to these bracelets when we get back to the physical plane. If they come with us, then the prophecy involving you has come a little closer and we're going to need to step things up."

She was dressed now, her arms at her sides. They clenched into fists and her mouth flattened into a thin line. "I can protect myself."

He gritted his teeth. *Add proud to stubborn.* "Yes, but there's always more to learn. And there's no shame in having others help you. Plus, we're bound now, you and I, so we work together. Don't forget you agreed to my teaching you in the binding ritual."

She scowled.

One thing at a time. The priority now was to make sure her Haven was secure. He needed to know she was safe when she was here. "I want to check you can travel between our Havens before we go back. It's the point at which you—and our Havens—are most vulnerable."

He'd approach the relationship issue again on the physical plane. Perhaps after he asked Tierra for some advice. He wasn't sure what was happening between them, but the sensible thing was to explore it. To plan ahead and to decide what to do with a little thought.

He pulled his own clothes on, and showed her how to guard her mind using a protection technique, before they moved to the arch.

"All you need to do is walk under the arch, protecting your mind as I showed you. You're vulnerable only for a split second, so there's not much danger, but given the situation, I'd rather be safe. Eventually it will become second nature to you to guard as you change locations in the dreamscape—and later, when you dreamwalk outside our Havens, you'll start your protection with this first technique, though you'll add others too."

She was all business now, body relaxed but alert. There was no trace of the wild abandon he'd seen in her a short while before. No trace of the softness, or the surrender. Her body language said she'd listen to him, but she'd make her own choices. Do it her own way.

"I'll walk through first. Follow me. Don't take long, or I'll be back looking for you," he said. He felt a sense of unease, but wasn't sure if that was down to Blaize's switch in behaviour, or a premonition. He didn't sense any potential danger, but he'd scan thoroughly as he stepped through to his Haven.

He proceeded through the archway, and moments later, he materialised in the gardens of his own tower. His heart thundered in his chest as he waited. Another few seconds, and she appeared. She looked a little disorientated, but she seemed fine.

"Great," he said, as his heart dropped back to its normal pace. "We'll return to your Haven and make sure you feel comfortable in both directions, then we'll head home." He waited until she nodded, then stepped back through the arch.

Cuinn took a second to look at the beautiful, rumpled bed. He hardened slightly as he saw an image of Blaize's lithe body writhing in the red silk. He turned his attention back to the arch. Where was she? What was taking so long? He dug his nails into his palms. Should he go back through? But what if he did and she came through at the same time?

Another minute passed.

Then movement and a shimmer in the arch, and he stepped forward with a sigh of relief.

Blaize fell through the doorway, bloody and unconscious, into his arms.

CHAPTER

30

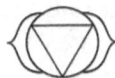

Blaize woke up in her own bed, a strange woman by her side. The woman offered her some water, which Blaize accepted gratefully, her throat dry and scratchy. As she tipped her head back, she felt a pull in the back of her hand, and looked down to see an IV drip attached to her. The woman's heart-shaped face exuded warmth and was surrounded by a honey-blond bob.

"Who are you?"

The woman smiled, and Blaize felt a little more at ease.

"I'm Cara, a good friend of Tierra's. I'm a Healer."

Blaize's heart turned to ice, the ease draining away. Her chest tightened and she raised her torso up a little. "You work at the Rogue Rehab centre."

"Yes."

"Have I ...?"

Cara tilted her head then laughed. "No, no, love, you haven't turned Rogue. You're fine. Sorry, I shouldn't laugh. But you're in no danger of that. You have an iron grip on your energies."

The ice in Blaize's chest melted, and she relaxed back against the pillows.

"We think you were attacked in the astral world, when you went between Cuinn's Haven and your own. You fought with something. But you made it back to Cuinn, and he brought you home. They called me because they wanted help, not because you were going Rogue." She looked at Blaize, assessing her. "Can I get you anything else? How's the pain?"

Blaize tested the various muscles in her body carefully. "I don't feel too bad. What're the bandages for?"

"You had a deep scratch across your arm. I stitched it up and it's covered while it heals. I've given you a lot of healing energy. I'm glad it's working. We have drugs too, if you need them, but we didn't want to add anything else into your system before we knew the effects of the attack." She went to Blaize's side and felt for her pulse. "The drip's just for hydration. I've been with you for a couple of days—it's good to see you awake and okay."

Blaize's eyes widened. "Days?"

"I'm afraid so. You were badly hurt. But you're on the mend now."

Blaize blew out a breath. "Thank you. You're a Healer? You have Anahata as your dominant Chakra?"

It was Cara's turned to nod. "Yes, and Manipura as my auxiliary. Not the typical Healer combination, but helpful at the Rehab centre."

Satisfied with Blaize's pulse, she plumped her pillows and helped her to sit up.

"I'll get Cuinn. He's been here as much as he could over the last couple of days, and spent the rest of his time trying to work out what happened."

She swept out of the door. Blaize was tempted to pull the drip out but thought she'd better wait. Cara didn't seem like someone to mess with.

Blaize rested her head on the pillows and looked up at the spotless white ceiling. She wasn't looking forward to seeing Cuinn. After they'd had sex—*great sex*—she'd been taken aback by his leap to a relationship. She hadn't expected that. *Wasn't our antagonism beforehand part of the reason the sex had been so great?* That didn't seem like a good basis for a relationship to her.

She frowned. She hadn't had any real long-term relationships in her life. She'd always been focused on her own goals. Developing her energy. Being the best at whatever she was working on. Her longest relationship had been a year, and she'd been the one to end it when she'd started training in Manipura. Since then, she'd only had the odd fling, which had been more like getting a workout partner than a relationship.

Could she persuade Cuinn to have more fabulous, sweaty sex to keep them both fit? She gave a small smile while she prodded the area around the bandage on her arm, trying to see where the scratch started and ended.

The binding ceremony had been magical. And white certainly suited Cuinn. He'd looked so ... powerful. Masculine.

She winced as she hit the start of the scratch. *Ouch.*

The door burst open and Cuinn rushed through, Cara and Tierra following at a more sedate pace. Cuinn sat in the chair by the bed, and took her hand.

"Blaize." He dropped a kiss on her palm.

Blaize felt something warm and liquid flare in her at the touch, but at the same time wanted to pull her arm away. She didn't want a relationship, and she didn't want him to think she did. There was nothing wrong with healthy sex between consenting adults—*lots of amazing, healthy sex*—but relationships led to trouble. She need look no further than her mother and father to see that. She was attracted to him, sure—*wanted him, badly*—but that didn't mean they were going to date, let alone get married. She needed to step back.

"How do you feel?" Cuinn asked.

"Stiff and achy, but not too bad. Not bad enough to need a drip." She looked at Cara. "Can you take it out?"

"After we've gotten a bit more food and liquid into you. Not long."

"Blaize, can you tell us what happened?" Cuinn leaned towards her, his focus locked on her as if she was something precious that was his to protect. His voice held a world of worry.

She found herself both wanting to soothe him, and at the same time, annoyed and guilty that her actions could be responsible for the pain in his voice. *I don't need this.*

"I'm not sure. I stepped forward to follow you through the gate, and instead of it taking a few seconds like the first time, something seemed to—to catch hold of me, and pull me in a different direction. I fought it—I'm not sure exactly how, or with what, and even though I know it must have been in the astral world, I felt it physically. But ..." She focused on Cuinn, puzzled. "How did I get these injuries? I thought that what happened on the astral plane wasn't real on the physical plane?"

Cuinn's weary gaze told her he knew her question also referred to what had happened between them.

"No. What happens in the astral plane is as real as what happens on this plane."

Well, that explained the need for the condom.

He held up their joined hands and she saw the bracelets from the dreamscape on their wrists. Her stomach lurched. *What the hell?* But she couldn't think about that now.

"It doesn't always translate into action on the physical plane, as it depends on the strength of the energy, but it's no less real either way." He put her hand down and sat back. "In your case, the Rogue, which is what we're assuming it was, was strong. Strong enough for your injuries to show up here too. But that may also come from your own strength. You were almost drained when you came through the portal, and unconscious. You must have expended a lot of energy in a short time to have that happen."

"I don't remember much more. I don't know how I managed to get through the portal. I tried to focus on my Haven, but it was blurry. I focused on you as well. I could sense your energy."

Tierra and Cara exchanged a surprised look.

"That's because we're bound as Maven and Adherent. It's rare that we won't be able to find each other." He frowned at the other women. Blaize made a note to ask Tierra what that was about next time they were alone together. But Blaize had other priorities right now.

"Was I really out for days?"

"Yes. And you seemed to be having bad dreams," Cuinn said. "Do you remember any of them? The dreams might help us with the prophecy. Or even just with what actually happened."

"The prophecy!" Blaize half sat up, then winced as her muscles protested. "I'm injured—this must be the prophecy that you saw fulfilled. And I'm fine."

She felt a sense of dread lift that she hadn't been aware of. *One thing less to worry about.*

Cuinn didn't say anything.

"Cuinn? I'm out of the water now. You can stop worrying." She stretched out her good hand to him, touching him lightly on the forearm.

"Maybe. I'm not sure. There may still be more danger. It doesn't match what I saw exactly—I need to do more research." Cuinn didn't move.

"You always need to do more research." Tierra came over to him and put her arms around him. "Right now, you need to take a nap. What with checking on Blaize and your own dreamwalks, as well as research, you've barely had any sleep in three days. Or a shower. Go, take a nap, and Cara and I will put some food together for us all."

Cara glided over to the two of them, and placed her hand on Cuinn's shoulder. Blaize was surprised by a bitter taste in her mouth. She drew her own hand quickly back.

"As your Healer, I agree," said Cara. She was elegant, composed, and feminine. "You need rest. If Blaize remembers anything about the dreams, she can write it down and we can share it later."

The advice was sensible, but Blaize was distracted. Really distracted. An annoying thought had lodged in her brain, and wouldn't get out.

Had Cuinn and Cara ever been lovers?

CHAPTER
31

Blaize wanted to be out tracking Indigo. Instead, Cuinn had disappeared, and she was under orders from Cara to rest.

Three days after waking, she was reading through prophecies in the library when a car drew up outside. Her heart lurched uncomfortably, and she walked downstairs, where she found an athletic blond with amused eyes, whose stubble-kissed look added to the overall picture of a surfer on his day off.

"Fintan!" Blaize smiled a real smile and gave Fintan an enthusiastic hug.

"Hey, Sparks." A friend of her Uncle's, Fintan had called her that since she was a teenager, as she'd loved the sparkles he'd created for her in the tropical night, distracting her from her nightmares soon after her parents had died. Her own personal fireworks show.

Cuinn followed a little way behind the others, looking bone-weary, and as if he'd lost another seven pounds since she had last seen him.

She stood awkwardly in front of him, Fintan's arm loosely around her shoulders. Cuinn looked at the two of them and smiled grimly.

"It's been a long few days, but I think we have a way forward. Fintan, you might as well fill Blaize in. I need a shower."

He didn't wait for an answer but disappeared back out of the door. Blaize took a half-step after him, and then shrugged, and turned back to Fintan. "Want to fight?"

Blaize squatted and kicked out with a low roundhouse sweep, and Fintan jumped back just in time.

"Nice."

"So what's the plan? Are you and I going hunting?" Blaize was eager to hear what Cuinn had agreed as a way forward with Minh, the Ajna-Muladhara Minor Circle member. Anything was better than hanging around the house. Thank Source Cara had agreed Blaize could train again, as long as she didn't overdo it. *Though it's possible we have different ideas of what overdoing it means.*

"Not exactly. You're going to be bait." Fintan sent a right hook towards Blaize's head. They were both sweating now, even though Blaize had turned the AC up high as soon as they'd hit the house's gym.

Blaize smiled as she darted backwards. "Sounds like my kind of plan."

"Cuinn's been at the books pretty hard since your attack. He found some references that seem relevant in an ancient prophecy that goes back to the fall of Atlantis, where a great evil was predicted that would upset the balance of the world and threaten our race. The prophecy says 'a full complement of Chakras' is needed to fight the evil."

Blaize struck him in the side of the leg with a kick, but he caught her foot and twisted, throwing her hard to the ground. *Ouch.* She landed face down and flipped herself, fast, to face him and at the same time kicked out with both legs. She hooked his ankle with one foot and slammed him in the knee with the other, and brought him down to the ground with a thud.

But he was quick to recover and scrambled up Blaize's body to sit on her in a Jiu-Jitsu mount.

"How can we use a full complement of Chakras when we only represent six? How would we include the Crown Chakra?" Blaize panted only slightly as he sat on top of her chest, his legs pinning her arms, his hands at her throat.

"The prophecy was put aside as incomplete centuries ago because of that very concern." Finn shifted to sit more firmly on her lungs, making it harder for her to breathe. "Whatever Cuinn's dusty books say, we need to capture the Rogue."

He put a bit more pressure on her throat, and she felt the blood build up in her head. Her cheeks heated, and tiny spots appeared in front of her eyes.

"For some reason, the Rogue wants you." He smirked. "Though if she could see you right now, she'd probably change her mind."

Blaize hefted her lower body, and dislodged Fintan enough so that he slipped slightly. It was enough for her to shift her hips again and twist her body so that he was knocked to the side, his hands away from her throat. She heaved a breath and coughed.

"Enough?" he asked from a horizontal position next to her. They'd been sparring for an hour now, and both were sweating with exertion.

She shook her head and pushed herself off the floor. She loved this. "Let's add energy. Protect the room."

He stood, and after a moment, a wall of fire caged them. It would keep any energy they used between them. She spooled a little Manipura energy, cautious.

"The plan is to get you to shine in the dreamscape like the tasty morsel of energy you are. When the Rogue comes for you, Cuinn will capture her on the astral plane, will find out where her physical body is, and Cara and I will go find it and take it to the Rehab centre. Simple."

Blaize frowned. "I need more time to learn about Ajna. She kicked my butt the other day. It was embarrassing."

Fintan's torso burst into flame. Out of the inferno, a handful of tiny daggers of fire flew through the air towards her. She dodged one and spread energy in front of her to absorb the rest. She created her own defensive fire and began to heat the ground under Fintan's bare feet.

His voice came from behind the wall of fire. "You have two days. We don't want to wait too long."

Her frown deepened. "Fine."

She'd be ready.

Fintan's flames disappeared and he danced on the spot as the heat seeped into his bare feet. "Tierra doesn't like it."

He ducked and rolled past Blaize and threw a fireball at her back from the floor.

She fell forward, the heat absorbed, but the strength of the hit pushed her to the floor, and her defensive fire flickered and went out. Her voice was muffled. "What?"

Fintan came up behind her fast, and before she could push herself up, he grabbed one of her arms and wrenched it up her back. *Ouch.*

"Using you as bait."

Blaize tried to shrug, but her arm was tight up against her back and she couldn't move. She heated up her own body hoping to dislodge Fintan.

"We can't leave the Rogue out there, or every time I draw power the Rogue could attack," she said. "And who knows what damage it might be doing at the moment? We can't leave it out there to ruin another family's lives."

"I agree."

The pain in her arm brought tears to her eyes. She used her feet against the ground to move her body forward, which took the pressure off for a moment, and was all she needed to twist her body around. She was still on the floor, but her arm was no longer trapped.

Fintan made a grab for her. "How are you getting along with Cuinn?"

She hesitated for a second, and he used the moment to catch her and pin her, one knee on her arm, the other arm secured by his hand.

"Fine. We're fine." She struggled to free herself, but he was well-built and drove all his weight down. She couldn't move either arm.

"And the binding went well?" He smirked at her.

She stopped struggling and scowled at him. "What did he tell you?"

"Nothing. But you just did." His bright blue eyes sparked with mischief.

His weight was high up her body, and her legs were free. She scissor-kicked, bending her body at a right angle, and caught his head between her feet. She yanked backwards, and he tipped back off her chest though he didn't let go of the wrist he'd been holding.

"There's nothing going on. We slept together, it was fine, he wants a relationship. I don't do relationships, you know that."

There was a brief struggle until they were both on the floor, limbs entwined. Fintan was on top, though by a slim margin. Neither of them had much wiggle room. The wall of fire around the room had gone.

"Maybe you should." Fintan sounded a bit out of breath.

She scowled harder and shoved her fingers into the notch in the centre of his collar bone, at the bottom of his throat, and forced him back.

"Not. Going. To. Happen." She struck him with each word, each blow driving him back off her. She kept hold of one of his arms, and stretched it tight, until he laughed and yielded defeat, tapping the floor with his free hand.

Cuinn knocked at Blaize's door. He'd told himself he wanted to check on her safety. That he needed to ensure that Fintan had briefed her properly. But what he really wanted to do was ask her exactly what her relationship with Fintan was. They'd seemed so …

natural together. Without any of the antagonism that he and Blaize seemed to share.

He scowled just as she opened the door. She narrowed her eyes and made no attempt to invite him in. "Yes?"

"I came to check Fintan had filled you in on the plan." He pushed past her and walked into the living room.

She turned, watching him, her arms folded. "Yes."

"And you're okay with being used as bait? Even though we can't be sure the prophecy I saw about you has been completed?" He swept a glance around the room as he waited for her answer. Blaize had only been here for a few weeks but she'd already put her mark on the house. The fire smouldered—he suspected given her fire energies it rarely went out.

A striking picture he'd never seen before hung on the wall, of a beach—but a beach very far from the usual tourist postcard version of a beach. In black and white, it showed an angry sea, where jagged lightning forked down from the sky to meet it.

A couple of her scarves were hung over the end of the sofa and the room smelled like her. Woodsmoke and ... what was it? Whatever it was, it sent a tiny jolt of arousal through him, which he crushed. He'd been away for days, in tiring meetings and lost in books and research. He'd looked forward to seeing her. But when he'd arrived, he'd come through the door behind Fintan, whose easy intimacy with Blaize had inspired pangs of both envy and hatred.

Cuinn turned around to see Blaize standing in the doorway still watching him. He met her eyes and raised one eyebrow.

"I'm fine with it." She shrugged.

He didn't see what she had to be annoyed about. He was the injured party here. "We'll start your training again tomorrow. But carefully. You can't overdo it. Mind energy is just as exhausting as any other kind."

"Good." She was polite, but wary. The heat that he'd seen in the dreamscape had gone. But he knew it was there under the surface, smouldering like the fire in the grate.

Ah damn. She's beautiful.

The night was hushed around them.

"I thought I'd examine the house's wardings and protection. To make sure you're safe."

Blaize frowned, but shrugged again. "Sure. Better safe than sorry."

Her body language was taut, her shoulders stiff, her arms still crossed tightly over her chest.

He walked through the tiny living room, checking that the back door in the kitchen was still locked, and taking a look round. He touched the wardings at the back door and windows. Each time he touched them with his energy, there was a flash of indigo. Satisfied, he came back into the living room. She hadn't moved. "Shall I check upstairs?"

Again, the shrug. It was starting to annoy him now. He was feeling very out of his depth. He brushed past her, her scent becoming stronger the closer he got, and his arm skimmed her soft burgundy sweater as he walked towards the stairs.

After a few seconds, he heard her footsteps on the stairs behind him.

What was he doing? What did he want to happen? He had promised himself he would give her time, time to realise how good they were together, how right. And not just for sex—though that was out of this world—but for so much more than that. She'd bewitched him, and although he wanted more than almost anything to consummate that relationship in the physical world, he'd decided that nothing else would happen between them until the Rogue was stopped.

So what, exactly, did he think he was doing, climbing up her stairs with an excuse as flimsy as any schoolboy's?

CHAPTER

32

Blaize was confused. Well, not confused exactly. She knew what she wanted, and what she didn't. She wanted hot sex with the gorgeous man climbing her stairs.

She did not want a relationship.

Unfortunately, his interest in the latter meant the former was probably a very bad idea. Not that you'd know he felt like that from the way he'd barged into her house. He'd been striding around her living room like he owned the place. Which she supposed he did. *But still. Rude much?*

And yet here she was, following him as if drugged. Although, of course, she was drugged. Did mild healing energy count as behaviour-altering? Perhaps she could blame that for what was about to happen.

She stood in the doorway.

They looked at each other, less than a yard separating them physically, but it felt like miles.

"We need to talk," he said. The scowl that had been on his face since she'd opened her door was still there. And something else. A dangerous edge she hadn't seen in him before. She didn't want to talk, though. If he was interested in more discussion, then he could piss off back to the house. She just didn't have the energy.

"Not tonight, Cuinn. I'm too tired. And you don't look so great yourself."

She went to the tiny dressing table, turned her back to him, and took her jewelery off. She was killing time. If she ignored him, he might go away and take that tempting body with him. She felt a tug low down in her body when she thought of it.

"About what happened in the dreamscape," he said.

He wasn't going away then. She turned back to face him and found him closer than before. This time only inches separated them, his breath warm on her face. She went on the offensive. Perhaps she could annoy him into leaving. "A lot happened in the dreamscape, Cuinn. Including me almost getting killed."

"One of the most frightening moments of my life."

"It wasn't great for me, either." She put a hand on one hip, and raised her chin. But the angrier she got, the more he seemed to relax, the scowl melting away to leave a more thoughtful expression on his face.

He reached for her, and with nowhere to go, her back against the dressing table, she couldn't dodge him without looking like a child. But he only took her hand in his.

"We're connected now, Blaize."

"I know." His hand felt cool, dry, and comforting. She wasn't sure whether to wrench hers away or to grab him with her other hand and pull him in tight.

"It's more than just the Maven-Adherent connection."

"Sexual attraction's a powerful connection, true." She refused to give an inch.

He moved a little closer. *Too close.* "It's more than that, Blaize."

His breath rifled through her hair. His scent was musky and male, and she felt light-headed. *To hell with it.* She'd made her intentions clear. If he wanted to pine for a relationship, that was his problem.

And anger made for heat. And she was in her element in hot weather.

She licked her lips, and looked up at him. She slowly reached to put a hand on his hip. His hair, messy as always, cast shadows on his face in the dim evening light of the room, and his eyes, almost lost in darkness, fixed on hers. Her hand slipped around to his lower back and dipped to touch the skin underneath his black chinos. He took an audible breath. His hands went to her head, cradling it in his hands. She shivered as one of his hands cupped her neck and drew it towards him.

She was transfixed. Hypnotised. Her nerve endings were on fire with anticipation. His body lined itself up against hers. He leaned down towards her mouth, and she closed her eyes and tilted her face up, ready. It was going to be a wild ride.

He dropped a light kiss on her mouth … and then, nothing. She opened her eyes in confusion. He'd gone. She heard him call back up the stairs, "We will talk, Blaize." The front door shut and the lock snicked behind him.

She was still in the same place minutes after his footsteps had died away.

What the fuck?

The next morning Cuinn concentrated on work, despite the fact that all he really wanted to do was talk to her about their relationship. Because, despite what she seemed to think, they were going to have a relationship—if they weren't already in one.

"We're going to stay in the room today; we're not going to dreamwalk," he said. "I'll put you in a light trance, and we'll see what you can remember about the Rogue. Any information we can pick up is helpful at this point for dealing with the Rogue later. But we'll go into your memories, and not into the dreamscape."

She nodded, one professional to another. He was impressed that she didn't seem to feel any fear for what they were about to try. It was unlikely to be easy.

"Just tell me what to do." She sat on the floor opposite him, both once more on their own mats.

"Lie down and relax." He kept his tone light and impersonal. He could do professional too. Though it had taken all the willpower he had to walk out on her last night. Right now he wanted to grab her, to shake and argue her into a relationship with him, but he kept those emotions locked down. She shot him a suspicious look, but followed his instructions, and lay back on the mat and closed her eyes.

Once she was relaxed, he said, "I'm going to ask you some questions. However those questions make you feel, remember I'm keeping you safe. Let any emotion wash over you without absorbing it. You don't need to take it on. Do you understand?"

"I do." Blaize murmured the words.

"Take yourself back to my Haven." He brought her mind back to the moments before she went through the portal and the Rogue attacked. He drew a careful breath. This was delicate work. He couldn't let any of his own fear or frustration show, because if she sensed it and became afraid herself, they could get nothing.

"You wait a minute or so, and then you step forward through the portal." A breath. "What do you see?"

Fear flickered across her face, and she shook her head slightly. Her hair pooled about her shoulders, and blended into the red tones of her mat. Her eyes remained closed and there was a tightness that hadn't been there before. But her voice was steady.

"I walk through and at first, there's—nothingness. I know it's only a breath between portals, so I take another step to get to my Haven. But as I lift my foot, I'm wrenched backwards. Strong arms are around me. I'm fighting them." A shallower breath. "She's a match for me here, where I don't know what's up and what's down."

"Remember, you're safe here, Blaize. Nothing can hurt you now."

Blaize's face was twisted though he wasn't sure whether it was in distress or anger. It smoothed some with his words.

"Can you feel her energies?" He sat crossed-legged at her side and leaned in closer, his elbows on his knees and his chin propped in one hand.

"I'm not sure. Her arms are squeezing me. I'm bending over, trying to throw her off me. Bear hugs should be easy to get out of. But she has me with something more than just her arms. And she's hot. Or at least, she's the same temperature as me, which is hot in this vacuum.

"I turn in her grasp, and her fist comes up and hits me in the face. It hurts! I fall backwards. She kicks me. The pain feels greater than just a physical blow. Each kick or punch has an energetic resonance. It's as if each time she touches me, I lose a little energy."

Cuinn's stomach twisted and he felt sick. He knew what the Rogue was. Something forbidden. Taboo.

Blaize came to the same conclusion and her eyes snapped open seconds later. "Oh, Source. She has the same energies as me, and she was feeding from me." Her gaze as it met his held a storm of emotion behind it.

"She's a Leech."

CHAPTER

33

Once Indigo had been bound to him as Maven and Adherent, a binding almost unbreakable, he'd introduced her to leeching. To help her be strong, he said. To live up to her full potential.

Her desire to please him had ensured that her initial shock at the forbidden practice had easily turned to curiosity. And then she'd experienced the almost sexual ecstasy of taking energy from another energetic. The fine line of pleasure-pain as you pulled energy not from the ether, but from another person.

And the power. Oh, the power.

Watching that other person, terrified, open before you.

Their face as you took more and more, and you became more energised, more powerful, while they wilted like a bloom picked days ago.

Indigo's body reacted to her thoughts, and even as she lay on her hard bed in the bare room on the outskirts of Merrow, she felt a thrill course through her, a pleasure almost sexual igniting her nerve endings. She let out a breath.

She longed to leech again. To take energy from an unwilling victim. To see the pride in her Maven's face as she drained that victim in front of him. It was worth every moment in this shitty town, in this shitty house.

Indigo still needed her Maven's help, or drugs, to overpower another person for leeching, and her Maven had been stingy with opportunities so far.

So far.

The trance had been unpleasant, despite Cuinn's efforts to make it as easy for Blaize as possible. The two of them had joined Fintan, Tierra and Cara for lunch afterwards, but Blaize only picked at hers, pushing food around her plate.

"Do you think it's Indigo?" she asked no one in particular.

"It could be. But geography means nothing in the dreamscape. Whoever it is could be anyone, anywhere in the world. It's likely, but we can't count on it," said Cuinn.

"The Rogue is probably an addict if she's leeching off Blaize. And it explains why she chose you Blaize, if you're her energetic match. It makes more sense now," Cara said.

Blaize leaned back in her chair and sipped at a glass of water. "So it might not even be anything to do with the prophecy. If she's just an individual Rogue who's addicted to energy and leeching from others to get it."

"Except that you're involved in the major prophecy," Cuinn said, as he put his knife and fork down. "You were in the line up with the other eleven. And if you were hurt, or worse, then it would still stop the prophecy from coming true, even if you were hurt through something else."

Blaize frowned. "I guess so. So we carry on as before? Especially now we know that I'm the best bait we have for this Rogue?"

Blaize wasn't sure about the major prophecy. Cuinn had refused to take her out into the wild energy in the dreamscape. He'd been adamant, saying she'd need a lot more training for that. But Blaize believed that the piece of the prophecy where he'd seen her hurt had been fulfilled by the Rogue's attack in the dreamscape, and she was itching to come up against the Rogue again.

Except that this time she'd be prepared.

But although Cuinn had agreed to using her as bait, he still wasn't keen.

"Maybe we should change the plan." He shoved away from the table and went over to the kitchen, coming back with another full mug of coffee.

He sat back down and his foot tapped against the floor under the table. Blaize thought maybe he'd had enough coffee for today. She decided not to comment on either his words or his behaviour, and silently congratulated herself for her unusual tact and diplomacy. She smothered a smile.

Fintan clapped Cuinn on the back. "Let it go. The plan's fine, and Blaize will kick the Rogue's ass. Blaize won't even need to charge herself with as much energy as we'd planned because the Rogue is looking specifically for her."

"Blaize is already powerful, considering she's only just started training. Especially as Ajna is her auxiliary, not her dominant energy." Cuinn took another sip of coffee. "I've seen energetics with Ajna as a dominant who were weaker than her."

Cuinn didn't look at Blaize as he gave her what was probably the first compliment he'd paid her. *Huh.* It boosted her confidence. If he thought she was strong, she had a solid chance of bringing the Rogue down.

"We'll spend the afternoon meditating and charging both your energies, Manipura and Ajna. And we'll spend the rest of the week practising for your trip outside our Havens on the astral plane. By then you should be almost well enough." Cuinn held up a hand to forestall Blaize's inevitable comment that she was already well enough. Blaize just wanted it done. But unfortunately, she wasn't in charge.

Cuinn was. "Cara gets the final say on when you're ready."

CHAPTER
34

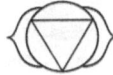

Cuinn was in Merrow with Tierra. She'd needed to stock up on supplies for the house, and he hadn't wanted her to go alone.

His cell phone rang, the discordant sound jarring. Very few people had his number. He held the phone up to his ear.

"Yes?"

"Mr. Ahern, it's Detective Davis. I'm sorry to tell you that the woman who attacked your friend came back. She broke into Sugar and Spice after closing and assaulted the owner. We've just sent Rosa to the hospital."

Cuinn grasped the cell tightly. "Rosa? Is she alright?"

"She'll live. The café's been pretty badly damaged. The assailant set some kind of a fire."

A wash of adrenaline hit him. One of a very small number of people he cared about had been attacked. He needed to find out what had happened, and see for himself if Rosa was ok. But this could be the break they needed. If they could follow the Rogue's trail, there would be no need for Blaize to act as bait. *No need for her to put herself into danger.*

"I'm in town. I'll be there in five minutes." He flicked the phone off and bolted out of the bookstore he'd been browsing in to find Tierra. He strode to the grocery store he'd left her in and stopped in front of her. She looked at him, surprised, a bag of cashew nuts in her hand.

"Rosa's been attacked by the Rogue. I need you to find out what Rosa can tell us about Indigo while I talk to the police."

"Whatever you need." Tierra, her eyes wide, followed him outside. "Shall I call Blaize?"

"Let's find out a bit more first. We can call her then. There's nothing she can do from home."

Everything was in position. The male and his weak sidekick were in town checking on Indigo's old boss. Indigo hadn't meant to hurt Rosa quite as much as she had. But it had been fun to burn down the café where so many patrons had looked down on her. Treated her like nothing.

Indigo looked around the clearing, which was about thirty yards across. The corpse of a homeless woman lay like a bundle of rags, propped against a large log. Indigo had burned the foliage a little to enlarge the clearing, so she had a good view on all sides. She was confident no one would be able to sneak up on her.

All Indigo needed to do was to get that bitch here. She got out her cell phone. Her Maven had given her Blaize's number – he had ways and means far beyond anything Indigo knew how to do. She dialled the number now.

As soon as she had Blaize's mind within reach, she was going to play a little game. She'd soon teach Blaize how little she knew about Ajna. That she couldn't trust her own senses. She was going to make the bitch feel like she'd won—and then bring her world crashing down around her head.

Because no one had ever told Indigo not to play with her food.

Blaize was in her cottage, working her way through a pile of combined prophecy books. Each collected the prophecies from farseer energetics in a particular place and time, and included such interesting titles as "1702: British Crown Colonies," and "1868: The Canadian Confederation."

Despite their boring titles, she'd been surprised to find herself captivated. They were like puzzle pieces. Each book was a collection of prophecies, and came with a handbook that was a commentary containing any thoughts on the individual prophecies other farseers had had. Blaize wasn't entirely sure what she was looking for, but Cuinn had suggested she use some of her downtime, before it was time for her to play bait, to get used to the feel of prophecies. She could see now that they were rarely clear cut.

Each prophecy came to a farseer energetic as a series of pictures. Some had audio, but not all. They might be a static picture or more like a film. It was different for every farseer. The stronger you were energetically, the more likely you would be to use all your senses to receive a prophecy.

And then the farseer had to describe the prophecy. This wasn't easy. Farseers were trained in observation, in noticing detail. She winced. That wasn't usually her thing. She was a big-picture person, though after spending the last few days training with Cuinn, she was learning, a little, how to notice more, and how to describe the world around her in richer detail.

They drilled the plan with the group at lunchtimes and supper. The work with Cuinn mainly focused on how she could shield her mind from Ajna attacks. But, as Blaize had admitted to Nixie that morning in a video conference call where they'd gossiped and caught up, it didn't come naturally to Blaize, which was just one more annoying thing about Ajna. Nixie had been more interested in the fact Blaize had had sex with Cuinn, and had teased that Blaize did seem to remember a lot of detail about that.

Blaize flushed a little.

The more detail the farseer noticed and was able to describe in a way others could understand, the more likely the farseer would be able to interpret the prophecy, alone or with others. Many of the Ajna farseers worked together at the Guild in Athens in order to connect prophecies together.

Even Cuinn had worked at the Guild, once upon a time. Apparently he even spoke fluent, if archaic, Greek. These days he wasn't an active farseer for the Guild and the prophecies he saw were almost accidental. He visited the Guild when he needed to, which was why he was away so often at the moment to discuss the prophecy that he believed put them all in danger.

She was deep in late 18th Century England when her phone rang, her mind full of the politics of war and revolution, and the prophecies that had tried to guide the energetics through the wars safely, while saving as many humans as possible.

She was jolted out of the book by the cell phone ringtone she used for unknown numbers. She frowned. She rarely received calls. Her family and friends overseas sent texts or emails, and the only people she knew in Canada were the energetics she was living with.

Her heart beat faster. What if there was an emergency at home? If Nix, Fai, or Marius were hurt? She grabbed the phone. "Blaize here."

Silence. Puzzled, after a few seconds she said, "Hello? Is there someone there?"

"I thought we might dance, you and I." The woman's voice had a sharp edge, along with suppressed delight. It was an unpleasant combination and Blaize's skin crawled as she realised who was speaking. "I have Rosa, your friend from the café. She's not feeling too good. Catch me if you can. You have thirty minutes to get here, or I start burning her. If you bring anyone with you? She's dead."

She ended with a map reference, a laugh, and the phone disconnected.

Blaize stared at the phone in shock. The Rogue had called her. How had she gotten Blaize's number? She needed to go find her, now.

But everyone else was out, and way more than thirty minutes from that map reference. Even if she called them, they wouldn't make it in time.

Fintan and Cara were in Vancouver, he following up a potential lead, and she checking in on an energetic patient. They were a couple of hours away at least.

Tierra and Cuinn were in town. Closer, but not close enough. She'd call them on the way and hope they'd be there in time to help. She seized her jacket and flew out of the front door. She couldn't waste any time. Indigo was clearly not in her right mind—who knew what she might do to Rosa, the friendly human from the café. Plus, this was an excellent opportunity to capture the Rogue. If Blaize waited, then she might miss it.

She ran out to the cars, chose an SUV at random, and shot off down the road. She plugged the map reference Indigo had mentioned into the GPS, and gunned the engine. She dialled Cuinn's phone as she shot onto the lane that led to the highway, juggling the steering wheel and the cell phone as she did so.

Voice mail. *Shit.* She left a message, the map reference, and a plea to come urgently. She tried Tierra. The same. Where were they both?

She called Fintan, who answered in his usual laconic drawl. "Yeah?"

Blaize filled him in on the call from Indigo. She really wished he was here.

"Sparks, under no circumstances go on your own," he ordered.

"What choice do I have? Tierra and Cuinn aren't answering their phones. Plus, I think I can take her now. I've been working on protecting myself from mind control attacks with Cuinn, and that was how she beat me last time."

"We don't know enough about her. Or who she's working with. What if she's not alone?"

Blaize frowned. She hadn't considered that. Why hadn't she considered that? She had a moment of self-doubt, then shook her head. "I don't think she's working with anyone."

The SUV purred, swiftly eating up the miles. She was less than five minutes away.

"Based on what exactly?" Fintan snapped.

"Uh … a feeling?" Blaize squirmed in the driver's seat, but she kept her eyes on the road. She glanced at the GPS. Nearly there. "Okay. I'll scope out the situation and wait for Cuinn to get here. I won't engage."

"Good. We're on our way back now. We'll be with you as soon as we can. I have the map coordinates. Stay away from the Rogue. Visual contact only." Fintan's voice was a little softer, but it was still an order.

They hung up, and Blaize pulled over to look at the map on the car's GPS. She was close to the coordinates Indigo had given her.

Will Indigo know this terrain any better than me? She had no idea if the woman was a local. Just because she'd been new to working at the coffee shop in Merrow didn't mean she was new to the area.

Blaize sat in the car and navigated around the area using the GPS, shifting the picture on the screen so she could get a good sense of where she was. There were some woods and a couple of barns marked. Not much in the way of housing, just a few cottages here and there. This wasn't well-travelled land.

Blaize checked her phone once more. Nothing from Cuinn or Tierra. She texted Cuinn: "Going to scope out the situation. Won't engage. Come ASAP."

She waited a moment, then switched the phone to silent and put it in her pocket. Her deadline wasn't far off. She got out of the vehicle, her body and mind now on alert. Indigo could be anywhere—and this was almost certainly a trap.

But Blaize was confident. Catching Rogues was what she was born to do. She decided to loop round and approach the meeting site from the opposite side. She didn't want the Rogue waiting for her.

She walked away from the car and into the woods that rolled over the land like a carpet. It was darker there, but she loved the smell of damp earth.

She picked up the pace, and breathed in deeply, her feet hitting the soft ground with gentle thuds. The pleasure of the physical activity was wonderful, despite her concern about what was waiting for her. Her chest lightened. She was finally taking action.

She slowed when, deep in the words, she saw a clearing and something slumped against a log in the centre. But Blaize was too far away to tell if it was a body, let alone if it was Rosa. She crept closer, staying low and hidden.

Blaize checked her cell. Still no message from Cuinn. She squatted on her haunches to wait. She trained her eyes on the body, glancing around every now and then to ensure there was no one else around. If nothing else happened, she could wait Indigo out here until Cuinn arrived. And then Blaize would meet the Rogue on her own terms.

Blaize breathed in and out to still herself, and put in place the shielding Cuinn had been teaching her for her mind, just as she might lock her Manipura shields over her body. This new type of shielding was harder to hold in place than her fire shields, but Cuinn had assured her that was just practice. And she had been practising. Practising until she was sick of it.

She had been there only a few minutes when she caught movement across the other side of the clearing. A thin figure with stringy black hair, wearing dirty jeans and a pink top, strode towards whatever was against the log. *Indigo.* Blaize managed to stop herself leaping to her feet and attacking. Just.

She gritted her teeth and watched the tableau play out. Indigo gave the pile a kick, the thud persuading Blaize that it was a body. But Blaize still couldn't tell if it was alive or dead.

Should she show herself? *What is Indigo doing?* Indigo seemed to be talking to the body on the floor, but there was a strange haze in the gap in the forest, and Blaize struggled to see clearly. *Is Indigo using fire?* Was smoke causing the scene to blur? *Is she burning Rosa?* Blaize shook her head to clear it. There were no flames, and she couldn't smell any smoke. Something wasn't quite right here, but she couldn't put her finger on what, exactly.

There was a movement to her side, and she tensed, ready to spring, to attack.

And then her whole body relaxed as she saw Cuinn, who crouched down next to her, his eyes on the clearing.

"What's going on?" he asked.

She filled him in. He stayed expressionless, listening. When she'd finished, he nodded, speaking in a harsh whisper.

"We can't take any chances. We'll go in from different angles. I'll work my way around the clearing. When you see me attack, follow me. I'll hold Indigo with my mind and you get Rosa. When Rosa's safe, I'll incapacitate Indigo, if I can."

"Surely it's better if I attack her?" protested Blaize in a low, urgent tone.

"You're not strong enough. She's too powerful." He moved off without another word through the forest.

Blaize felt a stab of disappointment in her belly. He hadn't even considered that she could attack the Rogue. And Blaize was a Warrior, not Cuinn. He was just a … a bookworm.

She scowled into the thick foliage between her and the gap in the woods, waiting. But following on the heels of annoyance was anxiety. He needed her to help him fight Indigo. He wasn't a fighter and had no wish to be. She was surprised by the thought that followed on from that: this was her opportunity to show him she was independent. That she wasn't Sophea.

She squinted across the clearing, which shimmered, the figures of Indigo and Rosa flickering in and out of sight. She tried to keep her focus on them despite the headache that pinched at her temples. Uncertainty filled her. What did she need to do? Confusion blurred her next steps.

Long minutes later, Cuinn broke through the woods the other side and shot towards the Rogue, rushing her in a physical attack. Blaize narrowed her eyes, the haze thicker now. Cuinn and the Rogue swam in and out of view, sometimes entirely obscured by the smog. Alarmed, Blaize exploded into action, and ran towards the body. If Indigo was going to burn the area, Blaize needed to get Rosa out now.

But as Blaize approached the struggling figures, the Rogue smashed Cuinn across the face with a hammer fist, and Cuinn fell to his knees, Indigo towering above him. The Rogue drew a knife from her hip, and slashed it across his throat. Blood sprayed across the clearing and spattered across the Rogue, whose triumphant gaze met Blaize's horrified one. Cuinn fell without a sound, his body disappearing into the thick haze.

Blaize sprinted the last few yards, torn between Rosa and Cuinn. But the scene was blurred, and Blaize's head felt fuzzy. She missed her footing as she got close and stumbled on a stray root.

She put her arm out to break her fall, and gasped as she hit the ground. On her hands and knees on the floor, she started to push herself upright, but confusion filled her and she couldn't remember what she was supposed to be doing. There was something urgent, she knew. Something life or death. She swayed on her hands and knees, her head drooping.

A strong arm grabbed her from behind, and pulled her head backwards and up by the hair, which stretched her neck out painfully. She felt a sharp prick where her neck and shoulder joined, and then—oblivion.

CHAPTER

35

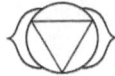

Cuinn didn't spend long with the police. After a short conversation, he left the police station and walked towards his car, pulling his cell from his pocket to text Tierra he was on his way back to pick her up.

The police, with whom he had a reasonable relationship, had let him read Rosa's statement. Indigo had come to see Rosa as she'd been closing up. Rosa had been worried about the other woman, explaining Indigo had looked even thinner than usual.

Rosa—*always too softhearted*—had invited Indigo in for something to eat, wanting to broach what had happened with Blaize. Rosa had told the police she'd never felt any need to be afraid of Indigo before, and she didn't intend to start now.

Rosa didn't remember much after that. An attack, pain, and then to her surprise, the arrival of the police. No one knew who had called the attack in.

The address the Rogue had given in her application form to the coffee shop had been false, and they had no way of tracking her down. The police were still making inquiries – which Cuinn felt was just another way of saying they had no idea where she was.

Cuinn had his hand on the car door when he saw the missed call from Blaize. His stomach gave a lurch, and he shook his head. He was jumping at shadows—the uneasy feeling would be nothing.

But once he'd listened to the voicemail and read her texts, Cuinn's stomach churned, and he gripped the phone in his fist.

What the hell was she thinking? Blaize was impulsive. Unpredictable. And the danger could be specifically directed towards Blaize—there had been a reason that Indigo had attacked Blaize and Cuinn still wasn't sure what it was. Until he understood if the leeching was the only purpose, or whether there was some darker purpose for choosing Blaize particularly, he wanted to keep her out of it. And, he admitted to himself, to protect her.

If only he'd answered the phone, he could have told Blaize that Indigo didn't have Rosa. That there was no need for her to go. By now the churning in his stomach had turned to a cold, hard rock.

He dialled Tierra on his way to the hospital, and her shocked voice said she would wait for him outside.

When he picked up Tierra, her face was paler than usual. He pulled away as soon as she shut her door, heading for the map reference at the northeast end of Kanaka Creek Regional Park. They'd both had messages from Fintan as well, who was well on his way back with Cara.

Tierra updated Cuinn on Rosa as they drove; she had been surrounded by white sheets and bleeping machines. The last thing that Rosa had said to Tierra had chilled him right down to the bone.

"She's damaged. She was like a junkie seeking a fix. I don't know what she's addicted to, but she's unpredictable. I've never seen anyone so out of control."

Cuinn and Tierra found the SUV Blaize had used and called Fintan and Cara to direct them there. There was no sign of Blaize or anyone else. Tierra had to threaten Cuinn with an energetic fight if he didn't wait for Fintan and Cara before he headed off into the woods to find Blaize. She closed her eyes to seek and track Blaize while they waited.

"She's not close by. I don't feel her within my range," she told him.

Cuinn paced up and down, grinding his teeth with impatience until Fintan pulled up almost an hour later, and he and Cara tumbled out of the car.

Cuinn updated the newcomers, and Fintan nodded before he spoke. "Okay. Tierra, can you work with me to track her? We can start from here and see where she went."

"Of course." Tierra pulled a coat from the car.

Fintan stopped Cuinn from joining them. "I think you should go back to the house. Check her Haven and the dreamscape. We'll take the cell phones in case she's injured. If she is, we'll call you. But the more of us out there, the more likely we are to obliterate any tracks. Tierra's our best tracker energetically and physically, so you need to let her work."

Cara nodded. "I'll stay with Cuinn until you need me."

Cuinn ran his hands through his hair. "I need to come."

"You'll do her more good at home, Cuinn. I promise. Now let us go and do what we're good at," Fintan said.

Cuinn could see the logic of his argument, but the emotions inside him threatened to overwhelm him. Cara put a hand on Cuinn's arm, and Tierra gave him a fierce hug. "You know I can do this, Cuinn, but Fin's right, I can't do it if there are too many distractions. It's going to be tricky enough when it gets dark. It's already six o'clock"

Cuinn nodded reluctantly. Tierra was good at finding things, but it wasn't a skill she had much use for these days. He hoped she'd had enough practice recently. "We'll stay at the car. But we're not going home immediately. You might need us. I'll see if I can find her mind in the physical area before I go to her Haven."

Fintan sent him one last sympathetic look and then he and Tierra were gone into the woods.

"Do you need anything else to be able to search for her?" said Cara.

Cuinn shook his head and got back into the car, putting the seat back so his long frame could lie down as much as possible. He relaxed and searched for her mind in as wide an area as he could. But he could find no trace of her. She was either unconscious, or she'd been taken out of his range—a range that was further than Tierra's. Neither was good. His stomach was a knot of tension, and all his muscles were tight. He couldn't stop thinking about the image from the prophecy, of her tied up, bloody and beaten.

After a couple of hours, with full dark outside the stuffy car, Cara's cell phone rang.

The noise felt shrill, intrusive after the quiet he'd been working in, but he welcomed it nonetheless. His eyes snapped open, and he put the seat back up as Cara spoke. Her end of the conversation didn't give anything away, and after a few "Okays" she turned the phone off.

"They've tracked her to a clearing where it looks like her trail ends. They think she's been kidnapped."

Cuinn wouldn't accept that. He opened the car door. Fintan had created a bobbing light with Manipura energy for them to follow. It led them to where Fintan and Tierra waited. A grave Tierra showed him the tracks they'd followed from Blaize's car to an overgrown area at the edge of a clearing where it looked as if someone had waited. The four of them then walked the tracks of someone heavy who'd left the clearing—possibly someone carrying another person. Those tracks went to a dirt track road, where Tierra thought a car had parked, before turning and leaving.

"Cuinn, I think we should call Adam. He can get us what we need to help us find her. Most of his work is tracking down Rogues," Tierra said. Her brother, Adam, Cuinn's cousin, was in a security team that worked across the Guilds to protect them from internal and external threats. He had access to tracking resources as well as being a powerful energetic tracker in his own right.

Cuinn felt sick. All his worst fears had come to pass. "They could be anywhere by now. They have hours of lead on us."

They would never find her.

Fintan nodded at Tierra, and she went to the side of the clearing to phone Adam.

"We'll find her Cuinn. If it's the same Rogue who leeched in the dreamscape, there are more of us, and we're smarter. We'll find her."

Cuinn punched a fist into the nearest tree. "I knew that the vision wasn't fulfilled by what happened on the astral plane. But I didn't want to believe it."

Slam. Slam.

"I wanted to believe it was over. I should have said something. Guarded her. Stayed with her. I've failed her, just as I failed Sophea."

Slam. The pain felt good. He deserved it.

Fintan grabbed his arm and gave it a shake, forcing Cuinn to give him his attention. "We'll find her. But you have to stay focused and present. We need you."

"Okay." It was easier to agree. He'd do what he could to help. The nausea in his stomach had stopped and everything felt numb. Switched off.

He couldn't bear it if he lost Blaize too.

CHAPTER
36

Blaize woke up, groggy and nauseated. Where was she? She tried to stretch her aching joints but found herself shackled, unable to move more than a few inches. That woke her more quickly. What had happened? She remembered the clearing. A haze. Rosa. Cuinn.

Oh, Source. Cuinn. He wasn't dead. He couldn't be dead. She refused to accept it as a possibility. She needed to find out what had happened, and now. But before that, she needed to get out of here.

She looked around her. She lay on a dirty bare mattress, in a small, dark room. It seemed like a basement, as there was only one window, high up in the wall, and a rickety metal staircase on the other side of the room, leading up to a solid looking door.

She had no sense of where she was, whether she was still in the woods or if she'd been moved.

She tried to use the power she had stored. But as she drew on it, she felt nauseous again and stopped. She gasped, and leaned her head to the side, not wanting to be sick while she was lying down.

The nausea receded after a few minutes, leaving her shaky as well as tired.

After an indeterminable amount of time, the door opened. Blaize shifted, ready to defend herself as much as the shackles allowed.

It was the Rogue.

Now thin to the point of emaciation, she had a hollow look around her eyes.

She sneered at Blaize.

"Good morning. For me, anyway. For you, not so much. And for Cuinn?" She laughed.

Blaize strained against the metal chains. She needed to get free. But how the hell could she do that without access to her energies?

Indigo laughed and ignored her struggles. She checked the bonds that held Blaize. "Didn't try to burn your way out yet? Shame. As soon as you pulled power, you'd have been sick. I was looking forward to seeing what you'd look like after you'd tried to call Warrior fire."

Blaize twisted her wrists as far as they'd go, trying to find some give in the chains. The sick feeling she'd had when she'd tried to pull energy earlier suggested Indigo wasn't lying about that, so Blaize would need to get free physically.

"Still, seeing you lying here surrounded by your own vomit would have been fun, you stuck-up bitch."

"Why are you doing this? And what did you do to Cuinn?" Blaize's body was no longer aching, the adrenaline energising her. Her heart tripped in her chest as she tried to understand what was going on. She was shocked by the poisonous ire that Indigo was directing at her.

"Cuinn?" Indigo shrugged. "He was nothing. To me, anyway. Others might say different. But I need what you have. Your energy. Tasty energy. You're just ... well, food basically."

The woman stepped away from the bed and closed her eyes. Energy swept over Blaize and her gut roiled. "Hmmm. Yes, you're still ready. Charged—you seem to have even more power than when we last met."

Indigo shook her head.

"I nearly took you then, in the dreamscape rather than here, but we—I—wasn't ready. I tried to get you to pull power in your dreams so I could tie you to me. But persistent thing you are, I couldn't make you though I had fun killing you over and over." She smiled.

"But that's in the past. I enjoyed our little game with Rosa and Cuinn. That made up for it a little. And now," she clapped her hands together, "now we're going to take a trip back to the dreamscape together where I can taste you properly, and I'm going to have me another snack. And that's really what life's going to be like for you for the next little while."

"Don't do this." Blaize tried to make her voice firm though she wanted to be sick. "We can help you, rehabilitate you. My friend works at the Rehab centre on the West Coast; she can get you over this addiction. There's no need to hurt me."

Fear mounted inside her as the woman talked. Indigo wasn't in her right mind. *How am I going to get out of this?* All her muscles were tight as she heaved against the chains at her hands and feet. Could she loosen any of them? Or was there enough give for her to strike Indigo when she came close again? Even a few inches might be enough to stun Indigo if Blaize was fast enough and put enough physical power into it.

"Why would I want to get over it?" Indigo's voice was amused. "It's such fun. And the taste … the taste of an energy like yours? It's hard to even put into words. It makes me feel … invincible."

She leaned over, and Blaize waited until the woman's face was inches away before thrusting her clenched fist towards it, putting every ounce of physical power she could into the movement. But Indigo was too quick and swerved easily to the side. Blaize caught a glimpse of something metal in Indigo's hand. Blaize flinched away, but where could she go?

"That's enough talking. Let's take a trip." Indigo grabbed Blaize's arm and shot something sharp into it.

Blaize winced at the stab of the needle, and then her eyelids became heavy as the drug took her under. Ignoring the nausea, she pulled power to try to burn it away, but the drug was faster than she was, especially in her current condition.

"No … wait."

And then, she went under.

When Blaize opened her eyes again, she was in an ornate room with a grand chandelier. She drew in a breath through her nose. No scent. She was in the dreamscape, though not Cuinn's Haven or her own. Her throat tightened. *Don't think of Cuinn.*

She was still tied down, but the chair and the chains were fancier. She shook her head, trying to dislodge some of the fatigue that had come over her. She didn't feel at all as she had previously on the astral plane. She felt dizzy, and it was hard to focus. Her vision swam.

Indigo appeared in front of her.

"No, no, don't get up." She laughed. "Really, all you need to do is sit there. I'll do all the heavy lifting."

Indigo stood behind her, hands on Blaize's shoulders. Blaize tried to shrug her off, but Indigo's bony fingers dug unpleasantly into her muscles with a bruising grip.

She felt ripples of power on her shoulders as Indigo leeched from her. At first it was just odd, like someone running her hand the wrong way along velvet. But then the feeling intensified and became painful as Indigo took more and more power.

And Blaize felt herself getting weaker, lassitude spilling into her limbs until her head lolled to one side, falling onto her shoulder.

Fintan and Tierra stayed in the park to see if there was anything else they could find. They'd agreed to go into Merrow at first light in case anyone had seen Indigo in the last couple of days and they could get a lead that way. Tierra hadn't been able to get through to Adam, who was still somewhere deep in Russia. Cuinn and Cara went home for Cuinn to work in his own environment.

He wanted to dive straight into the dreamscape, but while he was setting up the room, warding it with energetics shields one more time, Cara disappeared and came back with an energy drink. She handed it to him wordlessly, and although he grimaced, he took it and drank it.

Cara settled herself in the armchair, her eyes alert and watchful, and Cuinn sank onto his mat, arranging his position so he lay on his back.

Cuinn closed his eyes and took a few deep breaths before pulling the energy to go into the dreamscape, starting in his own Haven. He strode around the tower quickly in case there was any trace that Blaize had managed to come back here. He saw nothing.

Outside, he looked around before walking over to the green bower that held the portal between their Havens. The grass was soft underfoot and delicate roses had bloomed around the gate. His mouth twisted, and in response to the strong feelings and energy he was putting out, the sky started to boil. Thunder cracked and lighting streaked down. He nodded viciously, satisfied as the rain poured down on him, soaking him to the skin.

He stood in front of the portal for minutes, hoping when he stepped through he might find her there, and terrified that she wouldn't be.

Eventually, he gathered the courage to go through, the moment of disorientation before he stepped into her Haven making him blink. He scanned her garden, but she wasn't there. He paced over to the bed she had created the last time they were here, and dropped onto it, his hands grabbing the red silk. His breath came in heaves.

He tried to think what to do next. She wasn't in either of the two safe places for her in the astral plane, that was clear. He would need to go outside and seek her. Just as he had done fifty years earlier, seeking Sophea's mind.

He took one last look around her Haven and headed to his own to prepare for going out into the wild energies.

Many hours later, he opened his eyes in his own body. He was shaking. He had over-taxed himself on the astral plane, and for nothing. Cara was still sitting opposite him, watching him from the chair. She came over, lifted his head, and put a cushion under it. She offered him some water. He drank and let his body settle.

Cara looked at him questioningly. He shook his head.

"You need to rest. Still a few hours until Fintan and Tierra can go into town, and they're getting some sleep until they can leave."

He opened his mouth to protest, wanting just to replenish his physical energy with some food and then go in again. She caught his gaze. "There's no way you can go back in again straight away. You need sleep first, then food and drink. You can try again first thing in the morning. But you need a few hours of rest or your body will burn itself up."

Cuinn got to his feet with her help, and realising how exhausted he was, agreed. "But wake me for breakfast with the others. I want to talk strategy and see if there's anything they found that was unusual in the woods. Four heads are better than two."

She nodded, and helped him into his bedroom.

"I'll leave a note to ask the others to wake us."

"Thank you, Cara."

"Tell me what you found last night," Cuinn said, addressing Fintan and Tierra through a mouthful of toast early the next morning.

"Not much," Fintan said.

"We thought we'd go and talk to Rosa again. See if there's anything else she remembers." Tierra hesitated. "Do you think we should share more with the human police about Indigo? The non-energetic aspects?"

Cuinn shook his head, adamant. "It's too dangerous. Indigo's too volatile. She could hurt humans, or expose us. But see if you can find out anything else from the police as to what they have found out about the attack on Rosa. Fintan, you might have more luck there. Get Tierra to introduce you and play on your military background," Cuinn said. "I'll go back into the dreamscape."

"I'll stay with you. I can keep an eye on both you and the house," said Cara.

"Fine," said Cuinn.

"We'll stay out as long as we need to." Tierra addressed Cuinn directly. "Don't forget to eat."

CHAPTER

37

Blaize was woken by a persistent pain. She turned her head groggily to see a narrow plastic tube leading from a stand towards her arm, a nasty bruise forming around the entry point.

She tried to stay conscious. But flashes of memory, or dreams, kept intruding. Were they in her head, or was she in the dreamscape? The scenes were like pieces of a mosaic, flashes of colour that hurt her head, and nothing that she could focus on for more than a few seconds.

But the fragments, and the haze and fog that came with them nagged at her, trying to get her attention. There was something she was missing, something important. She moaned and shifted on the bed in an attempt to get comfortable in the restraints. She tugged on her wrists, and thought of a happier time when she had been willing to give up her control to an infuriating, rude, and inhospitable man who had gotten under her skin in a big way.

Her consciousness drifted over her accusation that he was the threat to her in the café. How wrong she had been. Her mind swam as snapshots from the fight with Indigo drifted through. How Indigo had beaten her. How hazy and confused she had felt.

How there had been a haze around them both, and how difficult it had been for Blaize to see clearly. A haze. Smog.

Blaize's eyes opened wide as she put the pieces together. Cuinn wasn't dead. The Rogue had torn through Blaize's mental shields like tissue paper and showed her an entire tableau that didn't exist. Anger warred with relief. *Cuinn was alive.*

The relief gave her some true sleep. But she soon woke again and drifted between fragments from the ether and consciousness.

Every time she woke up back in the basement, the renewed hope drove her to pull enough power to burn away the drugs that were being fed into her body through the drip. But they built up each time while she slept, and it was like trying to drain the ocean with a teacup.

As time passed, she became more and more agitated. Her fire energy was looking for a way out. Whatever combination of drugs and energy Indigo used had trapped Blaize's energy in her own body.

If she used energy, she'd be sick. If she didn't use it, eventually it could twist into a darker form, the sinister form that some energies could take when they had nowhere to go. She could become the thing she most hated: a Rogue.

She needed to get out of there. *Think. What are my options?* Her brain was mushy and fogged.

I need to contact Cuinn. And that was best done in the dreamscape. If he were alive—not if, there was no if; he was alive, she knew it—he would try to find her there. She just needed to send him a signal so he could locate her.

But she wasn't able to access the dreamscape with the level of drugs in her system at the moment. The only way she accessed the dreamscape was with Indigo. Blaize was trapped in the dreamscape just as much as she was trapped on the physical plane.

Her thoughts swirled round and round, and she fought against hopelessness as she swam in and out of consciousness.

What was her first priority? Get rid of some of the drugs in her system.

She burned them in tiny increments, increasing the amount in the moments of clarity she had and making her feel nauseous. She'd rest, then burn a little more, then rest.

After doing this for what seemed like hours, she passed out again. This time, it was a more healing sleep.

Blaize jolted awake with a sharp pain on her right cheek, which rocked her head to the side. When she opened her eyes, her face burned and she caught the movement of Indigo drawing her hand back. This new pain quickly blended into all the other pains in her body.

"Yeah, wake up bitch." Indigo's angry tones were back. "Thanks for supper." Blaize could see the hollows on Indigo's face were a little less pronounced than the day before. Blaize's energy clearly agreed with her.

Blaize stared back, exhausted. She aimed for a defiant sneer on her face. "I know what you did."

Indigo cocked her head. "What …"

She laughed. "Oh, you figured out my little game? Took you long enough."

"Why?"

"Why not? It was a good way to keep you occupied so I could catch you. And the look on your face when you thought your precious Maven was dead? Worth a little of my energy." She shrugged and put a box containing a greasy pizza on the bed next to Blaize. It smelled disgusting. "You need to eat."

Blaize stared at her.

"To keep your energy up," Indigo said. "You're pretty strong, but if you don't eat something—even with the drip—it will be hard to keep you alive. As I take your energy, your body will burn itself from the inside out. You'll lose weight and eventually your organs will fail."

Blaize blinked, and shook her head. She'd never been this close to her own death before. *I need to do something.*

"Why don't you just stop taking my energy?"

"Good one. You'll eat eventually. Because now you've worked out that Cuinn's still around, you have romantic notions of rescue. So I'll keep you alive and get to enjoy you for longer, and you'll lie there hoping someone will come and get you. They won't, of course. No one knows where you are except me and—" she stopped and put a hand to her mouth. "Except me. So, eat. Keep your hopes alive."

Blaize had to contort her body to reach the pizza box because of the chains on her wrists and ankles. But she managed to grab a slice of the pizza. The oil from the pizza made her stomach roil in protest. But Indigo was right. She wanted to stay alive. And she wanted to be rescued.

Well. No. She wanted to rescue herself.

But with horrible clarity, she realised that her pride, her extreme self-reliance, and her focus on doing everything herself, had played a huge part in getting her into this mess in the first place.

She might **want** to rescue herself, but she **needed** to get help. And she had an idea of how to do it.

She kept her eyes on Indigo as she ate, nervous of the strange energetic's unpredictability.

"Good work," Indigo said, once Blaize had eaten the slice of pizza.

Indigo walked towards the top of the bed, and Blaize flinched. But Indigo just checked the drip.

"I'll leave you with the rest." She went over to the door. As she opened it, she looked back. "You've been in training your whole life to be my battery, you know. You shine with power. And it's mine now. We're going to be spending a lot of time together. And don't worry, we're going to move to more comfortable conditions soon. We're still a little too close for comfort to that idiot, Cuinn."

So we're still close by.

Blaize felt relief and anxiety at the same time, and was unable to stop the conflict of emotions chase across her expression. Indigo cackled. "Ah, you still think he might find you and save you? I've been stalking you all since you arrived, and the only time you saw me was in the café. And he didn't even notice me then, did he? I'm protected. I'm not worried he'll find you. And even if he did, with the amount of energy I have from you, I think I could take him. You weren't hard, after all."

Indigo looked around the room, and her gaze stopped on a rickety wooden bookshelf in the corner of the basement, with a few damp books lying in piles on it. She narrowed her eyes, and the bookshelf burst into flames.

The heat was intense, and Blaize contracted her body on the bed and strained against the chains. The adrenaline from the fear burned more of the drugs in her system away. *Will she burn me to death?*

Blaize looked around the room, desperately searching for something she could do to protect herself from the fire. But the fire burned hard, and after minutes, books and bookshelf were just a pile of stinking ash on the floor.

"I don't think he'd have much of a defense against that, eh? Anyway. Enough fun. Eat your food." She turned away, and went to the door, and slammed it behind her.

It took Blaize several hours, but she managed to get the pizza down, no easy thing, given her bonds. Her neck ached by the end of it, and she lay back down again with a sigh of relief. Perhaps now, with a little rest, she would be able to burn away more of the drugs, which were just another poison, after all, from her body.

If she had less of the drugs in her system, the next time Indigo took her back to the dreamscape, into Indigo's Haven—which was what she assumed the trashy mansion was—she could break out and reach Cuinn with a message. He could then follow her and find her physically.

Cuinn was going to be very, very angry. Blaize had wanted to save Rosa and she'd rushed off, sure if it came to it, she'd be able to beat Indigo. Her impulsive and proud nature had gotten her into trouble again.

But with Cuinn, she'd held back. She'd kept her feelings under a tight rein. She'd been ready for spontaneity and impulse in terms of sex, but she'd been the opposite when it had come to a relationship.

She had thought she was like her father. That if she fell in love, her energy might twist, and she'd end up in a similar tragic situation. And she couldn't have borne it if that had happened to Cuinn.

If she survived this—when she survived—without her energy twisting, she would do things his way. They'd try a relationship. She felt a flutter in her stomach at the idea, and a new resolution fill her.

She closed her eyes, ready to try again for the dreamscape, but the door opened, and Indigo walked in with a fresh bag for the drip and another syringe.

"Don't get too comfortable, bitch." She changed the bag on the drip, giving it a satisfied tap, and then raised the needle.

Blaize, more alert this time, tried to flinch away, but the chains kept her well within Indigo's reach. "There's no point trying to get away. There's nowhere for you to go." She stabbed the needle into Blaize's tensed arm, and blackness crept over Blaize's vision. As she faded back into unconsciousness, Indigo said, "This is your life now. You, me, and the energy."

Despair flooded her as the drugs pulled her under.

38

Cuinn had spent most of the day in the dreamscape with nothing to show for it. He was exhausted. Cara had eventually forced him to come away from his rooms for a short period, making him eat. He was burning his own resources because of the amount of energy he used, and he already looked pounds thinner.

As he sat at the kitchen table with Cara, chewing listlessly on some stir-fried rice that Cara had put together, the front door opened. Tierra came in, her face tight, Fintan following behind her.

"Everything okay?" Cara asked them.

"Fine," Tierra's answer was terse, "but we didn't find much."

Cuinn's face focused on her. "But you found something?"

"Just a better sense of the Rogue's energy at the café." Fintan sat down wearily, and Cara put a plate of rice in front of him. "There was no question she burned the place, and Tierra didn't sense any other energetics there."

"We tracked the Rogue to where she must have had a car parked." She hung her head. "I'm sorry, Cuinn; I couldn't track it any further."

Cuinn put an arm out and touched hers. "No one could. I need to go back into the dreamscape." Cuinn stood. "That might be our only chance of finding her."

Tierra looked him up and down. "You're burning yourself up. You'll do yourself permanent damage if you don't rest a little. I wish we could track down Adam; this is much more his area."

"I can find her. There's no time for rest."

Tierra opened her mouth but hesitated.

"What's the matter?" Fintan said.

"I've had an idea. It's pretty ... unusual, and I don't think you're going to like it, but if you're going to keep searching in the dreamscape, then I don't think you have much choice."

Cuinn frowned. "What?"

"Promise me you'll hear me out."

"Get on with it, Tierra. We don't have time for games," Cuinn said.

"Let's blend energies. You can take some of my energy."

Cara gasped, and Fintan's eyes narrowed.

"It's an unusual situation, and I know you won't take too much," Tierra said quickly. "And no one else ever needs to know. I'm the only one here who can share energy with you; the others don't share either of your Chakras. It has to be me."

"This is a very bad idea," Fintan said. "Blending is forbidden other than between Mavens and Adherents. For good reason. People get addicted doing it. That's how you get Leeches in the first place."

"Cuinn and I are strong enough to do this. He's a Maven with experience of sharing energy."

"With his Adherents, maybe, but it's not the—"

Tierra gestured with a hand and cut across Fintan. "No one is going to get addicted. We can't stop him from going back to the dreamscape, but if he goes as he is, he either won't have the strength to deal with the Rogue when he finds her, or he'll harm himself. Cara's a Healer—as am I—and she can make sure we stop in time."

Cara nodded slowly. "I can do that."

Fintan jerked his head round to look at Cara. "You approve?"

She winced. "If the two of them want to do it, then I'll support them. I don't think it's the world's best idea, but I'd rather help them than have them do it unsupervised."

"Let's do it," Cuinn said. "Anything that helps me to search is good right now."

Fintan shook his head again but appeared more resigned. "Tierra, a word?"

She huffed, but the two of them went out of the kitchen together.

"Eat more rice," Cara said. "You need anything that will support your energy."

Cuinn took another mouthful. After a few minutes, Tierra and Fintan came back into the room, a frosty silence between them.

"We'll do it in a couple of hours. I need to prepare, as it's been a while since I worked with my Maven and shared energy with anyone. And you should rest, Cuinn."

"I'm too wired to rest."

"Well, you need to relax then. Wired isn't a good state to be in for the energy transfer."

"And you're sure you're okay with this?"

"You know I am." She took a forkful of rice and a drink of water. "Now, eat."

The four of them gathered an hour later in Tierra's workroom. The usually cosy room felt crowded to Cuinn with all of them present. He paced while Tierra prepared her sacred space. She had opened her glass doors to the evening air and surrounded her mat with plants. Cuinn had brought his own mat down from his room, and Tierra put handfuls of earth in the corners. He'd protested at first, but she'd reminded him he most often used the mat for Ajna work, and that this was Muladhara. She grounded his mat as best she could.

249

"You also need to get grounded," she said to Cuinn. "You need to relax."

"I don't feel relaxed."

"Sit and do some breathing exercises. This will be harder for both of us the further away from the earth you feel. At the very least, pace outside in bare feet so you connect with the earth."

Cuinn turned on his heels and stalked out of the glass doors. He shucked off his shoes and socks on the stone patio and stepped onto the cold, wet grass. At first the sensation was unpleasant, but as he dug his toes in, he felt his connection to the earth revive. He breathed in moss and damp soil. The garden was dark, the soft candles from Tierra's ceremonial setup behind him was his only light. He forced his breathing to deepen. He connected to the woods, to the earth, to the environment around him.

"The earth supports me, and it meets my needs." He repeated this mantra as he stretched out his arms, and thought of family, home, safety, security, and boundaries. And trust. Trust for the cousin who was more like a sister, and was prepared to break an energetic taboo to save another's life.

He grounded himself in his body, pulling a little energy from the earth around him. By the time he caught Tierra's shadow as she stood between the doors, he felt more himself.

A few minutes later he sat opposite Tierra in the space she had prepared. She took his hands. Fintan sat behind her, angled so he was able to see both her and Cuinn, and Cara was sitting behind Cuinn. They were energetic 'spotting'—making sure Cuinn didn't take too much energy and damage Tierra, or become addicted—both real possibilities, and the main reason that sharing energy between energetics who weren't Maven and Adherent was forbidden by the Circle. All of them could get into trouble for taking part in this activity, even if it went perfectly. For Cuinn, it was a risk he was willing to take for Blaize, but he felt a stab of guilt at involving the others.

Tierra had put on some low drumming music in the background, and the beat was rhythmic, hypnotic. He closed his eyes and centred himself in the element of earth, in Muladhara Chakra. Pine incense floated around him, further connecting him.

Each type of energy was shared in a different way. For Ajna elements, it was in the dreamscape. Fire energy was shared through an intense, unblinking gaze. For earth, it was through the power of touch.

He focused on his hands, and on the connection between himself and Tierra. After a few minutes of concentration, he could feel her energy like a prickling heat in his hands. This was an unusually fast connection, probably because of their relationship and the fact that they knew the feel of each other's energy so well.

He opened himself up to her energy, which pushed at him, eager to move from Tierra to him. He pulled a little, just as he would when pulling energy from the environment and astral plane, but this time he pulled from Tierra herself. He could almost see the strands of energy looping between them, replenishing his own dwindling stores.

The feeling created an endorphin rush, which was the reason it was easy to get addicted. It wasn't like pulling from the environment, which normally topped out at what each individual energetic could handle. When you drew from another energetic, there was no limit to the power you could take—until the other person died.

He tried to maintain his own Ajna activation while focusing on the Muladhara energy, a fine line to balance. But keeping his mind energy alert would give him the discernment to say stop.

It didn't take long for the rush to turn into a high, a euphoric feeling that had an unwilling smile edge across his face, though his eyes were still closed. The smile, more than anything, brought him back to the moment. He'd never felt less like smiling in his life.

The line between pain and pleasure at this point was delicate, and the connection between his hands and Tierra's smaller, more delicate hands felt intense. He could almost feel every individual whorl and line of her fingers.

"I think ... we should stop," he said, over the drumming. But he didn't break the connection, unwilling to let go of the rush quite yet.

Cara stood and touched Tierra and Cuinn on their shoulders, and closed her eyes briefly. When she opened them again, she nodded. "I agree. Enough, Tierra."

Nothing happened for a moment, and then Cuinn felt Tierra's energy cut off. He held back a groan as the pleasure left him. He rubbed his hands together, his eyes still closed. The incense hung heavy in the air around them, the drumming continuing. Everything felt suspended in time.

He opened his eyes just as Tierra let out a gasp, and Fintan moved forward to support her. Fintan scowled at Cara and Cuinn.

"She's fine, Fintan," Cara said, that hint of amusement back in her voice. "Help her into her room to lie down and get her to eat something light."

Fintan nodded and let Tierra rest in the crook of his arm for a while as Cuinn got up and stretched. He felt amazing. "I'll go back into the astral realm and see if I can make contact. She might be sleeping, so there's the possibility I might be able to connect to her dreams."

Cara rose. "I'm right behind you."

CHAPTER

39

Blaize woke up. And almost wished she hadn't. She was still trapped in the disgusting room, and her arms and legs ached from lying down for the last twenty-four hours. She felt better than the last time she'd been awake—perhaps the pizza had helped after all though she could tell she had already lost some weight. Indigo was right; taking her energy was draining her physical body quickly. She'd have to eat more if she wanted to keep herself going.

She lay, staring at the ceiling, trying to work out what to do. What she could do.

Part of her felt shame—shame that she had been captured so easily. Cuinn would be so angry with her. She winced, remembering Indigo's sharp comments about her own 'romantic notions of rescue.' *I have to hope. It's not naive to think I'll get out of here.*

She was strong, stronger than Indigo. But while Indigo was weak, she was also unpredictable, addicted as she was to the energy.

All Blaize needed was a moment. She didn't think she could break out of the shackles she had on, but if she could get control of herself in the dreamscape, she thought she could contact Cuinn.

And that had all better be done fast. Indigo was already talking about moving her.

The door opened again.

"Good morning, bitch." Indigo sang out the words. She walked jerkily to the end of the bed. Her eyes darted around the room and over Blaize, the pupils pinpricks.

Is she still high? Blaize shivered. It was hard to see how Indigo could be even more disturbed. She was already unpredictable enough.

"How are we today? A little thinner, I see. Ooops!" Indigo covered her mouth with a hand. "I took more than I meant to yesterday. But you, Blaize-bitch, are dee-licious. I'll have to keep myself in check in the future, or there won't be enough of you to go around, and I'll get into trouble!"

"What do you mean, go around? Are you working with someone?" Blaize's voice was scratchy.

Indigo froze for the smallest of moments, then laughed. "Just me, BB."

She put a can she'd been carrying next to Blaize.

"I brought you a protein shake. One of those meal replacement thingies. Enough calories to keep you going." She turned on her heel and walked out.

Blaize needed to drink it if she was to be well enough to take advantage of any chance that arose to get a message to Cuinn. She took a sip, grimaced, and started working on a new plan.

When Blaize hit the astral plane this time, she didn't wait. She knew what to expect, and as soon as her eyes opened in Indigo's tasteless Haven she focused the hottest fire she could create on her chains and broke them.

Indigo stepped back a pace, and her eyes widened. Blaize was able to land a backhanded blow across Indigo's gaunt face before she recovered from the surprise. But Indigo had the advantage health-wise, and even as her head snapped to the side from the blow, she came back with a hammer fist that just missed Blaize's cheek, catching her on the shoulder as she moved out of the way. Pain blossomed across Blaize's upper arm, and she staggered.

They fought in earnest, but Blaize had thought about this already. Physical fighting was only part of the tactics that could be used in the dreamscape. After a handful more blows were exchanged, she drew back from Indigo, bending forward slightly as if she was getting exhausted, but, in fact, creating space and distance between herself and the other energetic. She drew on the energy that she saw around Indigo, weakening her. The energy felt tainted, giving Blaize strength but also making her feel nauseous, so even as Indigo staggered, Blaize wobbled on her own feet.

Indigo fell onto her hands and knees and looked up at Blaize, hissing through her inky hair. She pushed off the floor and launched herself at Blaize, flying through the air with more height than Blaize could have managed in the physical plane. Her hands were grasping claws and the force of her landing pushed Blaize to the floor.

"You're nothing," Indigo hissed into her face. "You think you're somehow special. But you're nothing. You shouldn't have even been born."

Blaize was on her back with Indigo's hands around her neck and was perilously close to losing consciousness. But Indigo's words penetrated her brain. *What the hell?*

"You know nothing about me," Blaize panted out.

"I know your parents were told to stay apart. And look what happened to them. Your father became a Rogue, who killed your mother and himself."

When the anger washed over her body, Blaize didn't fight it, but she did hold on to her focus. She wouldn't let the anger control her this time. She would use it.

Blaize planted her feet firmly on the ground. She shifted her hip, ready, and took hold of Indigo's right arm. Blaize shoved and pushed her hips up at the same time, which tipped Indigo to the side, and Blaize used the momentum to switch places with Indigo.

Indigo fought under the influence, whereas Blaize fought for her life.

Once Blaize was in a sitting position she pinned one of Indigo's wrists with her knee, and the other with her hand. She held Indigo there while she took another moment, and then she pulled at Indigo's energy, which was flickering and weak.

Instead of absorbing the energy herself, she used it to build a cage around Indigo, throwing herself backwards as she closed the front of the cage. She then put a blindfold on the woman, pulling enough of Indigo's energy to render her unconscious.

She had the woman's astral body trapped. But for how long, Blaize didn't know.

She closed her eyes and focused everything she had on Cuinn's Haven. She sent out a pulse of energy that was as strong as she could make it, an energetic cry for help.

She repeated her message over and over. But her strength was limited. And it was failing.

Indigo stayed unconscious in her cage, her body stretched out on the floor. The prison Blaize had created for the woman's spirit held. For now.

CHAPTER
40

Cuinn was in the dreamscape, out in the wild energy. He was close to having to go back to at least his Haven, if not the physical plane, to rest. His fists clenched at the thought.

He wouldn't lose her.

He wouldn't let her down.

He moved his astral form through the untamed places, making and remaking the world as he proceeded through it. He sifted through pieces of dreamscape like an archeologist seeking shards of pottery from the past, looking for any trace of Blaize's distinct energy.

The inhospitable environment tested his strength, as he kept his own mind as focused as possible.

He especially didn't want to think about the vision of Blaize in the prophecy, dying.

He focused his mind on one thing only.

Finding her.

Staying receptive to any indications of her energy while broadcasting his own signal as a beacon and enclosing his mind in a strong shield, sapped his energy.

He would have to go back. He would be no good to Blaize if his own mind was caught in the dreamscape, lost to the influence of other, unknown energies.

He followed his trail of reality to his Haven. He was cautious, taking no chances, but his bitter anger at not finding Blaize infected the trail, his emotions changing reality as he jogged back.

A snarling dog appeared in front of him, and he stopped, using his black feelings to quickly shape some of the energies around him into a bigger dog. A hellhound. It sat at his side for a moment, before it threw itself towards the other dog—which didn't hesitate, but turned and ran.

Cuinn called his dog to his side.

It looked at him, eyes glowing, fierce teeth dripping saliva. He called it to heel and used the hellhound to chase away anything that tried to injure him.

He was close to his Haven when he felt something. A tug. A pulse of energy that felt familiar. It felt ... like Blaize. He span in place, trying to read where the energy was coming from. How had it reached him?

He put his hand on the dog, drawing the energy and the emotions that had created it back inside him, the hellhound disappearing like smoke.

He drew on the energy of the emotion, every single feeling that Blaize had ever caused him to feel. Anger, frustration, annoyance, irritation. Amusement, contentment, fun.

Love.

He wove this complex mix into an arrow. He created a bow and drew the string back, the muscles in his back and arm tense and straining. He released the string and shot the arrow into the air.

Find her.

The arrow disappeared from sight, and Cuinn followed its energy trail into the ether.

The wild energies flickered past him. Invisible hands grabbed at him as if he was being dragged through brambles and bushes, their sharp thorns scraping his skin and leaving him covered with long bloody scratches.

But finally the arrow connected to Blaize's pulse of energy in a stranger's Haven.

The Haven was warded, of course, he could see the energetic protection that surrounded it, but the wardings were as irregular as the Haven was misshapen. It had the appearance of a castle in a fairytale, but it was subtly wrong. Off.

He held up his hand, and the arrow flew back to his palm. His body shook from the efforts he was making. But he wouldn't give up now.

He hauled on his emotions again, putting everything he had into the arrow.

He drew the bow.

And released.

The arrow shot out, and twisted and turned, spinning in the air, a golden blur.

It found one of the weaker wardings and pierced it. Cuinn followed it in, expanding the weakness into an entrance.

And once he was in, he could feel her.

But her energy was faint. Fading.

He ran through the strange corridors, crystals and gold flickering at the edges of his vision.

He found a huge room and slammed through the doors. His gaze darted around the room until he saw her lying on the floor, her back propped up against the side of a bed.

Thank Source.

He got closer and saw she was battered and bloody. Next to her was an energetic cage. Holding the unconscious Rogue.

Blaize saw him and sagged in relief. "Can your energy follow me back to the physical plane? See where I am? Come find me? Indigo, the Rogue, said I'm not far from Merrow. But she'll move me as soon as she wakes."

Blaize started to fade, losing her connection with the dreamscape.

He clung to her energy and travelled back with her to her body. Once there, he looked around, trying to gauge where the property was. Blaize and her captor were unconscious in the basement, but he was unable to do much physically.

After what seemed like an eternity, he found a heap of abandoned junk mail thrown on a shelf. They all had the same address. Bingo. He noted the address and fled back to his Haven, gathering his strength and then dropping back into his own body.

It would be critical to reach her before the Rogue woke up. Source knew what damage the Rogue would do to Blaize when she did.

He'd never associated Blaize with the word 'fragile' before.

It was breaking his heart.

All four of them piled into Cuinn's rugged 4x4, Tierra to keep Cuinn calm, and Cara with medical supplies to help Blaize and restrain the Rogue. Fintan drove. On the way, Cara called the medical facility where she worked to request backup transport for the Rogue.

Each minute Cuinn spent in the car was agony. His body was rigid and stiff, and his every breath rasped from him like the noise of a saw blade. There was a metallic taste in his mouth.

He needed to get to her. Desperately. He couldn't let her down like Sophea.

They reached the address. Fintan dimmed the vehicle's lights and turned off the engine to coast onto the property as quietly as possible. They parked far away from the house and Fintan sketched out a plan. Despite Cara's Healer status, she'd also trained in Manipura and had fighting skills akin to Blaize's, so Tierra was the only one of them without any offensive training.

But Tierra's training meant she could spot any energetic shields the property had. "I'll walk around the house and check for wards."

"We don't have time for that," Cuinn said. "Blaize is in there, and who knows what shape she's in."

Fintan had a hand on Cuinn's arm, a reminder to stop him rushing off.

"It's more dangerous if we don't check first," warned Fintan.

Cuinn felt desperate. "See what you can find Tierra, and then we'll decide. Hurry."

He was so close, and still being held back.

They were crouched in the shadows of a thick set of bushes at the side of the house. Tierra drew in a breath and closed her eyes, and Cuinn felt the prickle of her Muladhara seep out. After a few interminable minutes, she opened them again.

"It's warded with Manipura and Ajna only. Cuinn, you should be able to get through the Ajna, and Fintan, if I show you the wards for Manipura by flaring them with my energy, can you destroy them?" Tierra said.

Cuinn went to work immediately. He opened up his energetic awareness and drew on his store of energy. The wards were sophisticated, but nothing Cuinn couldn't get rid of. He burned all three away, leaving nothing but Manipura. He gestured to Fintan and Tierra. *Hurry.*

Tierra closed her eyes and a ward flared over to the right. "Again, please," requested Fintan. It flared again, bright as a small sun.

A moment passed, and the ward exploded.

"One more. To the left." Tierra pointed. Another ward flared, and this time, Fintan was ready. The ward disappeared in a shower of energy.

"Now. For fuck's sake, let's go," said Cuinn, already moving. He went directly to the worn back door. It was locked. Fintan gestured to him to move and stepped back to give the lock a kick. The old wood shattered and splintered, the door slamming open but leaving the lock in position.

In the dirty kitchen, Cuinn looked around for the door to the basement he'd seen in the dreamscape. It was easy to spot, and he tried it. Locked again. Fintan came over. This time he put his hands on the door, and simply burned the lock out. Cuinn went through the door at a run, and threw himself at the bed, leaving the others to restrain Indigo, who thankfully hadn't yet regained consciousness.

Blaize lay shackled to a dirty bed, a tube coming from a needle attached to her hand. *Thank Source. She's alive.* He cradled Blaize in his arms while Fintan undid her chains. Cuinn felt sick, and he kissed away the tears drying on her face and wiped the hair from her forehead. He had nearly lost her. That wouldn't happen again.

She opened her eyes. "You're here."

He nodded. "I'm so sorry, Blaize. We found you as quickly as we could."

"Rescued myself, didn't I?"

He nodded, unable to speak because of the thick emotion that clogged his throat.

"But I thought I'd let you help. Now we're a team and all," Blaize finished, with some effort.

Cara looked at Cuinn, drawing his attention away from the exhausted woman in his arms. "The Rogue's fading. I don't know if she'll make it. Her body's okay, but her mind is—unstable."

"We could call a human ambulance; would that help?" said Tierra.

Cara shook her head. "I don't think so. It's her spirit and her mind, not her body. Not that that's in great shape, but she won't die from it. It's the addiction; it's eating her up."

"You need to check Blaize before you do anything with … that." Cuinn's tone was flat.

Tierra came over to Blaize. "I can check her. But you'll need to put her down."

Tierra stepped over to the bed, gesturing for Cuinn to move out of the way. Cuinn reluctantly and gently lowered Blaize onto the bed. Her hand came up and clenched around his, as Tierra softly touched her and checked her for injuries.

Cuinn could see a little colour return to Blaize's face as Tierra mended some of the worst injuries. Cara looked up, her eyebrows drawing together. "Tierra, be careful. You don't have much to spare yourself yet." Tierra nodded and stepped away, wobbling slightly. Fintan caught her. She frowned and tried to push him away. He settled himself more carefully around her. "Just until you get your balance back."

Cara was still working on the Rogue.

"How long do you think the evac team will be?" Fintan asked.

"Not soon enough. She's nearly gone. Her pulse is thready, and her energy is unstable."

"I want to talk to her," said Cuinn.

"I think Blaize's dreamscape cage is holding her mind. You'd have to talk to the Rogue on the etheric plane, and you'd be exposed if she got free. It's her Haven. She's strongest there," said Cara.

"She won't. I'm stronger. A lot stronger." Cuinn's firm stare dared Cara to disagree with him.

"It's a risk."

"It's not worth it, Cuinn." Blaize's voice came weakly from the bed, her fingers gripping his more tightly. "She'll live, or she won't. I'm sorry for it, but I wouldn't trade my life for hers. Or yours."

"Nor would I, but I still want to talk to her." He needed to find out what was behind her attack on Blaize—if it was anything more than a Leech who had found the perfect energetic to draw from. He needed to know if it was linked to the prophecy. It was worth the risk of going into Indigo's Haven once more.

He lay on the revolting bed next to Blaize and relaxed his body as fast as he dared.

He followed the energetic trail that he'd created earlier, and entered through the hole he'd torn in the Rogue's wardings.

Once inside he looked around at the decor, and pitied the Rogue. The environment was so far from the surroundings of the abandoned property where her physical body now lay, it was ridiculous.

He stood in front of the energetic. She lay on her side, restrained and caged. Her body seemed skeletal, her black hair hanging around her face like a shroud.

He nudged the cage. "Rogue. Wake up."

"No. No. I'm sorry. I'm hungry. I'm tired. Let me sleep," she muttered, and he had to strain to hear the words. She didn't sound rational.

"Rogue. Tell me if you were working alone or with someone else." He spoke louder, squatting so he was closer to her head. She opened her eyes slightly and squinted up at him.

"Indigo, I'm Indigo. Where's my tasty dinner? I kept her alive, the redhead." Her face shifted quickly to anger. "The bitch. Thinks she can Queen Bee me. I'm the queen of the castle here, I am."

"Blaize is far away from here where you can't hurt her any more." Cuinn resisted the urge to kick the cage. Instead, he gripped the bars and put his face to hers.

She spat at him, and he jerked back, wiping at his neck where the spittle had landed. The Rogue was out of her mind. But he needed to be sure that she was the end of this. That this wasn't related to the main prophecy. That Blaize was safe once the Rogue was dead. As he could see she soon would be.

"You are Queen Bee, I can see. Queen of the flowers and of your beautiful Haven."

She laughed. It was an unnerving sound. Her face rubbed against the floor like a cat.

"Hmmm. I love my house I do. Safe here." Her face turned sad. "Usually safe. Not today. Not today."

"Indigo, were you working with someone else? Was anyone helping you?"

"Secrets, secrets. I know some secrets. Secrets about your friends. Friends now, and future friends. Prophecies come to all with Ajna you know, not just the good ones."

His frustration built, and one of the jewelled lamps across the room exploded.

"Naughty boy! A temper on you despite your energies. You're not the only one with a temper either. Your cousins have challenges ahead. Did you know they're part of the prophecy? And that friend of yours. He has a temper on him too, the blond one. Likes to play. Ah, so many of you caught up in the web. Some you know; some you don't. Surprises in store." She laughed again and more glass broke.

Adrenalin pumped through Cuinn's tired body as he looked around him. *She knows about the prophecy.*

"What are you talking about? What prophecy are you talking about?" He wanted to shake her.

Her Haven was starting to break up as she lost control of her mind and faded.

"Nothing's set in stone," she sang, her voice grating. "Thought I'd win this one; didn't. Maybe you think you'll win the next one; won't. Who knows? Whoknows? Whoknowswhoknowwhoknows?"

The room was breaking, falling and exploding around him now. He put up a shield to protect himself from the flying pieces. He needed to get out of there.

"What else do you know, Indigo? Who were you with?"

Her eyes opened and fixed on his. "More than you, smarty-pants. More than you. Send my love to your father."

The life went out of her eyes and her head slumped, blood trickling from her nose. Wild energies seeped into the room, savage and unpredictable.

He fled.

CHAPTER

41

He sat quietly on the patio of the large house far from the city, staring out at the countryside around him. The earth was green and fertile, but no birds sang, and no insects chittered. The air was paused around him. Waiting.

The destruction of Indigo and her Haven had affected him badly. No matter how much power he had leeched from the flotsam and jetsam of the energetics—because no matter what the Guilds said, not every energetic was part of a happy family—no Maven could lose an Adherent and not suffer.

He clenched his fists. *Indigo should not have failed me.*

It took him a moment to rein in his anger, but he was a practical man, and his anger took energy from him that he could ill afford.

He breathed in and out, slowly, carefully, and drew on a little power from the ether each time, replenishing himself.

A tall, graceful blond woman came out from the house and stood next to him. "How are you feeling?"

"Fine," he said. "I just need to rest."

"If there's anything I can do, let me know." She played with the silver teardrop necklace that she favoured.

"I will. Perhaps you could send Dagon to me at some point. I need him to attend to some business. We'll visit the house in the city in a day or so too."

"Do you think you'll be well enough?" She sounded concerned.

"I'll be fine." At least he would after he'd had a chance to leech from the energetic match that Dagon would procure him.

She patted his arm and walked back to the door. "Just shout if you need me."

He didn't move when she had gone. He sat and thought for a long while. About Indigo, Cuinn and Blaize, and the prophecies. They chased the same prophecy, but he had more clarity about the stakes than them.

Unlimited power was within his reach. All that prevented him from gaining it was twelve energetics. Not only that, but they needed to be in six very specific couples. All he had to do was prevent one couple from bonding, and the prophecy would fall apart.

Prophecies were tricky things. They mattered—but they could be changed. Nothing was set in stone.

So he'd been unsuccessful the first time. That was fine.

He had five more chances.

Blaize woke up with a gasp. She snapped her eyes open and checked her surroundings. She was in a bright, clean room. She breathed a sigh of relief as she realised she wasn't in the vile basement.

But where was she?

The pristine white room seemed to be in a high-class hospital. Had she dreamed about the rescue? Had she been taken somewhere else? Her stomach clenched.

The door started to open, and she tried to sit up, but the change in pressure caused dizziness to crash over her, and she fell back onto the pillow.

"Blaize, Blaize, honey, it's okay; it's me, Cara. Everything's fine." Cara hurried over to her and stroked her forehead. "You're fine."

"Where's Cuinn? What happened to Indigo?" Blaize shuddered.

"Cuinn's fine. He's in a different room. He tried some heroics of his own and only just escaped in one piece, so he's resting too."

"Where are we?"

"We're in my Rehab centre out on the West Coast. It was the best place to bring you and Cuinn. And the Rogue."

Blaize shifted in the bed. If the Rogue was here, then Blaize was going to prepare herself for another fight. Just in case. *Although…* "Did she … Did she survive?"

Cara shook her head. "She was a long way down the addiction path—you weren't the first energetic she did this to. I'm sorry."

Blaize breathed a guilty sigh of relief. "I'm not. I'm sorry I killed her, but I'm not sorry she's dead."

"I understand. We'll talk more about it later. My experience says this won't be the last time you'll think about her I'm afraid." She poured a glass of water and handed it to Blaize.

The water was cool and refreshing.

"Do you think you could eat something?"

Blaize's stomach shifted and growled. She laughed. "I guess so. But no fast food. I won't be eating any more of that for a while."

As the days passed, Blaize became more and more suspicious that Cuinn was avoiding her. *Why isn't he here? If he loved me, wouldn't he be here? I nearly died, for Source's sake. But I survived. And I didn't turn into a Rogue.* She was safe to be around.

Her heart broke a little bit more every day he didn't visit her. She'd been ready to agree to his terms, but hadn't had the chance to tell him.

Eventually, she was allowed to move around a little in the facility, going outside for the first time, and standing in the gardens, which overlooked the pebbled beach and restless sea.

"You're seeing it at its best," said Cara, coming out to sit next to her and passing her a cup of hot tea. "It's nearly summer now, and the weather's good. It can be a real bitch in winter when we get snow."

"Where's Cuinn?"

Cara sighed. "He's back home. Tierra, Adam, and Fin are with him. Something came up that he needed to deal with. Once you're ready, you can go back there and see him."

"I'm not sure I want to." *Lie.*

"He didn't leave because he doesn't want to be with you, Blaize. He has a strong connection to the energies there, and we thought it would help him recover more quickly. And other information came up when he was interrogating Indigo—"

Blaize flinched at the name.

"And he's gone back to look into that too."

Blaize was sure Cuinn had realised she was a liability, her impulsive nature one that would put them all at risk, time and time again. And yet her confinement and ordeal had made her see that Cuinn was the most important person in her life.

Cuinn felt empty. Despite the infusion of energy from Tierra, he'd overextended himself to break into Indigo's Haven, and it had taken him a while to recover.

But Indigo's final words had galvanised him to get back to his books and dreamwalks—as soon as Tierra and Cara had allowed it.

He had told the others he had more information, but despite their probing, he hadn't yet revealed to them that he suspected several of them were also involved in the prophecy. He needed more information before he dropped that bombshell.

His single-mindedness was all designed to keep Blaize, and his family, safe. That was what he told himself. As he returned this time from seeing the Circle members and filling them in on what had happened with the Rogue, he forced himself to admit there was more to it than that.

He'd made a mistake when he'd compared Blaize to Sophea. When he'd seen how Blaize had caged the Rogue and called to him in the dreamscape, he'd realised Sophea and Blaize were nothing alike.

Blaize was independent. Self-sufficient. She was a grown woman who was a match for his own inner strength, while her passionate nature balanced his own logical calm. She had enough power to protect herself. She was going to be a hell of an Ajna energetic once she'd been trained.

Seeing her lifted him. She made him laugh. She annoyed the hell out of him.

He was in love with Blaize.

And he didn't know what he would do if she didn't love him back. He could wait if he had to, but every moment of the coming years would be a living hell, being Maven and Adherent and not lovers. She pushed his objectivity, the stability that usually came from his earth energies, to their limit. What if she never admitted she loved him? He was sure she did. Sure of it.

But he was worried—terrified—that he had messed things up irrevocably. He'd let her get taken, for Source's sake. She hadn't been in contact as she recovered, and he'd respected her privacy. But now she was at the house, and he was heading home to see her for the first time since her capture.

Cuinn's dreams had changed as well. Thankfully, he'd stopped dreaming the prophecy of Blaize's death, and now he dreamt of her with him, but just out of reach.

In his dreamwalks, more of the twelve had faces.

Tierra and Fintan were there, as well as Adam and Cara. Other figures were still shadowy. The fact that some of his family and friends were involved had made him work even harder on the problem.

He opened the front door to the sound of voices in the hub of the house, the kitchen. He walked to the room, feeling as if he was on death row. In a few minutes, he would find out if Blaize returned his feelings.

There were five of them in the room: the three women, Fin, and Adam.

But he only had eyes for one person.

Her hair curled gently around her face, and her green eyes looked at him. Her face seemed pale, and she hadn't put back all the weight that she'd burned off through Indigo's leeching. Still, she was beautiful.

Cara moved in front of her, greeting him warmly, and the room filled with the sounds of people. He took his place at the table. Tierra filled his plate, this time with pancakes, fruit and a lot of syrup, and handed him a cup of coffee.

As he ate, he was acutely aware of Blaize sitting quietly opposite him. She still seemed so fragile, as if something in her had been damaged by her experience with the Rogue. Which, of course, it probably had. He wanted to take her in his arms and hold her against him.

It seemed like hours before everyone had finished eating and started drifting to other parts of the house. Blaize stood, saying she was heading back to her own cottage for some peace and quiet.

He jumped at the chance. "Let me walk you back."

She tilted her head and frowned. "Don't be silly, Cuinn. It's a hundred yards. Indigo's gone."

"I insist." He put out his arm for her to take. She sighed and took it, her hand in the crook of his elbow. He swallowed as he pulled his arm in toward his body, her hand hot against his side.

They reached her door with no words yet exchanged. He felt tongue-tied, but as she opened her front door, he had to say something.

"I'm so sorry, Blaize."

She turned to him. "For what?"

"Everything."

Her eyebrow rose. "Everything?"

"You getting kidnapped, me not managing to save you sooner. Your injuries. Everything."

"I'm sorry I got caught. I was careless. Stupid. Proud." She looked away. "She took me by surprise."

"But it's not your fault," they said simultaneously.

They regarded each other in silence.

"Huh," said Blaize. "Where have you been? Why didn't you call?"

"I thought you would want some time alone to heal. Without me."

"I wouldn't want to see you?"

"Did you?"

She didn't say anything for a while, as she examined his face with a scrutiny that made him feel as if she was examining his soul.

Finally, she sighed. "I did."

His stomach flipped, and a tiny spark of hope flashed inside him. He stepped forward slowly and took her hands.

CHAPTER
42

Blaize was afraid to move. Cuinn was in front of her, living, breathing. She could smell mint on his cool, sweet breath, and the mixed male scent of his sweat and deodorant. It reminded her of moss and recently chopped firewood.

She breathed him in, as his cool, dry hands took hers. She loved the feel of his long fingers as they wrapped around hers. His firm but gentle grip gave her butterflies as he pulled her towards him. She didn't lift her eyes from his chest as he brought her slowly closer.

One of his arms snaked around her, and his hand came to her chin to tilt her head up. Her gaze trailed from his chest up, past his strong collarbones to his elegant neck. His five o'clock shadow added to his usual aura of rumpled geek chic. She felt a surge of tenderness, delighting in his touch.

As she finally met his eyes, which today were dove grey, she saw a hint of vulnerability. Vulnerability that she suspected would be reflected in her own eyes. This was the start of something different. Something she'd never allowed herself before.

She put her hand on his cheek, enjoying the roughness of his facial hair, and rubbed her hand backwards and forwards. He tipped his head to one side, resting it more fully on her hand and placed his hand on the back of her neck.

"We have a lot to talk about." His voice was pitched lower than usual.

"But perhaps we should talk later? I've heard we both need a lot of rest." She stepped back into the house, pulling him inside with her, their hands still in place, locking them together.

"I agree. You can't take chances with the injuries we've had."

"A lot of bed rest." She advanced up the stairs but stopped when she was a step above him, his hands now on her hips. He cocked an eyebrow at her, which shot higher as she stripped off the sweater she was wearing and dropped it beside her.

When she put her hands on his hips and tugged at his sweater, he raised his hands above his head, his eye contact solid. She smiled.

She drew him after her, and they stumbled up the rest of the stairs, eyes locked and their hands keeping contact with each other's bodies.

When her legs hit the bed, she fell backwards, taking him with her. Their mouths met, tongues tangling in a passionate joining.

They struggled with each other's clothes, laughing at their efforts to strip each other as quickly as possible.

She threw an arm out to grope into her bedside table for a condom, barely taking her lips off his as he used his own hands to remove her delicate underwear.

Finally, they were skin to skin, their bodies moving together in time.

<Blaize?>

Startled, she looked up at him. She frowned, figuring it out. Huh. *<Yes?>*

He grinned as their connection deepened further.

<Great, now we discover this! Would have been useful last week> she sent with her mind.

<You should have had sex with me on the physical plane before>

She narrowed her eyes at him, and then reached down between their bodies to add her hands to everything else that was going on, and he stopped talking in a hurry.

Much later they lay together, sheets and limbs entwined, in her little cottage bedroom. She felt happier than she had for a long time as if her two energies had blended as she relaxed. She was warm and confident from her Manipura, but also insightful and perceptive from the Ajna.

She propped her chin on her hand and looked down at him. Her other hand traced circles on his stomach; then she trailed her fingers through the arrow of hair that led from his belly button down to other, more fascinating things.

"To be clear," she said. "I'm not going anywhere. I'm with you now. Whatever's to be faced, I'll face it with you. I don't need protecting. Or, sometimes I will, and sometimes I'll protect you."

He nodded. "I know. I also know that's a very distracting view." His gaze flickered to her breasts, which given their respective positions were presented quite close to his face.

She laughed.

"I also know that I love you, Blaize Blackfire."

She flopped down next to him and snuggled into the crook of his outstretched arm. "Well. I still think this is all a bit fast, but hey, who am I to fight it? I love you too, Cuinn Ahern."

He let out a relieved breath, and with his free arm he groped for a condom where she'd left them the night before. He slid it on and rolled on top of her, causing her to gasp. He moved again, slowly and smoothly, and the next sound she made was a moan.

The two of them spent the rest of the day making sure each of them got a great deal of bed rest.

Cuinn didn't leave Blaize's cottage that day or night, and they were late to breakfast the next morning, coming in holding hands. Blaize met the other women's eyes, a hint of colour in her cheeks, and they smiled back—Tierra with love, and Cara approvingly. Fintan opened his mouth to say something, but Cuinn narrowed his eyes at him and shut him up before anything came out.

After heaping his plate with food that Tierra and, to his surprise, Fintan, had put together, Cuinn got everyone's attention. He made eye contact with each of them.

"I need to share some information with you all. But it has to stay in this room for now. It's incomplete, and I don't yet know the meaning of it."

He talked them through Indigo's last words, and what he thought the implications were—mainly that most of them in the room appeared to be involved in the prophecy. There was silence for a while after this, as each of them digested the information.

"I spent much of the day yesterday back at the house where Blaize was held, because my team had suggested some disturbing findings when they went through it the first time." Adam, a large, solid man, with the same dark hair and eyes as his sister, had no problem commanding the room.

Cuinn frowned. The situation was already bad and Adam wasn't prone to exaggeration. Cuinn braced for more bad news.

"I don't think Indigo was working alone. And worse, I believe the other person was the driving force. Indigo was just the patsy."

Blaize squeezed Cuinn's hand tightly, her face sombre. "You're probably right. It's hard to remember everything clearly, but a couple of times she seemed to hint that there was someone else involved. And one time, she looked almost frightened by the fact she'd implied it."

Adam nodded. "There's someone else."

"This attempt to take Blaize was almost certainly tied into the prophecy. And now, so are all of you." Cuinn met each of their gazes again. "I need your help. This prophecy is a threat not only to us as individuals—because, make no mistake, Blaize's experience tells us there is personal danger here—but to our whole race. The enemy, whoever that is, seems to know more than we do. We may be the only thing standing between our race and its extinction."

The others around the table looked at him after his speech, their serious faces reflecting back his words. He was sorry to put this burden on them, dumping them in this mess without asking.

Despite the guilt, he was also glad, glad to share the burden with the people he trusted most in the world.

"I'm here. I'll see this through with you. Where you go, I go." Blaize lifted his hand to her soft lips and kissed it.

Tierra was next. "Whatever you need, I'm here."

Her brother just nodded his head, as if it were a given.

Fintan, his face graver than Cuinn had seen it in many years, the usual mischievous twinkle in his eye absent, said, "Whatever you need, Cuinn."

Cara's warm, soft voice added her assent.

Something inside Cuinn relaxed. With the people in this room, he had a much better chance of working through whatever was to come. He hated putting them in danger, but he couldn't solve this puzzle on his own. Their combined energies and efforts would give them a real advantage in whatever was to come.

He hoped that it would be enough.

The Guilds and Circles

The energetics power structure is Guild based.

There are six Major Guilds, one for each of the six Chakras:

Muladhara (The Root Chakra – Earth Element)
Svadisthana (The Sacral Chakra – Water Element)
Manipura (The Navel Chakra – Fire Element)
Anahata (The Heart Chakra – Air Element)
Vishudha (The Throat Chakra – Ether (Space) Element)
Ajna (The Third Eye – The Mind)
  (Sahasara, the Crown Chakra, does not have a Guild.)

Each energetic has two activated Chakras, one dominant and one auxiliary, and it is the combination of these that influences their power, and to some degree, their personality.

Because of the huge differences between an energetic like Blaize, who combines her Manipura dominant with Ajna auxiliary, and one like Fintan, who combines Manipura dominant with Anahata auxiliary, a system of Minor Guilds also developed. There are thirty Minor Guilds representing each combination of powers (for example, Manipura-Ajna is a separate Guild from Ajna-Manipura).

Each individual energetic therefore belongs to two Major Guilds, and one Minor Guild.

For example: Cuinn has Ajna dominant, and Muladhara auxiliary. He therefore belongs to the Ajna Major Guild, the Muladhara Major Guild, and the Ajna-Muladhara Minor Guild.

The Major Circle is the highest form of government with one powerful energetic representing each Major Guild, making decisions on behalf of the race. The Minor Circle, the second tier of government, is made up of the thirty energetics who lead each of the Minor Guilds.

List of Minor Guilds:

- Muladhara-Svadisthana
- Muladhara-Manipura
- Muladhara-Anahata
- Muladhara-Vishudha
- Muladhara-Ajna
- Svadisthana-Muladhara
- Svadisthana-Manipura
- Svadisthana-Anahata
- Svadisthana-Vishudha
- Svadisthana-Ajna
- Manipura-Muladhara
- Manipura-Svadisthana
- Manipura-Anahata
- Manipura-Vishudha
- Manipura-Ajna

- Anahata-Muladhara
- Anahata-Svadisthana
- Anahata-Manipura
- Anahata-Vishudha
- Anahata-Ajna
- Vishudha-Muladhara
- Vishudha-Svadisthana
- Vishudha-Manipura
- Vishudha-Anahata
- Vishudha-Ajna
- Ajna-Muladhara
- Ajna-Svadisthana
- Ajna-Manipura
- Ajna-Anahata
- Ajna-Vishudha

Want More?

The story of the energetics continues in Tierra and Fintan's story, **Tierra and the Warrior**.

To be first to hear when it's out, visit my website, EllenBardAuthor.com/sign-up and sign up for updates, giveaways and inside information.

Discover Your Energetic Profile!

Want to know what your dominant and auxiliary Chakras would be? Which Guild you would belong to? What your archetype is?

Take the Chakra Quiz, and find out!
http://ellenbardauthor.com/chakra-quiz/

Help Spread the Word

If you loved the book and have a moment to spare, I would hugely appreciate it if you had time to leave a short review where you bought the book, and/or on goodreads. For instructions, go to the link below.

EllenBardAuthor.com/
how-to-leave-a-review

Your review will help other readers discover the series, and is greatly appreciated in spreading the word. Authors like me rely on amazing readers like you.

Thank you!

About the Author

Ellen is a fiction author who writes paranormal romance full of enchantment, intrigue and action. Her writing blends a background in psychology and her experiences travelling the world with a love of magic, fantasy and a (mostly!) happy ending.

She's also an entrepreneur and has a website where she shares actionable advice about personal development to support readers in making small changes so they can shine a little brighter in the world.

She's a Chartered Occupational Psychologist with the British Psychological Society, and continues to work as an international management consultant, which she has done for the last 15 years. She's worked all over the world including far-flung places such as China, Saudi Arabia and Malaysia.

Her passion for other lands and cultures helps inform her writing, as does her desire to try new things – from art classes to Krav Maga, the self-defence system.

She's a passionate and dedicated reader, working her way through between 100-150 fiction and non-fiction books a year – find her on goodreads to read her reviews.

Born in the UK, she currently lives in a tiny house in Chiang Mai, Thailand where the main feature is a hammock.

Connect with Ellen:

Facebook: facebook.com/EllenBardAuthor
Twitter: @ellenbard
Pinterest: pinterest.com/ellenmbard/
Goodreads: www.goodreads.com/ellenbard
Instagram: www.instagram.com/ellenbard

Acknowledgments

I feel so incredibly lucky to have wonderful family and friends who have supported me in plenty of crazy endeavours, this book being just one!

Mary Bard, my mum, has especially gone above and beyond, acting as alpha reader, first editor, cheerleader, and so much more. I can't thank her enough for all her love and efforts to support me on my journey. My sister, Sarah, is an incredible beta reader with great attention to detail, and is also a huge support on the artistic side, helping with websites, visuals, graphics and many other things.

My sprawling family – Dunnes and Bards – thank you all for your support and love over the last few years.

My developmental editor, Lynnette Labelle, thank you for such constructive advice on bringing the story to life. My copy editor and friend Angela Anderson, who did a great job at American-ising ('-izing'!) my usually very British style! Erin Dameron-Hill, thank you for such an amazing job with the cover – I love it. Simon Hartshorne, thanks for your help bringing the visuals of the archetypes and the Chakras to life on the website.

NaNoWriMo 2013 was the event that clarified I wanted to write fiction, and I'm grateful to the Thailand group for getting me through that first book, but I got so much more out of the month because Nyla Nox, the Thailand moderator, became a friend who I have had many 'writing races' with since. She was at the other end of Skype writing her own books for a number of the pages of this book. I hope we continue to motivate each other through future works.

So many elements from things I've learned in life have gone into the book. My Krav Maga teacher, Matt, is a hero of mine, for all the things he has taught me – resilience, inner strength and just never-give-the-f**k-up. I hope I never have to use any of his teachings in practice, but it's been fun to use them for Blaize and the gang. He also checked over the fight scenes for me – all mistakes are my own!

For Professor Cowie, who taught me self-hypnosis and Jungian theory – I never thought that the tower would come in handy quite in the way it has, but I love exploring my inner world and bringing a little of that to life has been fantastic.

I'm grateful to all the yoga teachers and meditation teachers over the years, especially my most recent community in Thailand where I've spent two seasons so far, and will probably return again soon. There are too many to mention here, but Amitayus, thanks for brainstorming archetypes with me in our little island café, and Grace Bryant, who was both a beta reader and has worked with me on many other behind the scenes activities, thank you.

My other beta readers and friends, Laura Quinn, Catherine Bedford, Katie Bullas, John Mansfield and Debbie Hantusch, thanks for the great suggestions and support. I'm so grateful to you all for taking the time to read the book and give me your feedback – I think it's very courageous and was a great help. Thanks also to my aunt, Ellen Dunne, who helped do the final proof of the paperback version of the book.

Caroline Leon, who was instrumental in helping me to change my life by encouraging and supporting me in Thailand, thank you – keep being amazing.

Justin Morgan and Ed Clarke – I love you boys so much, thank you for always being there for me. Graham Morley, thanks for helping to keep me sane and grounded. Helen Blackie, Ray Glennon, Sam Blackie, Ann Curtis, Alan Gardner, Samia Khan, Ian Newcombe, Tom Sandman, Sally Gold and Tessa Kelly, thank you all for your support, accommodation, meals, coffees and chats as I wrote sections while in the UK.

Finally, Dad, I miss you every day and I wish so much you'd been here to see this happen. Cuinn's golden arrow was for you (it was a longbow).

Ellen Bard, September 2015